ABIGAIL A

CW00965767

R. J. KINNARNEY

Cover design by Sarah Robins

For all the friends who have loved with me; for all the students who have laughed with me and for all the animals who have been with me.

Thank you.

Chapter A

Brakes squealed. Metal crunched against metal. There was the sound of tearing tarpaulin and the car came to rest half under the lorry and half under the lorry's load which had been released by the force of the accident.

The lorry driver had sat at the junction for at least ten minutes before there was even a small break in the rush-hour traffic. The wipers were set to their fastest speed to try and clear some of the rain which seemed to be gushing rather than pouring down the windscreen. He had carefully eased the lorry out onto the main road not wishing to disturb his cargo in any way.

Some minutes earlier the lorry had pulled out of the big gateway of the army barracks where it had filled up with some of the town's finest and most pungent horse manure and the driver was understandably nervous about losing such a load.

Unfortunately for all concerned, the side window of the lorry was not equipped with wipers and the driver was unable to see the large black car bearing down on him at breakneck speed. The car driver was equally ill placed to see the lorry because not only was he handicapped by the weather but also by the heavily tinted windows of his vehicle.

Hence the crunch.

Small amounts of this horses' 'by-product' weigh little but ten tonnes of it weigh…ten tonnes. The car was almost completely flattened and it was fairly clear that whoever had been driving would have suffered a similar fate.

Despite it looking unlikely that an ambulance crew would be any use whatsoever, a call to summon help was put through to the emergency services. It was more than a little difficult for the switchboard operator to make out what the caller was saying at first and she had to get him to repeat his location several times before she could reliably send the crew on their way.

"Ever such a funny voice, he's got," she told Polly, one of the ambulance crew, over the radio. "Sounded foreign but just like he was holding his nose too. Wouldn't leave his name either. Aren't people funny? Over."

Polly had been having a very late lunch when the call came through and she now swallowed the last bit of the sausage sandwich which she had taken along with her. "Sure are. Not clear how long it's going to take us to get there. Traffic's appalling and this rain's really not helping. Over."

The journey was slower than even Polly could have imagined and she was amazed that, in spite of blue lights flashing and sirens blaring like it was the end of the world, they still did not manage to get to the scene of the accident before one of the large cars from Unwins Undertakers.

"How do they do it?" she asked Dan as they both opened their doors to leap out. Dan, however, was unable to answer because he was overwhelmed by the appalling smell which greeted them.

"What on earth is that? What was on the back of that lorry anyway?" It did not take long for it to dawn on him that the job they were about to deal with was maybe one of the most unpleasant of his career to date. "Great! I'm so glad that I agreed to cancel my leave for this, I must say."

"One thing's for certain," Polly put in, "there is no way that *I* am going to dig him out of there.

"If this rain keeps up you won't need to dig. That stuff will have completely turned into slurry in about half an hour."

"Yes, and if the driver's alive now, he sure won't be after swallowing eight pints of slurry. Someone's going to have to get him out. But who, because it took *us* long enough to get through here with the traffic?" As she spoke, they heard the sound of boots pounding behind them. They both turned to see roughly forty soldiers running towards them in formation, brandishing not guns but shovels. "Aha!" said Polly. "The cavalry's arrived." She was never one to miss a joke, no matter how inappropriate the circumstances.

The soldiers made short work of the digging and before long the car was exposed enough that the fire brigade were able to prise open the driver's door like a can of tinned tomatoes.

3

Polly poked her head into the car and realised that the car resembled tinned tomatoes in other ways too. "There's blood everywhere in here," she called back to Dan. "Nasty head wound. And would you believe it, the guy was wearing dark glasses. On a day like this, he had it coming to him, I'd say. What an idiot!" Polly had been in this job for just under seven years and it had created in her, what other colleagues called a 'sympathy bypass'.

Once the car had been opened, it didn't take long to load the patient into the back of the ambulance and they were soon nudging their way through traffic on the way back to the hospital.

In the recovery room, Doctor Dennis Dobbing, the registrar in charge that evening soon established that the patient's life was not at risk but that because of the severe blow to the forehead at the point of impact and the subsequent crushing under the weight of the 'material' it would, in his professional opinion, be a very long time before the patient recovered consciousness. It was also not possible, in his professional opinion, to estimate the amount of long-term damage caused by the injuries.

The patient, now known as Patient A, was quickly transferred to the Intensive Care Unit – mainly to free up space in an increasingly crowded Accident and Emergency department. It was a Friday evening and there was a big football-match on television. This combination always resulted in a great deal of alcohol being consumed and a great strain being placed on hospitals all across the country.

At this stage, the patient could only be named Patient A because there was absolutely nothing either on him or inside the car with which to identify him. No driving licence, no credit cards, no receipts even. Not one scrap of paper, not one thing.

The police investigating the incident, naturally pursued the matter of the car registration. They immediately put a trace on the car number plate and found that it was registered to a Mr. Zoltan Zappa of Zappa Towers.

They prepared themselves to deliver some very bad news and went round to Zappa Towers to see if they could find anyone home. The house was on a terribly exclusive road and was approached through immense black gates topped by a fearsome looking crest complete with obligatory hook-beaked eagles. A huge gravel drive led up to the rather ostentatiously large front doors.

The police banged the huge eagle doorknocker and, after a short wait, an incredibly tall man answered the door. They were so taken aback by the man's extraordinary height and imposing demeanour that trying to see the top of his head they both nearly fell backwards onto the gravel.

"Erm, good...afternoon...sorry, I mean good...evening, sir. Are we at the home of one Mr. Zoltan Zappa?" said a very flustered Constable Christine Campbell.

"I am he," boomed back the man in the deepest voice it was possible to imagine. It was difficult to tell from just those three words, just exactly where the man's accent was from. This, however, was really the least of the police officers' problems since they had left lying in Intensive Care the man they had thought to be Mr. Zappa.

"Do you, Mr. Zappa, own a large black Range Rover, registration number ZAP 1Z?" squeaked a now trembling Constable Campbell. This was not giving the best impression possible of the local force but it was difficult for Christine to remain composed when confronted by a two metre giant who she thought to be currently in a coma.

"Dat is no longerrrr my vehicle. I have sold dis some tvelve monsss ago. Vot is dis all about, anyvay?" growled back Mr. Zappa in an increasingly irritated tone.

"Your vehicle, sorry, erm, ex-vehicle has been involved in a serious accident and the driver is currently unconscious in the Intensive Care Unit of Hope House Hospital. Could you...do you think....shed any light on the possible identity of this, erm, gentleman?"

"How vood I know. I juss tol you dat I solt it von year ago ent I solt it to a dealerrr. Now please go avay and leave me alone. I am a verrry busy man and do not have time for such games."

With that, he retreated into the house and slammed the door in the faces of the police officers, who did, of course, feel rather disgruntled at being treated in such an ignorant fashion but who were also incredibly relieved at having the excuse of retreating from that rather scary establishment with its more than scary resident.

Inspector Ian Irving decided that now, having let poor Constable Campbell take all the flack from a very angry Mr. Zappa, he would assume command of the situation. "Right, Campbell, well it looks like it's back to the station and back to the drawing board with regard to our nameless patient. By now, the boys should have gone over that car with a fine tooth-comb and maybe, just maybe they'll have discovered something vaguely useful."

Inspector Irving did not value highly the abilities of his colleagues in forensics but, actually, a fine-tooth comb had not been needed at all for the discovery which they unveiled to the Inspector the following day at the station.

Just as expected, when the team had opened up the boot of the car there was nothing. No bits of rubbish or empty shopping bags, but more significantly, nothing useful in case of emergency. No car-jack, no warning triangle, no blanket or box of tissues. This was becoming more and more mysterious. Never had the team seen such a clean and empty car before; it had to be deliberate.

"Spare tyre must be under the carpet, sir", Sergeant Spencer called out to his superior who was combining supervising the operation with drinking a large milky coffee, eating an extremely messy doughnut and telephoning a drinking pal to arrange the evening's entertainment. He was also using the opportunity to show off to his team that he had got one of the first new-fangled mobile phones on the market.

Two of the officers in their white plastic boiler suits stood on the other side of the car watching him. "What an idiot! Look at him, the big 'I Am'. Does he know he looks like he's holding a brick to his head and talking into it?"

His colleague whispered back, "Maybe it *is* a brick. Ibbo would buy anything if it meant that he could flash some cash about." There was no love lost between the Inspector and his team.

Ibbotson barked at Spencer. "Well, get the tyre out then Sergeant! Honestly, do I have to do everything around here myself?!....Are you still there, Dave? Right the Red Lion at eight, then?"

"Guv, guv, you'd better come and have a look at this!"

"What is it now, Spencer? Do you think I've never seen a spare tyre before? What, has it got a flat, or something? Quick run to the guy's bedside and book him for it!"

"Not 'a flat' exactly, sir. More 'a float'."

"Listen, Spencer, *you* might be into the cryptic crosswords in the posh newspapers you read in the canteen in the desperate hope that someone will think you are intelligent. *I* on the other hand would rather have my information given to me as straightforward as possible. Now what the blazes are you talking about?"

"I'm talking about the biggest stash of money that I've ever seen in my life, sir. It's right here, stuffed inside the well for the spare tyre."

The doughnut, coffee and telephone crashed to the floor as Inspector Ibbotson went dashing over to inspect this 'stash'. This being a big car, it was a big tyre well and it was absolutely full of £50 notes. It was indeed a vast sum of money.

"Get it out, Spencer, get it out. Let's count it!" Ibbotson shouted in his excitement.

"Don't you think that we ought to check it over for fingerprints, traces of drugs, anything like that before we actually count it? After all sir, we *are* the forensic squad." Sergeant Spencer, who had always had his doubts about the skill and integrity of Ibbotson, spoke with more than a hint of condescension, flavoured with a large amount of suspicion.

"Well, obviously, Spencer, I didn't mean count it before it had been checked over. Honestly, sometimes I think you've just got no idea at all. I have to spell out every little thing." With that the inspector retreated to pick up his now slightly battered phone. "Somebody clear up this mess! This place is such a tip! There's coffee and jam everywhere. I'll be in my office. Don't disturb me unless you've got something half way useful to report like where in the hell all that money has come from." And he left, leaving his grateful team to get on in peace with the task in hand.

It took hours to find out that there were no useful prints on the money. "These are all used notes," Spencer told the team. "They've probably been through hundreds of hands by now."

The sniffer dogs came in and found no trace of narcotics, explosives; nothing untoward at all in fact.

Naturally, the next step was to check the serial numbers on the notes to see if it was stolen loot. This was another lengthy operation because there were just so many of them and every single one had to be entered into the police computer. It was made all the more difficult by the fact that it was now the middle of the night and all the data entry clerks were, understandably, at home tucked up in bed. Sergeant Spencer was a bright lad and had many skills but, sadly, typing was not one of them, which made the task extremely laborious.

Finally at 8.30 the next morning, Spencer reached his conclusion about the stash. It seemed that this money was clean. In no way was it related to a crime of any description and it looked like it would have to be handed over to Patient A, when and if he ever recovered. Ibbotson was not going to like this and, unfortunately, he was often guilty of 'shooting the messenger'.

"You lads better head on home now and get a good 'morning's' sleep unless anyone fancies helping me break the news to the Inspector?" He looked around at the worried, silent faces. "Thought not. Well, wish me luck, anyway!"

At least Spencer knew he'd got a good two hours before he had to hand the information over because the Inspector could be relied upon never to be in the station before half ten, particularly after a night on the tiles. The sergeant was going to use that time to investigate further the small brown packet found tucked in among the £50 notes.

———————————

Down in the basement, where the station's rather underused and dusty library was located, Sergeant Spencer had a great deal of difficulty locating the book he was looking for. He eventually found it tucked away among books on Passion (crimes of) and Pottery (antique and modern). "How could 'Botany (a comprehensive encyclopaedia of)' end up in the 'P' section?", Spencer thought to himself. "Of course, silly me, P for plants not B for botany." Not all the officers in the station had Spencer's education.

The book, which Spencer had pulled off the shelf, was gigantic and, as he flicked through its seventeen hundred pages, his heart sank. Police work was really nothing like as glamorous as he had seen on the television when he was growing up. No fast cars rushing to arrest the leader of an international drug trafficking gang for Spencer. Oh no, just a trawl through some very dusty books to establish the nature of a small packet of seeds. For that is, indeed, what was in the packet – just seeds. Twenty-six seeds to be precise. Fairly large seeds but nothing extraordinary. They would actually have attracted very little attention had they not been tucked in among the one million three hundred thousand pounds of used notes in the boot of a crashed car.

Luckily for Spencer, in the encyclopaedia there was an entire section on seed identification. He trawled through the whole lot but could find nothing which exactly matched those in the packet. Either the size was not quite right, the shape was slightly off, the colour was a marginally different tone. 'It's no good,' he thought 'I shall have to take these along to the Botanical Gardens and consult an expert. Meantime, I'd better go up and give Ibbotson the 'good' news!'

While he was down in the basement, Spencer had lost track of time and it was already eleven fifteen when he entered Ibbotson's office, having stowed the seed packet back in with the money for safekeeping. The inspector was not exactly pleased. He had, after all, been at his desk for all of forty minutes and had expected to be given the results of the investigation immediately. His mood was not helped by the information which was given to him.

"Right, thanks for nothing, Spencer. You'd better get back on to that case of the jewellery shop robbery. Let's see if you can come up with something more interesting about that, eh? I'll take this one from here and write up the report for the super," Ibbotson mumbled between sips of the liver salts which he was drinking in the vain attempt of making his stomach feel vaguely normal.

"But, guv, there's one more thing…", Spencer began.

This time it was not a mumble, which Ibbotson produced, but a roar. "Did you hear what I said, sergeant? *I* will take it from here. Now, get out and do as you're told!" Clearly Ibbotson had missed every session on the ten-week course in 'People Management – Getting the Best out of your Team'!

Spencer knew that it was utterly pointless trying to deal with his superior when he was in this sort of mood and left briskly, allowing the door to slam just a little harder than he might normally do. 'I do hope that that doesn't make his headache any worse,' the sergeant thought, sarcastically. 'Funny though that he should offer to write up the report. He's never done that before.' This was only a fleeting thought in Spencer's mind because he was, quite frankly, glad to have one less job to do.

Inspector Ibbotson left his office ten minutes later, having hastily compiled his report. He hurried along to the property office to pick up three extremely large bags of money. It appeared that he had to attend to a call of nature before proceeding on to Inspector Irving's office to deliver the report and the one million two hundred and fifty thousand pounds. It seems that, since the money had been depleted to the tune of fifty thousand pounds, Spencer's doubts about his inspector's integrity were wholly justified.

Having unceremoniously dumped the money and the report in Irving's office, Ibbotson headed back to his own room to call his superior and report himself too unwell to work the rest of the day. He then picked up his hold-all and rushed out but, of course, just had to pay another quick visit to the Gent's before dashing off home!

Chapter B

To say that Inspector Irving had been looking forward to receiving the forensic report would be to overstate the matter a little because he clearly had no faith whatsoever in the ability of that particular team. So, he was not disappointed when he skimmed over the single side of A4, which had been almost thrown on his desk by Ibbotson.

He opened one of the huge sacks of money and began to dream about jacking in this awful job to retire to a desert island somewhere all by himself. His idea of heaven was not to have to speak to anyone from one week's end to the next and his reputation for unsociability went before him.

Still, he knew that he wouldn't really take any of the money – after all, that would be dishonest and that would never do for a police officer.

His dreams were rudely interrupted by Constable Campbell coming in, carrying the extremely greasy looking bacon and egg sandwich, which she had smuggled out of the canteen for him. Regulations about food consumption in offices and elsewhere in the station were very strict at the time because the superintendent was only just getting over having his best uniform used as a nest for fifteen mice.

"Any news, sir?" she asked, although she knew from the look on Irving's face that whatever news there was, it was not good.

"As ever, the forensics guys have come up trumps…I don't think! They reckon there's nothing on the car at all. And what's more there's nothing on the one and a quarter million they found in the boot."

Campbell's eyebrows nearly shot up through her hairline. This was the first that she had heard of the money. "One and a quarter million? Where on earth does anyone get that sort of money? It must be dodgy, sir, mustn't it?"

"Well, they reckon not. There's no trace on it, so we have to assume it's legit."

"It's a bit hard to believe. What do we do now?" Campbell asked.

"Not much we can do, Campbell…except dream, of course! We'll just have to hand over the dough and move on to something else. But I tell you what, I am going to put that guy down for Dangerous Driving and Failing to Register a Vehicle. Let's face it, if he ever does recover, he's not exactly going to find it difficult to pay the fine, now, is he?"

"I suppose you're right there. Do you want me to help you count it or anything, before you close up the case?" Campbell offered.

"No, you're all right. I think we've wasted enough time on this already. Just dump the bags in the station property office and run the property slip over to the hospital. They can leave it with the bloke's clothes and stuff…Sarnie would have been better with more brown sauce, by the way. Try to remember that next time."

'Some people do not know the meaning of the word 'gratitude'!' thought Campbell. She was sure that she would never be like that herself, when she finally got promotion. Still, for the time being she knew that she just had to bite her tongue and get on with doing all the menial, boring tasks that no-one else wanted to do.

Down she trudged to the property office, which was next to the library in the basement. She had to make three trips since the bags, full of so much money, were extremely heavy but none of her fellow officers who she passed seemed in the least inclined to help her out. Especially not that, to-her-mind, snooty Sergeant Spencer from forensics. In her opinion, he really did think that he was a cut above the rest just because he was a bit more educated than your average policeman.

As usual, it took the property sergeant ages to fill out the slip. He always seemed to need about three attempts to get it right. The matter was further complicated by the fact that there was no name to put with the goods. This was almost too much for the sergeant but Campbell managed to persuade him that it was sufficient to put the goods down under the name of Patient A, since that was the name attached to the whole case file.

By the time all the paperwork had been finished, it was already early afternoon and Campbell thought that she would combine her trip to the hospital with a little light retail therapy at her favourite shop on the High Street. If all her senior officers could take advantage of their positions, then she was going to do likewise.

She was, however, later to regret deeply the purchase of that turquoise towelling jumpsuit and not only for the reason that it was a complete fashion disaster!

While all this action had been taking place at the police station, Patient A, lay languishing in Hope House Hospital. His condition was deemed to be "poorly but stable". This is what friends and relatives would have been told, had he had any, or had those which he had been remotely interested. As it was, the nursing staff on the Intensive Care ward took only one call regarding the unknown patient, from a man with a rather indistinguishable and indefinable, yet very strong accent. Sister Simons did remark to her colleague that the caller had sounded somewhat put out when he had learnt that the patient was stable and that the medical staff were hopeful for his eventual recovery.

Ever inquisitive, Sister Simons was anxious for a visit from the police so that she might have more information about the enigma, lying in Bed Seven. This was curiosity from a purely professional standpoint, of course. "I need to know who he is so that I can find out whether he's got any previous medical history or allergies, you see," she told her somewhat disbelieving staff.

She had, in fact, expected that a police officer would be at the hospital long before four thirty in the afternoon. After all, it was now getting on for 24 hours after the accident. She assumed, wrongly, that there was nothing terribly special about this incident and that the police had got more pressing matters to deal with.

Indeed they had. Would it be the fuchsia two-piece or the turquoise jumpsuit, which Christine Campbell was going to buy for her first date with Eddie Eccleston on Saturday evening? This was a very important decision because it was a very important date. She had adored Eddie since they had ended up in the same Maths class in the sixth form. That was six years ago now and he had never so much as looked at her until last week when she had pulled over a very flashy looking sports car, which was going rather faster than the speed limit allowed. At the wheel was her heartthrob. He suddenly seemed to want to chat to her and it was during this brief chat that he asked her out for dinner. She was so excited that it was only as the red Mazda was driving away that she realised that she had completely forgotten to take the details from his licence and write out the speeding ticket. "Oh well," she thought, "thirty miles an hour over the speed limit is not too excessive, really." She cast from her mind the fact that the limit was only thirty miles an hour in the first place

She must have tried on numerous outfits that afternoon, in a desperate attempt to find something which would render her truly irresistible. The changing room in MissFits, the fashion emporium of her choice, was piled high with clothes, bags, shoes, scarves. So much so, that it was even quite difficult to locate her own things when she had finally made her momentous decision and, in the confusion, she dropped the entire contents of her over-stuffed handbag all over the floor. A member of staff kindly came to her rescue telling her not to worry because she, the assistant, would tidy up the mess and put all the rejected items back on display.

Christine wrote out a cheque and, as she did so, gave a huge sigh, of both relief at having finally chosen something and concern at the amount of money she was spending. Still, she was sure that it would be worth it if Eddie were even remotely impressed.

She glanced at her watch as the cashier was wrapping the purchase and realised that she had really spent rather too much time "taking advantage of her position" and if she didn't get a move on she might not have a "position" to take advantage of for very much longer.

As soon as her package was ready, she was out of that shop like a shot and running up the High Street towards Hope House. She arrived, panting, at the Intensive Care reception and was greeted by an officious Sister Simons.

"Have you come to tell me who my mysterious patient is, Constable?"

"I'm afraid not, Sister. I've just come to deliver a property slip for the goods discovered in the boot of his car. I'd be grateful if you could put it with his clothes so that he can claim the items when he is able," Campbell replied, hunting frantically in her bag for the slip in question.

"Of course I will…. Just leave it here on this clipboard. I can't stand around all day waiting for you to find it. I do have patients to attend to, you know."

"I…I…realise that, Sister. I just can't seem to…". It was at this point that she realised that it must have been one of the many pieces of paper, which had fallen out of her handbag in the changing room. She had thought that they were only old receipts and had left them there for the sales assistant to clear up. That would teach her not to be lazy and untidy.

'Oh no,' she thought. 'I need to get back to that shop, and quickly. If that slip goes in the bin, I'm sunk. I'll never be able to explain it away to the property sergeant and he'll report me to Irving and I'll never be trusted again and I'll never get a promotion and my whole life will be ruined and...' Tears filled her eyes as she began stuffing everything back into her handbag. Her experience in the shop had still not taught her to pack her bag neatly.

She thought, at the back of her mind, that there would surely be time to recover the slip because the shop would not put their rubbish out until closing time, which was another hour away.

Unfortunately for Campbell, however, as she was running back along the miles of hospital corridor, the police station receptionist was putting a call through to Inspector Irving from one Amanda Anderson, assistant at MissFits fashion emporium in the High Street.

Irving was waiting for Constable Campbell when she arrived back at the station having dashed into MissFits to pick up the slip. Of course, she had no idea of the trouble that she was in because Amanda Anderson had simply handed over the slip, assuming that Campbell had been sent by her superior officer who sounded like a very grumpy individual, in Amanda's opinion. Christine then hurried back to Hope House, dropped the slip off at the Intensive Care Unit and ran like mad to tell the inspector that the mission had been accomplished.

No warning of what she was about to face had been given to the constable but, as she entered Inspector Irving's office, the bells started to go off in her head like a hundred thousand churches on a Sunday morning. Irving's face was as dark as thunder.

"Nice shopping trip was it, Campbell? You know, you really ought to wait until you're a sergeant to take advantage of your position like that. Oh, but wait a minute....I was forgetting, you're never going to make sergeant, are you? Not while I'm working in this station, you're not anyway!"

"But, inspector, I can explain everything..." began Campbell, although she actually had no idea at this point what excuse she was going to give.

"No explanation needed, Constable. You abandoned your job, wasted time for which you are well paid – that's tantamount to theft in my book. Get out of my sight now, I need to concentrate on the report I'm going to write about you for Superintendent Strange."

Campbell left the office on the verge of crying. As she was hurrying down the corridor, she managed to see, through her tears, that stuck-up Sergeant Spencer who was staring at her in, what she considered to be, an extremely rude fashion. 'You might have a load of brains,' she thought, 'but you're a bit short in the old 'manners department'!'

She went into the Ladies' and locked herself in a cubicle. She was just contemplating how her life was over and how she would be a boring old constable for ever and how she had nothing in the world to look forward to, when she remembered her date on Saturday with the lovely Eddie Eccleston. Maybe life wasn't too bad, after all. She would concentrate on this and nothing else for the next few days and maybe that would take her mind off the disastrous developments in her career.

A couple of days later and it is nine o'clock on Saturday evening. Constable Campbell is dressed to kill in her turquoise towelling jumpsuit, sitting in Rumours, the bar where she and Eddie had agreed to meet before going off for their romantic dinner. She is sipping her third gin and orange and feeling a little woozy, having had nothing to eat all day because she was saving herself for the lovely Italian meal they were going to have together.

Now, there is only one slight problem with this image – no Eddie! He was now ninety minutes late and Christine, having gone through 'pressure of work', 'car broken down', 'horrific road accident', 'inability to decide what outfit to wear', was running out of excuses to make for his unpunctuality.

Suddenly she saw him coming out of the Gents' at the other side of the very crowded bar. She began the difficult task of pushing her way through the crowd on four-inch white plastic stilettos. Just as she was nearing Eddie, she noticed his arm around a tall, bottle blonde who was wearing rather less than Christine thought was proper. From the way they were talking and touching each other, she knew that this was certainly not his sister and that the only thing left for her to do now, was to get out of there as quickly as possible.

She turned to run but, as she did so, the heel snapped off her right shoe and she went crashing to the floor in a heap of indignity. She hoped against hope that Eddie had not noticed and he might well not have done, had she not crashed into three lads drinking beer from bottles. Each bottle had a piece of lime wedged in the neck of it. The bottles, the men, the limes and Campbell lay in a heap on the rather sticky bar floor.

By the time that she had removed her shoes and been helped to her feet, Eddie's was the only laughing face that she could see among the crowd of hyenas surrounding her.

This had indeed been a black week for Constable Campbell.

Black week it might have been for Constable Campbell but it was an even blacker week, and indeed black few months, for Patient A. He lay in a very deep coma for some five months during which time, as he was no longer considered to be in danger, he was moved from the 'tender' ministrations of Sister Simons and placed in a small side ward on his own.

One evening late in December, Nurse Nelson was moaning to her colleagues about her fate. "Why should *I* have to work tonight? It's the Hope House Hospital Christmas Ball tonight and I really wanted to go." She had designs on that very handsome Doctor Dobbing and thought that the Ball might be the ideal opportunity to make her dreams come true. She was forgetting, of course, that everyone she was talking to was also missing the Ball but, in her usual selfish fashion, she did not see this as at all relevant.

Gradually Nurse Nelson noticed that everyone appeared to have stopped listening to her. She felt that this was more than a little rude but, oddly enough, it seemed to keep on happening to her. Eventually she gave up speaking and it was at this point that she was able to hear what had distracted them all from her riveting tale.

"A...B...C...D...E...F, no good, I just can't remember. G...H...I...J...K. Really this is too tiresome. L...M...N. N! Yes that's it, N! Nurse! Nurse! Nurse!"

Patient A was awake. All the staff left their station and rushed into his side ward. Even though none of them expected him ever to come round because, after all, five months is an awfully long time, they had all agreed that whoever was in charge at the moment he awoke would get a magnum of champagne. Nurse Nelson, for it was indeed she who was in charge, was unaware of the inadvisability of drinking an entire magnum of champagne by herself in one go and was extremely ill for the entirety of her off-duty the following week!

Back in the side-ward, the staff were pulling tubes out of Patient A and giving him a thorough examination. "Sir, sir, can you hear me? Can you hear me?" yelled one of the nurses.

"Of course I can hear you. There's no need to shout!" replied the disgruntled patient.

"Can you tell us what your name is, sir?" asked Charge Nurse Challoner.

"I can't tell you anything until you bring some….what's it called? Clear stuff. You drink it."

"Vodka", answered Nurse Nelson.

"I think that the patient might be referring to water, nurse", said a voice from over her shoulder. It was Doctor Dobbing. He had been summoned from the Ball by a thoughtful member of the ward staff since he was on call that evening and had also been present at Patient A's admission to hospital. Nurse Nelson, for once, was absolutely speechless both because Dr. Dobbing looked utterly gorgeous in his tuxedo and because she realized that she had just made a complete and total idiot of herself. To say nothing of rather giving the game away about her drinking habits.

"O…Of course. I was just kidding around, doctor. I'll run and get some at once." At which point, she scurried off very much with her tail between her legs.

"Well, my good man," said Dr. Dobbing turning back to the bed, "I was beginning to doubt that I would ever have this conversation with you. Five months is an awfully long time to be in a coma, you know."

"Five months? Five months? Do you mean to tell me that I have been in this… this..A..B..Bed for five whole months?" croaked Patient A.

"Indeed you have."

"Here's the water, sir", said Nurse Nelson, offering a plastic cup to Dr. Dobbing.

"Well, nurse, I think you'd better give it to the patient as I'm sure that his need is greater than mine!"

This was going from bad to worse as far as Nurse Nelson was concerned. Could she really make herself look any more stupid in the eyes of her hero, she wondered. And as she wondered, she tripped over the doctor's quite sizeable feet, resulting in the cup full of water being emptied over the patient's head.

"I think that the patient was intending to drink the water, nurse, rather than bathe in it. Perhaps the excitement of his recovery has been too much for you. Why don't you return to the station and be there in case the other patients need you. Meanwhile, we'll attend to the patient in here. Charge Nurse Challoner, would you get the patient some water and then maybe we can have a proper conversation with him."

"Certainly, sir. Right away, sir", Challoner replied.

He attended to the task swiftly and Nurse Nelson went back to the station to prepare the next month's rota. "Charge Nurse Challoner, a month of night duty, I think", she said to herself. Nelson was nothing if not vengeful.

Once the patient had drunk the water so kindly provided by Challoner, Dr. Dobbing began to question him. His first and most obvious question was the same as that already posed by the charge nurse.

"Can you tell me what your name is, sir?"

"Do you know, I really don't think I can. I haven't the foggiest idea who I am!" smiled back Patient A.

Chapter C

This was going to be more complicated than Doctor Dobbing had previously thought. The professional opinion which he had formulated over the five month period had been that the patient would either never regain consciousness or would come round with all his faculties in tact. Faced with the developments with Patient A, he was beginning to question his 'professional opinion'.

"Are you sure that you have no idea whatsoever about your name, sir?"

"Well, I think that if I wasn't sure, I'd have told you, wouldn't I?"

"Quite so, quite so" mumbled Dobbing. Turning to Challoner, he said "I think that we have a rather serious case of amnesia on our hands, charge nurse. I might add that it would appear the gentleman's spirit and 'sense of humour' are remarkably in tact!"

"They certainly seem to be, doctor. Is there anything special that we should do to help the gentleman recover his memory?"

"Ahem, ahem," came from the bed. "I am still here, you know. You might have been talking across my unconscious …A…B..Body for the last five months but I am most definitely awake now and would appreciate being included in discussions about my condition and treatment."

"So sorry. You are quite right, of course. Is there anything that you feel you need or anything which might help you?" asked Dobbing.

"Well, I'm sure there are things but, do you know, I can't for the life of me remember what they are" laughed Patient A. Unfortunately, the laughing brought on a dreadful coughing fit in the patient. Dr. Dobbing fitted him with an oxygen mask and then suggested that they all leave the room and let the patient recover from what must have been an ordeal.

"One thing before you go, doctor. Would you mind switching the..the..oh rats, A...B...C...D...E, now what is it called? F...G...H...I...I? Is that it? No, I don't think so. J...K...L...Aha, L...Light off, please?"

"Certainly will. Good night, er, Patient A."

Outside the door of the side ward Dobbing turned to Challoner and said, "That's most interesting. Did you notice how he is going through the alphabet to jog his memory on common words which he is having difficulty accessing? I must question him about that tomorrow. This really is a fascinating case."

"Oh yes, sir. Yes indeed. I shall be here tomorrow and would love to hear what the patient has to say, if that's O.K., sir?"

"Certainly, Challoner. But won't you be exhausted having worked through the night."

"Not at all. Not at all. I am so keen to learn and can't think of anyone who I would rather learn from."

Nurse Nelson, who at that moment was passing on her way to the lavatories to empty a rather full bedpan, heard this little exchange. She wished that the bedpan had been empty because Challoner's sickly tone made her feel inclined to vomit. 'You'd never catch me sucking up to the doctors in such an obvious way', she thought. Nurse Nelson's self-awareness was not one of her greatest assets.

"Right you are, Challoner. See you tomorrow then" and at that he turned on his heels and headed back to the Ball where he had left at least a dozen disappointed nurses.

He really did look very handsome in his dinner jacket.

The next day dawned bright and clear, which is more than can be said for Doctor Dobbing who, when he returned to the Ball, had completely thrown himself into the spirit of the party – and had thrown quite a lot of party spirit down his throat.

When the doctor finally arrived, clutching a very large, very black coffee, Charge Nurse Challoner was waiting at the entrance to the ward.

"Your patient is awake and well, doctor. Shall we go on in and see him?"

"If you don't mind, Challoner, I'd just like to finish my coffee. I think I'm going to need a clear head to deal with the gentleman this morning. Incidentally, any change with regard to his memory?"

"None at all, I'm afraid, Doctor. We're still no closer to knowing who this mystery man is," replied Challoner.

"Oh well, that was just as I feared. I've got a feeling that we might never know his true identity."

There was a moment's silence while Dobbing drained the last of his coffee; a silence only interrupted by the sound of the double doors to the ward banging as Nurse Nelson headed off home after one of the longest night shifts of her life. For once, Dr. Dobbing noticed her leaving and looked enviously after her. The thought of going home to get some rest was an incredibly attractive one. Instead, he was facing his usual hectic twelve-hour shift.

"Right, let's go and see our man, Charge Nurse!" the doctor called out as he was heading off down the ward. He had obviously been considerably revived by that coffee.

"Good morning, sir and how are you this morning?" Dobbing said in his most cheerful manner.

"How refreshing of you not to ask 'How are 'we' this morning?' That's all I've had from the nursing staff since I woke. How on earth am I to know how *they* are? I do wonder about the education system these days, if people don't know the simple difference between 'you' and 'we'. What is the world coming to? Anyway, in answer to your…what's the thing called? A..B..C.. Oh blow, another word I can't remember. D..E..F.. you know, when you ask someone something and they give you an answer? What's it called, now? G.."

"Is the word you are looking for 'question', by any chance?" asked Dobbing.

"That's it, that's it. Question. In answer to your question, I'm very well thank you, Doctor, though I can see that the same is clearly not true for you! Hard night, was it?" replied Patient A.

"Well, sir, you know how it is at these Christmas parties? One feels obliged to socialize, doesn't one?" replied the doctor.

"Oh yes, 'obliged', of course one is!" the patient said sarcastically.

"On to more important matters, I must ask you about your means of remembering words. This chanting through the alphabet really is most interesting. How did you come to realize that this was a useful tool in helping to jog your memory?"

"I have a vague recollection, from when I was very young, of someone rather irritatingly going through the alphabet to aid them in remembering people's names. As far as I can recall, I thought that this was just a silly and annoying habit but last night when I was desperately casting about for words I decided to give it a go. After all, I had nothing to lose, did I? I could hardly look more of a fool than I look already. Incidentally, I have been going over and over the alphabet all night trying to remember my own name but I've had no luck at all. Not a thing. I neither know how many names I've got nor what those names begin with."

Challoner was unable to keep quiet any longer and had to make his presence felt. Laughing, he said: "It's quite true, Doctor. We heard nothing but the alphabet all night long to the point where I was jokingly calling the patient 'Mr. Alphabet'."

Dobbing looked at the nurse sternly. "Charge Nurse, I really don't think that that is the most tactful way to discuss someone in our care, do you?"

"You're doing it again," Patient A shouted from the bed. "I am awake and able to speak for myself now. Anyway, I quite like it – Mr. Alphabet. Mr. Alphabet, yes. It has quite a A..B..C..D.. you know, it's the sound that telephones and bells make? E..F.."

"Ring, sir?" suggested Challoner.

"That's the one, 'ring'. I think that, in the absence of anything better and until such time as I remember my own name, I shall be known from now on as Mr. Alphabet."

"It's somewhat unconventional but as you wish, sir…sorry, 'Mr. Alphabet'!" agreed the doctor.

As each day passed, Mr. Alphabet continued to make a swift and steady recovery. It seemed like hour by hour his vocabulary grew and, along with it, grew both his desire to escape his confinement and his ability to express this desire. He was really becoming most tiresome for the nursing staff. So much so that after only two weeks, everyone was begging Dr. Dobbing to discharge him and put them all out of their misery.

"I really don't feel happy about discharging him while he still can not remember any details about his former life, about the accident which brought him here, about who he actually is," Dobbing told the ward staff as he began his ward round one morning, early in January. "After all, the man has not got a penny to his name. Would you really just cast him out onto the streets to fend for himself in the depths of winter?"

The answer which most of those present would have liked to give to this last question was a resounding 'yes' because they had all had about as much as they could take of the grumpy Mr. Alphabet and his incessant chanting of A..B..C…

Over the next few days, the pressure on the doctor continued to mount until he was forced to concede defeat and discharge his patient. As Mr. Alphabet had made a complete physical recovery, there was no reasonable excuse for keeping him in hospital any longer.

"I am going to discharge you on condition that if you have any problems at all, and I mean *anything*, you contact me immediately. It's slightly unconventional not hand you over to an outpatient consultant but somehow I need to feel sure that you are re-adapting well to life in the outside world. Six months is a very long time to be in one place, you know."

"I do indeed know, Doctor. Incidentally, how long have you been locked up in this prison? I mean, how long have you been working in this hospital?" enquired Mr. Alphabet.

"Five years."

"Oh, you should be let out soon on the grounds of good ..good..A..B..B..yes, Behaviour!" laughed the patient.

"Very funny, very funny," the doctor grinned back through gritted teeth. Actually, he, too, was tiring of Mr. Alphabet's somewhat grim and unusual sense of humour. "I have brought you all the property which you came into hospital with. It's not much I'm afraid. Really only the clothes you stood up – or should I say, lay down?! – in."

A shadow passed over Mr. Alphabet's face as it often did when he was about to recall something important.

"You have a very odd look on your face, Mr. Alphabet. What is it? Have I reminded you of something?" asked Dr. Dobbing.

Mr. Alphabet saw the look of excitement on the doctor's face and thought that, if he was not careful, the doctor, thinking that he was on the verge of a great discovery, might change his mind and banish him back to his bed.

"Oh no, nothing. I was just pulling a face due to a touch of wind!" lied the soon to be ex-patient. "If you don't mind, I'll just put my clothes on and get ready to leave."

"Of course, go ahead. I'll say goodbye now. It really was fascinating meeting you and I hope that we meet in the future some time, under less difficult circumstances. When you're dressed, the nurses here will give you help on where to go when you're discharged, etc."

"Right you are, Doctor. Oh and thank you for everything."

"Pleasure!"

Before Dobbing had left the side-ward, Mr. Alphabet had already put on his trousers. He reached down into the pockets to straighten them out and his hand touched a neatly folded, very thin piece of paper.

'What's this? 'Police property slip'? I certainly don't remember that,' Mr. Alphabet thought to himself. This came as no great surprise to him as there was a great deal he 'certainly did not remember'. However, there was no time to ponder the matter further because he could still hear Dr. Dobbing's voice out on the main ward and Mr. Alphabet knew that if Dobbing saw this slip, the excitement of a breakthrough on the amnesia front might just be too much for him. 'It's kinder all round to keep this bit of information to myself for the time being, I think.'

He dressed hurriedly in the clothes which he had been given. Thankfully, some kind soul had taken the rather smart suit he had been wearing at the time of the accident to the dry-cleaners. This act of kindness was motivated above all by the over-powering smell of horse excrement which seemed to be clinging to every fibre of the suit and which had begun to seep its way out of the patients' property cupboard.

Mr. Alphabet could not get the suit on fast enough. "I'm not hanging around here, waiting for those nurses to give me, no doubt fairly useless, information about where to go now. They might change their minds and keep me in here. Heaven forbid!"

It certainly felt odd being out of hospital pyjamas for the first time in almost six months. This odd feeling was nothing, however, compared with what he felt as he finally walked out of the hospital into the fresh, if slightly polluted air of the town. "Now what? Where am I going to go? I can't even afford a bus ride anywhere. No-one is going to pick up a stranger from outside a hospital and give them a lift somewhere. Even if they did I would have no idea where to go."

As Mr. Alphabet stood pondering his dilemma, a police car came past at quite a rate and suddenly screeched to a halt a few feet up the road from him.

"Charming," he thought. "I was released from captivity a matter of minutes ago and I'm about to be arrested for loitering with intent!"

He started to move down the road towards the bus stop when he heard a voice calling out behind him. "Sir, sir. One minute please, sir."

'There we are. I bet she's got her little book out already, writing down my A..B..C..D..description in case I make a run for it! 'Sir', though? That at least sounds reasonably respectful', he thought.

"I can't believe it's you, sir. What a coincidence," said the police woman.

"Do you know me, officer?" asked Mr. Alphabet excitedly. This could be a clue to finding out who he really was.

"Of course, I do, sir. You're Patient A. I am Constable Christine Campbell. I was one of the officers on the case when you were taken into hospital three months ago."

The disappointment on Mr. Alphabet's face was plain to see. "It was nearly six months ago, actually, Constable."

"My goodness, how time flies when you're…. Yes, well. How are you getting on, Mr…Patient…I don't really know what to call you, sir, sorry."

"My name is Mr. Alphabet, Constable and I'm not. 'Getting on', I mean. I've only just been freed from my incarceration and I really don't know where to go now. I've no idea who I am, where I live. Nothing. All I've got to my…all I've got to my..Oh bother, all I've got is this 'Police property slip'. Not much, really, is it?"

Constable Campbell smiled. "Sir, if you will get in my car and come along to the station with me, I'll show you just how much that small piece of paper is worth!"

Chapter D

On the short drive to the police station, Constable Campbell could barely contain herself and was nearly turning inside out with excitement. When they arrived, however, the property sergeant was not exactly inclined to share in her enthusiasm. These whippersnappers always arrived just as he'd made a nice cup of tea and they wanted everything done yesterday.

"It's going to take me a while to find this, Constable. Why don't you come back in half an hour? Take the gentleman off to the canteen for a nice sandwich," the sergeant said.

Campbell had learnt through bitter past experience that when the sergeant was in this sort of mood, there was absolutely no point in arguing with him. So off she went with an extremely curious Mr. Alphabet.

The canteen was packed, but they managed to find one empty table.

"I see that our streets are safe and in good hands…provided that it is not lunchtime!" said Mr. Alphabet.

Campbell just smiled. She was used to this sort of behaviour from 'Joe Public'.

They munched on their sandwiches in silence for a while until Mr. Alphabet could stand it no longer. "I must say that '*nice* sandwich' when referring to this particular canteen is somewhat of an oxymoron, Constable."

"It's a *what*moron? Do you mean that the people who made it are a bit thick, because if so…" began Campbell.

"No, Constable. An oxymoron is a contradiction in terms, when two words put together have opposite meanings."

"Ooo, aren't you clever, sir. Were you a school teacher or something? Oh, sorry. I don't suppose you know, do you? Well I think you must have been, anyway."

"Maybe you're right. Who knows?" replied Mr. Alphabetus, realizing that his joke about the sandwich had gone completely over Campbell's head. "Anyway, I'm sure that half an hour must have passed by now. Shall we go back and see what the property sergeant has to give us."

"Okey doke!"

Half an hour had indeed passed, in fact the queue had been so long in the canteen that it was forty minutes later that they arrived back at what was loosely termed 'the property office', although 'cupboard' would have been more appropriate. Still, the property sergeant made them wait a further ten minutes before he was willing to hand over three rather large and very dusty sacks.

Mr. Alphabet was not the most patient of men and he found the extra delay almost impossible to bear.

"What's the hold up sergeant?" he almost barked.

"Well, that ticket you gave me was not exactly easy to read, was it? It looks as though someone had chewed it up."

Constable Campbell remembered the awful day that she had had when she almost lost the slip and could, at that moment, have happily chewed the sergeant's head off. Still, being the professional that she was and continuing with what seemed to be her endless task of trying to redeem herself, she smiled politely, heaved the bags from the desk in front of the grumpy sergeant and handed one of them over to Mr. Alphabet.

"This weighs a tonne, constable, what on earth can be in it? When you said 'worth' earlier, I assumed that I was going to be picking up a small package because everyone knows that the smallest items are usually the most expensive."

"Sir, if you wouldn't mind coming along the corridor with me, there's a vacant reporting room and we can take a look at the contents of your bags. I can assure you that you won't be disappointed."

"No problem, constable. I really don't want to waste any more of your time. I'll just head off now."

"No really, sir, I think you should come with me." Campbell was anxious to get Mr. Alphabet away from the prying eyes of the property sergeant who was by now beginning to smell a rat.

27

There must have been an unusual note of assertiveness in the constable's voice because the perplexed Mr. Alphabet agreed to her request without further hesitation.

When they got to the empty office, he heaved the bag which he was carrying onto the desk and began untying the knot at the top. The suspense was almost too much for both him and Campbell. It seemed that whoever had tied up the bag wanted to be sure that it was not easily opened again and examined. For some strange reason, that weird Inspector Ibbotson came into Constable Campbell's mind. Wasn't it odd how he just went off sick like that and never came back to work again? Apparently, when the human resources guy from the station had gone round to see him at his flat, he was greeted by a very irate landlord who said that Ibbotson had gone off leaving three months of unpaid rent and bills. Bizarre! Still, there were more important things to think about right at this moment.

Finally, Mr. Alphabet worked the knot loose and opened the bag up. There in front of him sat approximately one third of the total one million two hundred and fifty thousand pounds although he clearly did not know that right then. He just knew it was more money than he'd ever seen in his life. Or was it? How would he know?

" There you are, sir. What do you say to that? Worth the wait, I'd say, wouldn't you?"

"Quite so, Constable, quite so. I can't quite believe my eyes. Is this really all mine? How did I get it? Where's it from?"

"Good questions, sir. I was hoping that maybe seeing the stash would jog your memory but it looks like I was wrong. We weren't able to find any trace of where it came from but it was in your possession when the accident happened so I can tell you that it is most definitely yours."

"Oh my, oh my. What on earth am I going to do with it?"

Campbell couldn't believe her ears. 'That much money and he doesn't know what to do with it! I could think of one or two things to buy with it – that gorgeous purple Smucci trouser suit that I've had my eye on for weeks, for a start.' Christine had clearly learned nothing from her fashion disaster with the turquoise jump suit.

"Well, for starters you won't have to worry about not having anywhere to live now, will you?"

"You're right, of course. What's the name of the best er..erm..Oh blast! A..B..C..D..Big place, lots of rooms, you sleep there..E..F.."

"Hotel, sir?"

"Yes that's it, Constable, thank you. Hotel. What's the name of the best hotel in town?"

"That'll be the Skwitz, sir, on Park Road. I'll drop you round there if you like because, for one thing, you're never going to manage all this on your own, are you?"

"You're so right. Thank you very much, constable. To the Skwitz then."

———————————————

The staff on the reception desk of the Skwitz were used to their clients arriving with a matching set of luggage but were far from used to that set being made up of three black bin-liners. Yet more perturbing was the fact that the gentleman holding one of the bags had no form of identification and they were on the point of calling security when Mr. Alphabet asked "How much will you charge for a suite for one month?"

The chief receptionist smirked and said "Sir, that would be the small sum of £5500." By this time, quite a crowd of staff had gathered within eavesdropping distance to see how quickly this 'bag-person' could be dealt with.

"Will you give a discount for cash in advance?" Mr. Alphabet inquired reaching into the sack and pulling out a large pile of notes.

Suddenly, there were a dozen pairs of hands reaching out to take his coat, offer him a chair, bring him a cup of tea, polish his shoes. It's amazing what a difference those little pieces of green paper made.

"Will you place two of my bags in your safe, please, until I can make other arrangements?" asked Mr. Alphabet.

"With the greatest of pleasure, sir," grovelled the receptionist.

Very soon he found himself settling down into his extremely plush and luxurious penthouse suite with a view over the whole town. 'This beats looking at the four walls of Hope House Hospital, I must say,' he thought to himself. He could see all the buildings, old and new, tall and small, glass and brick. There was one building which particularly caught Mr. Alphabet's eye because of the state it was in. It was big, ugly, run-down and old and appeared to have nothing but wilderness around it. 'Ugh, I'm glad that I'm up here in this warm and luxurious hotel room and not living in that draughty looking old place. Now what though? What an odd situation – all this money and I have no idea what to do with it. Only one thing for it – a ..oh, what is it now? A..B.. that's it B.. bath and a sleep in this lovely soft bed. Maybe that will clear my head and I'll be able to think more clearly tomorrow.'

So, having bathed and undressed, Mr. Alphabet climbed into bed thinking 'First thing tomorrow morning I really must sort the business of my clothing and oh..no.. what on earth are those things called that you wear in bed? A..B..C..D.. Oh bother, I'm too tired to work it out now. How on earth am I going to be able to sort my life out when I don't even know what basic things are called?'

In spite of being a bit annoyed when he got into bed, he was so tired out by the excitement of the day that he went to sleep almost before his head touched the goose-down pillow. All night long he had dream after dream after dream and every one of them seemed to feature that big old ugly building which he had seen from his hotel room window. His dreams were finally broken by the sound of a bell ringing and he shot up in bed wondering what on earth was happening and thinking that it must be break time. 'Break time? What is that all about?' he thought.

Finally, he realised that it was only the telephone and when he answered it the desk clerk said "This is Daz, speakingggg. There is a young lady waiting in reception to see you, sir."

"Would you tell her that I have only just awoken and will need to perform my ablutions before coming down to see her?"

"You're going to do your what?" replied the puzzled clerk.

"I'm going to have a wash." , er..D…What did you say your name was, young man?"

"Daz, sir. It's short for Darren.""Ooo, sir, don't you speak beautiful, like. Are you a teacher or something? Only I wish I'd been a bit more into school and less into sport. That way I might not be stuck on this desk. And I wouldn't have got it in the neck so much from me Mum and Dad and teachers."

"Er..D…What did you say your name was, young man?"

"Daz, sir. It's short for Darren."

"Well, Darren, that's very interesting and thank you for sharing that with me but I really feel that I must press on and not keep the young lady waiting any longer than is strictly necessary. Maybe we can talk about your situation at another juncture..er, another time."

"Oh, yes, right. Sorry, sir. I'll give the lady your message."

Mr. Alphabet put the phone down and set about getting ready to go downstairs. All the time he kept hearing Darren's voice: "Are you a teacher or something?" and Constable Campbell's: "I reckon you must have been a school teacher".

As quick as lighting, Mr. Alphabet made a decision. 'That's it. That's what I'll do with that money. I'm going to set up my own school.'

Mr. Alphabet came downstairs into the hotel lobby to find Constable Campbell waiting for him. She was dressed in her own, somewhat unusual, clothes and he almost did not recognise her.

"Sir, it's me, Christine. It just occurred to me that maybe you'd need some help buying things and organising yourself a bit. So, as it's my day off and I've got nothing better..I mean, er.."

"It's all right, Christine, I understand exactly what you mean and actually I'm very grateful because it is going to be a bit tricky not knowing half the words for the items which I need to purchase."

"Ooo, shopping! There's nothing I like more. I know some great clothes shops."

"I can see that Christine. You must bear in mind, however that I must be nearly twice your age and my taste might be slightly more traditional than yours."

"Purple flares are out then, are they?"

Mr. Alphabet had such a look of utter horror on his face that Christine burst out laughing. "I was only kidding Mr. A. I go shopping for my Dad all the time so I know what the score is."

"Very good. You had me completely fooled and that doesn't often happen. I think we're going to get along very well."

"Let's go then. I've got my car outside but we might be better off on the bus because the parking's rotten."

"Bus it is then, Christine. Do you think that I should make a list before we go?"

"No need for that, I don't think. We'll just go to Dorrid's department store, they've got everything there. Come on let's go." It seemed that Christine was as eager to spend his money as she was her own.

They did not have to wait long for the bus and were soon hurrying through the big revolving doors at the front of Dorrid's.

It took Christine only about one hour to completely kit him out for daytime formal, daytime casual, evening dress and nightwear 'Pyjamas, that's what those night things are called!', Mr. Alphabet said to himself. He had a full complement of toiletries, shaving gear and, most importantly, a set of designer matching luggage to put the whole lot in. Never again would he need to put up with the disdainful looks of hotel receptionists.

Mr. Alphabet really was most impressed with both the skill which Christine showed in judging his taste exactly and the speed at which she accomplished her mission. 'If she can weigh up the criminals as quickly and effectively as she has just weighed me up, then she should have a very successful career in the police.'

"Right, Christine, time for a spot of well deserved lunch I feel, don't you?"

"I'll leave you to it then, Mr. A."

"You most certainly will not. I am inviting you for lunch and it's not just to thank you for your help this morning. I've got an idea that I'd like to discuss with you."

"Oh, right you are. Thanks very much."

"Where do you suggest we go? It needs to be somewhere really quite special. Remember that this is the first proper meal of my life since I can't remember those which went before and I can't count that turned-up sandwich in the police station canteen as a 'meal'."

"Weeell…there is somewhere really lovely close by but it's a bit pricey."

"Christine, I have pockets full of money. I really don't think that a 'bit pricey' is much of a problem, do you?"

"I suppose not. Right let's go to the restaurant at Harridge's Hotel. A new chef has recently taken it over. He's supposed to be really good. A vile man by all accounts but he can't half cook up some lovely nosh!"

"That sounds good to me."

They left Dorrid's and set out down the back streets towards Harridge's. Mr. Alphabet was very glad that he had Christine with him because this old part of town seemed to have so many winding little back streets.

They turned up one particularly gloomy looking street and there in front of him was the ugly old building which he had seen from his window and which had been haunting him all night. Attached to the railings and almost hidden by the heavily overgrown bushes was a sign.

'For Sale. All Enquiries please contact Ezey and Enfer Estate Agents.'

"Do you have a pen, Christine? I'd like to take down the number of these agents."

"You're not serious are you, Mr. A? That place has been deserted for years. No-one in their right mind would buy that place, not with all the stories going round about it."

"Well, I think that we both know that a man who can not even remember the word 'pyjamas' can not be said to be in his right mind. So, it sounds like I fit the bill perfectly, wouldn't you agree?!"

Over lunch at Harridge's, Mr. Alphabet told Christine about his plans for the school.

"You can't be thinking of opening a school in the old Grauen building? There hasn't been anyone living there for as long as I can remember. Apparently it used to belong to some strange foreign bloke who just upped and left one day. There was all sorts of talk at the station about what had gone on there but we never really found out. No-one is going to send their children there, for goodness sake."

"Well, we'll see about that. I think that it has great potential. I mean it's spacious, solidly built – if in need of a little modernisation…"

" 'A little modernisation'?! Tell you what, why don't you give up on the school idea and become an estate agent instead. I mean, you're already starting to sound like one!"

"Now, now, Christine, there's no need to be sarcastic." Mr. Alphabet replied with a smile. " Time's getting on anyway. Shall we get the..oh rats..A..B.. that's it B. Bill?" He signalled to the waiter that he was ready to pay. "I might also ask if I can use the hotel's telephone on the way out. Maybe the estate agents could take us around the house since we're in the area."

"Us? Us? Have you taken leave of your senses? If you think that I'm going round that creepy old place on a gloomy afternoon like this, you've got another thing coming!" Christine replied.

" 'Think' Christine. It's 'you've got another *think* coming', not 'thing'." He corrected her.

"Yes, well whatever. Think or thing, I'm not doing it."

"I quite understand your concern. I'll just have to go alone." At which he put down what Christine guiltily viewed as a rather large pile of notes and got up from the table and began to head for the hotel lobby. "Don't look so worried Christine. It was a wonderful meal; a once in a lifetime experience…I think! Anyway, if I'm going to go ahead with my plans I shall be a little more parsimonious from now on."

"Meaning?" Even though she had not known Mr. Alphabet for very long at all, Christine had got used to needing to ask him this at regular intervals.

"Careful, cautious with money"

"Oh, I see. I'll have to tell my Dad to use that when he's talking about his brother. Seems better than saying 'he's so tight that he squeaks when he walks'!" At this, she burst out laughing and it was the second time in as many days that Mr. Alphabet had been on the receiving end of some interesting looks from hotel staff.

"Well, Christine, if you're really sure that you can't be persuaded to do some house viewing, I'll let you get on with what's left of your day off."

"Okey doke, Mr. A.. Rather you than me though. Let me know how you get on," Christine shivered.

"I certainly will, my dear, and thank you once again for all your help today. It really has been invaluable."

"No problem. See you soon." With that Christine pushed her way out of the revolving doors almost sending flying a very smart young lady carrying what looked like a dog in her handbag. 'Whatever next?!' thought Christine. 'I think it's a nightmare cleaning out *my* bag. Heaven only knows what she has to shovel out of hers! Ugh!'

Mr. Alphabet meanwhile was putting a call through to Ezey and Enfer. It did not take long before an eager young voice answered.

"I'd like to view the house I believe to be called the Grauen place, please. I am in the area at the moment and was wondering if you could take me around there now," Mr. Alphabet launched in.

The voice no longer seemed quite so eager. "The Grauen place sir? I'm not sure if we have the keys for that at the moment. I'll just look into it. Hold the line please." The line clicked and Mr. Alphabet was treated to a jazz beat rendition of Chopin's Funeral March played on a child's electronic keyboard. 'Well, they really know how to put their clients at ease,' thought Mr. Alphabet.

Suddenly the torment was interrupted by the young man's voice coming back on the line, "I have the keys here, sir, but are you really sure that that is the property you wish to view? It does require quite considerable modernisation and has been uninhabited for years. There is a question of rising damp in the cellars and dry rot in the attic and…"

"Are you actually trying to sell this house or not? It is indeed the property which I want to see and, if you are available, I'd like to do it NOW, please."

"Very well, sir. But there are also one or two more properties which I can show you that might be of interest and…"

"No thank you, young man. I have no desire to see two bedroom starter homes where there is no room to swing a..oh what are those animals called? Furry, snooty, drink milk?"

"Cat, sir?" The young estate agent was beginning to have his doubts about the mental state of his potential new client.

"That's it. Cat. I wish to see one property and one property only. Now are you ready and willing to take me or do I have to approach this through another channel?"

"No, sir. There's no need for that. I can meet you there in about twenty minutes. How does that sound?"

"Perfect. I'll be waiting."

"Right ho. On my way. Oh, incidentally, sir, my name is Eddie Eccleston. May I take your name for our records?"

"You certainly may. My name is Mr. Alphabet."

"Right…yes… of course it is!" Any doubts which Eddie had had about this curious gentleman were now confirmed.

Chapter E

Twenty minutes later in the gloom of the late afternoon outside the Grauen building, Mr. Alphabet stood and waited for Eddie. Only a couple of seconds late, a rather smart looking red sports car came speeding around the corner and screeched to a halt in front of him.

'Well, they might not be able to sell this place but business is clearly booming elsewhere,' Mr. Alphabet thought to himself.

Eddie climbed out of the car clutching a flimsy sheet of paper.

"Mr...er..Alphabet? Nice to meet you, sir. I have brought the particulars of the property with me for you to have a look at."

"That's very kind of you, thank you," Mr. Alphabet replied, taking the crumpled sheet from Eddie. "For such a large building, the particulars seem to be 'particularly' small."

"Well, the fact is, sir, that we have been rather busy over the past few months and have had to prioritise our work in order to concentrate on more..well... more.."

"More saleable properties, perhaps, Mr. Eccelston? Incidentally, exactly how long has the property been on the market?" As he was asking this, Mr. Alphabet was studying the particulars, which appeared to have been typed on a dilapidated Corona portable typewriter, circa 1965. " 'A excelle t property which would be efit from some moder isation'? It would appear that we have here the interesting case of the Missing Consonant! I sincerely hope that you have managed to invest in some new office equipment since the time when this was typed, Mr. Eccleston."

"Sure we have," Eddie replied. "Shall we head on inside anyway while there is still some light." He was already beginning to get very irritated with Mr. Alphabet and was keen to avoid spending any longer with him than was strictly necessary.

"Certainly. Let's get on with it."

It took Eddie some time to locate the keyhole in the gate because the bushes which must once have lined the walls of the property, now seemed to be trying to force their way out through the bars. Eventually, he managed to get the key in the lock and used all his force to turn it. "Should have brought some oil, I think, shouldn't I?" he joked. "It's a while since the gate's been opened."

" 'A while' is rather an understatement, I'd say, wouldn't you?" Mr. Alphabet frowned. He was beginning to have his doubts as to whether Eddie had ever actually set foot inside the property which he was now going to try to sell. Really, this was most annoying because Mr. Alphabet felt sure that there were going to be a huge number of questions to which he would need the answers and he felt equally sure that Eddie would not be able to provide him with the information.

They trudged through a carpet of wet, black leaves up the driveway to the huge front doors of the property where the charade with the keys took place again. Mr. Alphabet would normally by now have lost his patience but on this occasion he was too busy looking at the crest set into the brickwork above the doors. Something about those hook-beaked eagles stirred his memory but, as usual, the more that he tried to force himself to remember, the more his memory locked up.

Eddie gave the door one enormous heave with his shoulder and almost flew into the cavernous hallway within. "There we are, sir. Won't you come on in?" he said, as though inviting Mr. Alphabet in for a nice cup of tea. Before Mr. Alphabet could open his mouth, Eddie launched into his estate agent patter. "As you can see, there is huge potential in this hallway. You will notice the large stone fireplace which I think you will agree is really a feature of this room. Note the full-length leaded windows which…"

"Much as I appreciate the running commentary, Mr. Eccleston, I think that we can maybe do without it, don't you? If I have any questions, I will be sure to put them to you."

Silence was not something that Eddie was terribly comfortable with since it was his job to talk for England but he realised that with this client he had better respect his wishes.

Mr. Alphabet led the way from the hallway into a huge room which must once have been a ballroom. All that was left of its former glory were four extremely dusty and disintegrating chandeliers hanging from the ceiling twenty feet above their heads. Eddie did not like the look of the rusty old chain holding the chandelier which he was standing under and quickly hurried back to the doorway out of harm's way.

"I'll just wait out in the hall for you, sir. I'm sure you'd like some time alone to view this really quite splendid space which could be…"

Mr. Alphabet shot such a stern look over his shoulder that Eddie almost ran through the doorway leaving his client to view what was indeed a 'splendid space' and a space ideal for a school assembly hall.

The viewing of the whole property took about an hour and a half because it was so vast, was on three floors and had so many bedrooms that Mr. Alphabet lost count after 26. By the time that they finally came downstairs into the hallway, it was almost dark and Eddie, who normally prided himself on his courage and fearlessness, was now beginning to get more than a little spooked by the place.

"Right, sir, are we ready to go then?"

"You might be ready Mr. Eccleston. I on the other hand am not since I haven't yet viewed the..oh..no..what on earth's that thing called? Outside, flowers grow in it."

"Plant-pot…Window-box?"

"No, no. Usually has grass in the middle. Oh, what is that thing called?"

Suddenly a gruff voice came from behind them. "Would that be a garden you are talking about, mister?"

Both Eddie and Mr. Alphabet jumped half out of their skins as they turned to the doorway to see an extremely ancient, very grubby looking man almost bent double and leaning on a gnarled old stick for support.

"And who, may I ask, are you?" enquired Eddie, making a big show of being courageous and unflustered.

"Yes, you 'may ask', my lad. I'm the man what deals with that 'thing outside' as your friend put it. I am Grey. Gardener here. Been here 65 years, man and boy. Man and boy," the stranger replied in what, to Eddie, felt was a voice more suited to the middle of a field or cow-shed than to the elegant surroundings of this part of town. "Now," Grey continued, "what's more to the point, who are you?"

It occurred to Mr. Alphabet that he needed to keep on the right side of Grey because he could be very useful. So, before Eddie could get a word in, Mr. Alphabet strode over to Grey, took his mud-encrusted hand and shook it firmly. "I am Mr. Alphabet. Pleased to meet you, Mr. Grey."

"What kind of a bloomin' name is that? Mr. Alphabet? Sounds like you just made it up!"

Eddie was glad that someone else had raised this point with his client because it was certainly what he had been feeling from the start.

"It's rather a long story, Mr. Grey…"

"Just call me Grey. Just Grey. I never been a Mr. in all my life and I ain't about to start now."

"Right, of course, Grey. Well…Grey, do you think that you could show us the wonderful garden which has kept you busy for…how long was it?"

"65 years, mister, man and boy. Man and boy."

"Marvellous, marvellous. 65 years. My, you must know some stories about this place," replied Mr. Alphabet.

"Why? What 'ave you 'eard? I 'ope you ain't another one of those snoopers." Grey was really most put out.

"Not at all, not at all. I just thought that you might be able to help me. You see, I'm hoping to buy this property and renovate it." Seeing Grey's worried expression, Mr. Alphabet was quick to reassure him, "Oh, don't worry. I'm not one of those awful property people who's going to come along and rip the heart out of the building to build 45 'highly individual luxury flats' decorated in various shades of beige and that look like every other 'highly individual' place you've ever seen. I'm going to use the property for my own purposes and I will certainly be needing the services of an excellent gardener who knows the property inside out."

Grey seemed relieved, if still somewhat suspicious. "Well, mister, to be honest the garden is not looking its best at the moment. I've been here on my own for 26 years and I've sort of run out of will and money. I'm sure I could soon have it back right for you though, mister."

"I have no doubt about it, Grey." Mr. Alphabet turned to Eddie, "Look, I think it's really getting a little too dark to see the exterior of the property and we've kept Grey for long enough. How about if we come back tomorrow morning and have a look at things in daylight?"

In one way, Eddie was delighted because as dusk was descending he was beginning to get more and more nervous in this old house – not that he'd ever admit it of course because that would not really do much for his street cred, would it? He did not, however, relish the thought of having to come back tomorrow and put up with more from condescending Mr. Alphabet and creepy Grey. 'Still,' he thought, 'that's my job and if the weird guy is going to cough up the money for this old pile, I'm going to be in for a big fat commission. Might even be able to splash out and upgrade the motor.'

"Whatever you say, sir. What time were you thinking of?" he asked Mr. Alphabet.

"9 o'clock sharp, I think, don't you? Does that suit you, Grey?"

"Always up with the lark, me. Always have been, man and boy. Man and boy," Grey replied.

"Good, that's settled then. We'll let you get back to your…incidentally, Grey, where do you live? I didn't notice that any of the rooms had signs of habitation."

"Oh no, mister. I wouldn't dream of living in the big house. I've got a little cottage in the grounds by the back gate. Lived there 65 years, I have, man and boy…"

"Yeah, we know, 'man and boy, man and boy'!" Eddie laughed. His laughing was immediately cut short, however, by Mr. Alphabet who shot him the most reprimanding look he had ever received in his life.

"There is a time and a place for joking, Mr. Eccleston, and this is neither the time nor the place. Shall we go and leave this good gentleman to his evening? Grey, we will see you first thing tomorrow. Thank you so much for your help."

"That's quite o.k., mister. I'll get back to preparing me rabbit stew – I was half way through gutting the beast when I saw the light up here."

The information about the rabbit was a little more than Mr. Alphabet would have wished for, particularly following his large lunch with Christine and he was glad to take his leave quickly and find himself back out in the fresh air.

"Can I give you a lift somewhere, Mr. Alphabet? Where do you live?" asked Eddie.

"I am staying at the Skwitz and yes, I would be very grateful to be dropped off there, thank you."

"The Skwitz, eh? Not bad!" Eddie whistled. He was beginning to wonder if maybe this strange gentleman was actually not as crazy as he had thought at first. The idea of that gleaming new sports car came flashing into his mind. 'What a date magnet, that'd be,' he thought.

"Well, Mr. Eccleston, are we going to stand around on this damp, cold pavement all night or shall we get a move on?"

If he was going to earn a big commission, it was certain that Eddie was going to have to work for his money.

On the drive to the hotel, Mr. Alphabet made verbal notes into Eddie's dictaphone of all the details and documentation that he wanted to see at their meeting the next morning. Eddie was clearly not going to be home in time to watch the football on telly with his mates as planned.

It was a relief to both driver and passenger when the Mazda screamed to a halt outside the hotel. Mr. Alphabet had found Eddie's driving a little hair-raising, to say the least, and he was extremely relieved to be climbing out of the sports car at last.

"Well, thank you once again Mr. Eccleston. I look forward to being able to expedite this ..oh.. no.. what is that word? Business transaction…between two parties. A..B..C.."

"Deal, sir?"

Mr. Alphabet was not at all surprised that that was one word which tripped very rapidly off Eddie's tongue.

"Correct, 'deal'."

"By the way, what's 'expedite'?"

Mr. Alphabet was equally unsurprised that this was not a word in Eddie's vocabulary. "It means to cause something to be achieved or resolved with speed."

"Oh right, yes. No worries on that score, sir. We at Ezey and Enfer pride ourselves on the speed and …"

"Spare me the sales patter, Mr. Eccleston. If it were not for the fact that the property I desire is only on your books, then you could be almost certain that we would have no business relationship. I will see you here at 8.35 tomorrow morning. I assume that you have no objection to picking me up?"

"No. No objection at all," Eddie replied. "Except for the fact that I think you are a stuck-up boring old pain in the whatsit!" he mumbled under his breath.

"What was that?"

"Oh, nothing, nothing. See you tomorrow then. Have a good evening."

"Thank you, I will," said Mr. Alphabet turning to go through the hotel door which the doorman had been holding open since the car first pulled up outside.

"Good evening, sir. Lovely evening!" the doorman said as Mr. Alphabet passed by.

Mr. Alphabet just looked out at the grey, damp drizzle and half-smiled back at the man. Irony was clearly alive and well in this hotel.

As he entered the lobby, Darren the desk-clerk, or 'Daz' as he liked to be called, rushed over to greet him.

"Are you still here, Darren?" enquired Mr. Alphabet. "Isn't that rather a long shift because you were here first thing this morning when I left, weren't you?"

"I'm doing a bit of overtime, sir, because I'm saving up to go on a book-keeping course when the colleges start back in September," Daz replied.

"Well good for you, young man. There's nothing I like to see more than someone keen to educate themselves. Incidentally, did my.. oh, not again! What are those things called? Normally all wrapped up in brown paper and string. Things inside. Oh..A..B..C.." It had been a long day and Mr. Alphabet was too tired for this.

"Packages, sir? Parcels?" Daz suggested.

"Oh, Darren, you are marvellous. That's two words I've learned now."

" 'Learned', sir? I don't get it."

"I'll let you in on a little secret, Darren, I was involved in an accident and I've lost my memory. I've no idea who I am, where I'm from, what I was. That's annoying enough, as you can imagine, but it's not being able to remember just simple words I find really difficult and frustrating. I really am most stupid." If Mr. Alphabet could be critical of others, it was nothing compared with the criticism he was prepared to heap on himself.

"Oh, sir, I wouldn't say that at all."

"Well, that's very kind of you. By the way, I'd be grateful if we could keep this little secret between us. I don't really want to have to explain myself to all and sundry."

"Sure. And yes, your packages stroke parcels did arrive," Daz said with a smile. "They're up in your room and unpacked. I saw to it myself."

"Excellent job. One day, you'll go far, my lad, and I hope that I'm there to see it," Mr. Alphabet told Daz. "Meanwhile, I'm off to bed. It's been a very exciting but equally long day and I'm just about fit to drop. Good night, Darren, and thank you again."

"Good night, sir. Have a good night's rest."

"I will, Darren. You too. Oh, just in case I don't wake up of my own accord, could you arrange for a wake-up call for me at 7.45 tomorrow morning. I have a very important meeting and I don't want to be late for it."

"I'll see to it myself, sir."

"Thank you again."

Mr. Alphabet could barely drag himself over to the lift and up to his room. It was a matter of only twenty minutes before he was showered, changed into his lovely new pyjamas and asleep.

Chapter F

There had been no need to arrange for the wake-up call. Mr. Alphabet woke at 6.30 the following morning, having slept a sleep completely uninterrupted by dreams – or at least, uninterrupted by any dreams that he could remember. At 7.45 exactly, the telephone rang. It was Darren, "Good morning, sir, your wake-up call, as requested. Also, I have a message for you. Your young lady called yesterday evening at around 9.30. I didn't put her through to you as I was sure that you wouldn't want to be disturbed."

"That's very thoughtful of you, thank you. Incidentally, I'm flattered that you should refer to Constable Campbell as my 'young lady' but it would be more accurate to describe her as a friend."

" 'Constable', sir? No trouble is there?" Daz enquired in a worried tone.

"None at all, Darren," Mr. Alphabet reassured him. "She has been helping me considerably since my discharge from hospital. Did she leave any message when she called?"

"She just asked if you could call her this morning and she left her number." Daz read out the number to Mr. Alphabet.

Mr. Alphabet thanked Darren, hung up and immediately redialled the number which had been given to him. The phone rang a number of times before a sleepy voice answered.

"Christine, it's Mr. Alphabet. I'm sorry, did I wake you?"

"Oh, don't worry about it. I've got to get up anyway. I've got another off-duty day today but, like an idiot, I promised my Mum that I'd take her to the supermarket because her car's broken down. I'm supposed to be meeting her at 8. What time is it, by the way?"

Mr. Alphabet looked at the smart new watch which he had purchased the previous day in Dorrid's. "It's 7.52 now."

"Saints alive. I've got 8 minutes. I've got to go. Rats, I wanted to hear all about the House of Ghouls!" Christine joked.

Mr. Alphabet replied that his viewing had been very positive and that he had another appointment to view the property at 9. "It's a wonderfully bright morning, Christine. If you can face it, why don't you come over after your shopping trip?"

"What a great way to spend a day off! First the supermarket, then a haunted house. Is there no end to the fun?!"

Mr. Alphabet sounded hurt, "I quite understand if you'd rather not and I'd just like to thank you for all the help which you have given me."

He was about to conclude the call when Christine said, "Oh all right then, why not? I can't really meet anything or anyone too awful in broad daylight, now can I?"

Mr. Alphabet cheered up considerably at this. "I don't know about that. You haven't seen the estate agent yet!" he joked, little knowing how close to the mark his throw away comment was going to prove to be.

They both laughed and Christine rushed off to get ready for an exciting trawl along the butchery counter.

Not many minutes later, Mr. Alphabet, unable to contain his excitement, was in the lobby awaiting Eddie's arrival. 'I wish I could drive myself and not have to rely on the execrable Mr. Eccleston. How on earth do I know, come to that, that I can't drive? What a to-do!' Mr. Alphabet exclaimed to himself.

Eddie, however, may have many faults but being late was not one of them. Lateness, of course, might have indicated some inadequacy in his driving technique which would never do. So, at precisely 8.35, as arranged, the red Mazda arrived at the entrance to the hotel amid a shower of spraying gravel.

"Good morning, Mr. A. Sleep well, did you?" Eddie enquired through gritted teeth. Clearly, as predicted, his had not been a long night's sleep.

"Very well, thank you. Shall we press on?" countered Mr. Alphabet, anxious, as always, not to enter into any small talk with Eddie.

"Right. The papers you want are all here. You might want to have a quick look through them on the way there." Eddie handed over an enormous pile of papers, some of which looked like they might have been around when the Magna Carta was first being drafted.

"Judging by the speed at which we returned from the Grauen place last night, Mr. Eccleston, I'd say that I'll probably just about have time to peruse the top sheet before we arrive!" Mr. Alphabet was attempting to make a joke but this morning, unlike the previous night, Eddie was in no mood for pleasantries and was already revving the engine as Mr. Alphabet lowered himself into the not-too-comfortable bucket seats. 'Bucket!,' thought Mr. Alphabet. 'A bucket, or more appropriately a.. oh, no, not again…'

"Eddie, what is that thing called where you put all your rubbish, things you don't want? You know, often big, round…you get them in kitchens…"

" 'Bin', would that be?"

"That's it, bin."

"Why?" enquired Eddie, puzzled.

"Oh, no reason," Mr. Alphabet quickly replied, realising that he was almost thinking aloud. He'd have to watch that one. It could prove to be very dangerous.

Mr. Alphabet was unable to say much as Eddie was treating the traffic lights on Park Road as if they were the lights on the starting grid at Brands Hatch. There was no way that the expensive looking white limousine in the next lane was going to get away from the lights faster than them, try as it might. They took off so fast as the lights changed to green that Mr. Alphabet wondered whether a) he was going to end up in the back seat with the force of it and b) whether he was going to be able to hang on to the rather lovely scrambled eggs on toast which Daz had had sent up to his room for breakfast. Now, that would make a fine mess of the inside of Eddie's precious car.

A matter of moments later, they arrived outside the Grauen building which in the light of the bright winter morning was barely less intimidating than it had been the previous twilight.

Eddie, this time, had had the foresight to bring some oil with him – engine oil, obviously – and so they were soon through the gates. It was five minutes to nine and there was no sign of Grey.

"Perhaps he has overslept, sir," Eddie said with a slight hint of sarcasm in his voice.

"I doubt that, Eddie, but maybe we should go around to his cottage at the back gate to see that he is all right. I mean to say, he is rather old…"

"Good idea, sir, follow me." Eddie marched off as if he knew exactly where he was going which, naturally, he did not.

As they approached the cottage, they saw a tall man walk briskly up the side path to the cottage talking to a little black and tan dog who was trotting on his heels. "Comb snail! Snail!" they heard him call.

"Snail?" said Eddie. "That's a funny old name for a dog. Doesn't look that slow to me."

"I don't think that he was saying 'Snail', Mr. Eccleston. I think that maybe he wasn't speaking in English."

"Oh, I see. I'll bow to your superior knowledge on that one." 'Good idea!' thought Mr. Alphabet.

"What I'd like to know though is who the bloke is and what he's doing here," exclaimed Eddie.

"My thoughts exactly, Mr. Eccleston. My thoughts exactly."

Mr. Alphabet strode up to the front door of the ramshackle cottage and rapped firmly on the knocker. There was that eagle again, how strange!

There was silence from inside the cottage. He knocked again. Still nothing.

Finally, he and Eddie heard Grey's voice coming from somewhere at the back of the building.

"'Old yer 'orses. I'm not as young as I used to be." It seemed to take an age before the door creaked open and there stood Grey, bent over his stick and wearing a tweed jacket which definitely looked like it had seen better days. "What do you want to go knocking so bloomin' loud for? Enough to frighten a body half to death, that was!"

"Good morning, Grey. Sorry to have rushed you. I think we may have been a couple of minutes early. I do apologise."

"No matter, mister. It just takes a lot longer to do things these days than it used to. And another thing – I'm not used to having anyone round me or knocking on my door. I been on my own here so long now."

"But when we were walking through the grounds from the big house, we saw…" Eddie began but was stopped in his tracks by the heel of Mr. Alphabet's new brogues hitting him sharply on the ankle. "Oy, what was that for?" Eddie cried.

"What's that, my lad? What did you say you saw?" asked Grey.

Before Eddie could reply, Mr. Alphabet interrupted, "We saw how much work there must have been here for you, with the upkeep of your own cottage alone, never mind the work on the big house." Mr. Alphabet had quickly realised that the mystery of the stranger in the garden was probably not one which ought to be tackled head on with Grey and that a much more softly, softly approach was going to be the best way to get all the information he needed.

"Oh, aye. There was work enough. Work enough for the half dozen fellas who used to be here, never mind one poor old soul slaving on his own," Grey informed them.

"Perhaps you could tell us more about it as we look around the grounds, Grey?"asked Mr. Alphabet.

"Right you are, mister. I'll just get me wellies on."

"I'm beginning to think that it wasn't such a good idea wearing my brand new Italian suit I bought in Dorrid's sale and which cost me the best part of two weeks' wages," Eddie grumbled.

As they moved around the acres of grounds, stumbling over half buried tree roots and the remains of the herb garden's stone walls, Grey pointed out to Eddie and Mr. Alphabet the various plants, exotic and native, which he had propagated and nurtured. Finally, they came to a very secluded area of the garden in the corner furthest from the big house.

"You'll 'ave to push back them branches to get through to the other side," Grey said indicating a creeper which had tied itself in knots across the path. "Used to flower really beautiful that did, in summer, but it got too much for me."

Mr. Alphabet was the first to push through the overgrown plant and could not believe his eyes when he got to the other side. There was the most magnificent greenhouse, or rather 'hot house' as it would have been called at the time that it was constructed. It was as tall as a two storey building and was, obviously, mostly made up of glass panes, the majority of which were amazingly still in tact. Both ends of the greenhouse and several panels in the middle were made of stained glass with pictures of exotic and tropical plants, some of which Mr. Alphabet thought that he recognised.

"This is just incredible! And it's all so well preserved. It looks as if that creeper has made a protective …oh what is it now? A..B..C.. Soldiers carry them, boxers have them in their mouth. Oh this really is too bad!"

" 'Shield', mister?" asked Grey.

"That's it 'shield'", replied Mr. Alphabet looking around the greenhouse. "Whoever built this house must have had an extremely keen interest in botany," Mr. Alphabet addressed Grey.

"That they did, mister. Do you want to have a look inside? Course I got no idea what's going on in there. I haven't been in it for donkey's years."

"Yes, let's take a look." Mr. Alphabet could barely contain his excitement.

Eddie was first to the door of the greenhouse. He pushed it back and strode in, almost immediately regretting his rash act for he plunged above the knees into the dark green mossy slime which made up the floor of the place. "Oh, that's just great, that is. Ruined my suit, that has. And I'm supposed to be having lunch with a very important lady client who I was hoping would become a bit more than a client. What's she going to say when I turn up looking like the monster that just crawled from the deep?"

"If she has any sense, she will tell you that business and pleasure do not mix," Mr. Alphabet said with a smile.

'I'm beginning to think that this 'business' doesn't mix with anything,' Eddie thought to himself. Addressing Mr. Alphabet and not returning the smile, he said "Give me a hand to get out of this mess will you?"

Mr. Alphabet tried to help Eddie out of the slime but it was not an easy task because it seemed to be a bit like quick sand and the harder that Eddie struggled, the further he sank.

"Funny thing," said Grey, "This floor in here's never been right in all the years I've been here. We used to have walkways made from planks across it but it looks like they've either rotted away or sunk. If you just gets your suit ruined, you can count yourself lucky, lad. There's many a tale I could tell you about fellas coming down here to check out the plants and never being seen again."

This, understandably, did nothing to ease Eddie's panic.

"'Old on lad, I always used to leave a rope here, just in case." Grey turned around and picked up a large blue tow rope which he skilfully looped around Eddie's waist and he and Mr. Alphabet eventually managed to haul the angry estate agent out of the quagmire.

"It might have been an idea to tell me about that stinking mess," Eddie shouted at Grey.

"Well, maybe next time you won't just rush into things without thinking. There's a lesson in that, boy."

"Yes well, I think I've had about as much as I can take of lessons for the time being. If you'll excuse me I'm going back to the office to clean up and put in my insurance claim." With that he stalked away so quickly that Mr. Alphabet did not have the time to warn him about the green slime ruining the upholstery in his lovely sports car.

Chapter G

That day, Grey was keen to show every nook and cranny of the old building and its grounds to Mr. Alphabet and that final viewing, for indeed it was final, took the best part of six hours. Grey really need not have bothered, in fact, since the minute that he set eyes on the strange hot house, Mr. Alphabet had decided that this was the place for him.

It took a mere ten days to complete the purchase of the property which, as anyone who has ever been near an estate agent, or indeed a solicitor, knows is about as usual as going to a coffee shop and being served in under thirty minutes! Still, miracles do happen. The renovation of the building and the conversion into a school with all the necessary associated paraphernalia took somewhat longer, however.

Some four and a half years, or precisely fifty-two months later, Mr. Alphabet was almost ready to start considering the intricacies of the admission procedure to his new school. Of course, his first major problem was that without an admissions secretary, there would be no admissions procedure. But who was he to employ? He needed someone who was honest, reliable, trustworthy; someone who would be sympathetic to the parents and pupils but who, at the same time would take no nonsense and who would be able to sniff out dishonesty and disorganisation at five hundred paces. Where on earth to find such a person was a problem which kept Mr. Alphabet awake many a long night.

The great difficulty was that, in spite of living in the town for the previous fifty-two months, he had actually made friends with next to no-one. In point of fact, he was barely even acquainted with anyone, never mind on 'dinner over a nice glass of Californian Chardonnay' terms. So, he had no-one to ask.

"This really is a dilemma, Grey," he complained early one morning when the two of them were making their daily tour of the hothouse and garden. "You're about the only person I know in this town."

"What about that nice police lady who used to come over to see you? We 'aven't seen 'er in a long time 'ave we, mister?"

"I didn't think of Christine because she's been so busy with her sergeant's exams but I think that they must be coming to an end soon anyway. I'll give her a call right away. Grey, you are an absolute genius."

"Aye, I know that, mister," Grey replied modestly.

Mr. Alphabet could not wait to return to the house and get straight on the phone to Christine.

After five rings the telephone was answered. "Hello."

"Christine, it's…" "We are unable to take your call right now, but please do not hang up," the voice went on.

"Confounded machines!" shouted Mr. Alphabet. He had still not come to terms with the wonders of technology. When the voice stopped, he left his rather halting message. "Er..Christine, it's Mr. Alphabet. I was..er.. wondering how you had got on in your exams. And…er…I also have a slight dilemma which you might be able to help me with. Perhaps you could give me a call when it's convenient. I..er.. look forward to speaking to you and…" "Beeeep," interjected the machine. Mr. Alphabet slammed down the receiver, once again cursing modern gadgets, or more accurately, cursing his own inability to deal with them.

"Problem, mister?" came a voice behind him.

Mr. Alphabet jumped up as though he had been shot. "Grey, I have known you for more than four years and yet I don't think that I will ever get used to the way you are able to creep around so silently. And in answer to your question, my only problem is being stuck in the past, which is ever so slightly ironic because most of the past I can't remember anyway!"

Grey smiled knowingly and shuffled away on his stick. As he moved away, Mr. Alphabet watched his slow progress and thought how Grey's condition never seemed to alter. He never got any better or any worse. Come to think of it, he never appeared to be getting any older either. How on earth did he manage that? Mr. Alphabet knew that he personally was unable to look in the mirror without seeing yet another indication of the onset of old age. If it wasn't more grey hairs that he noticed, it was the fact that his forehead seemed to be getting higher and higher every day which could mean only one thing – receding hair! "I must ask Grey about that when I have a chance, but right now, I have more pressing matters to attend to like sorting out the paperwork in the cupboard under the stairs."

"The-cupboard-under-the-stairs-great-clearout" was something which had been hanging over him for a couple of years but the situation had latterly become critical because it was now only possible to keep the door closed by propping one of the heavy oak hall chairs against it. Each time that the door was opened, there was a risk that the whole jumbled mess of paper would come spilling out all over the hall floor. It was not that Mr. Alphabet was disorganised but he had just had far too much on his mind for the past few years to be able to think about something so seemingly trivial.

He had decided, however, that should the day dawn grey and miserable, today would be the day for starting the job. He had been somewhat crestfallen, therefore, to wake to dismal rainy weather which looked set to continue for the entire day. "No excuse for procrastination now," he thought.

Once he had begun the task, he actually found it incredibly satisfying to throw away so much rubbish – catalogues from companies for whose goods he had absolutely no use, take away pizza menus, bank statements indicating a depressingly diminishing balance. Some five and a half hours and thirty-two large bin bags later, he came across a small brown packet.

He opened the packet and found some rather odd looking seeds. Twenty-six of them to be precise. "Oh, I remember these. They were in with the money when Christine gave it to me. I must ask her if she knows anything about them."

"Let's 'ave a look at 'em, mister," Grey said from where he was standing in the doorway. At that, the packet shot up in the air and the seeds scattered over the polished wooden floor of the hallway.

"Grey, this has got to stop!" shouted Mr. Alphabet. "One of these days I'm going to be holding something a bit more dangerous than a packet of seeds, like perhaps the large meat cleaver from the kitchen and I might be forced to hack your stick in half with it!" They both laughed and Grey got down on his hands and knees to collect the seeds. 'There you are,' Mr. Alphabet thought to himself, 'how, at his age and in his condition does he crouch down and jump up so easily?'

53

"'Ain't never seen nothing like these, mister. They's whoppers, ain't they?" he said holding up what was indeed a very large seed.

"They do look quite interesting, but I'd say that having been sitting around for at least five years to my knowledge they're probably as dead as a..oh what is it..A..B.."

" 'Door nail', mister," replied Grey.

"No, no. It's a bird, I think. C.."

"Oh, that's a 'dodo' you're talking about." Grey had got used to Mr. Alphabet's difficulties with his memory and it had become rather like a game between them to see whether Grey could guess the word before Mr. Alphabet prompted his mind by arriving at the correct letter in the alphabet.

"Ah yes, 'dodo', that's it. Funny looking creature. Anyway, as I was saying, let's just bin the seeds along with all the other rubbish."

"Not so sure, meself," Grey replied. "No harm in trying 'em out now is there. I'll put 'em up the back in the hothouse where we've got that bit of spare ground. If they don't come through, nothing lost is there?"

"I suppose not. Go ahead then." Mr. Alphabet had learned not to argue with Grey who for a relatively easy going man could certainly dig his heels in when he felt strongly about something and was inclined to get his own way.

"I'll do it now before it gets dark."

"Oh, I don't think another day will matter, since they've been lying here neglected for such a long time. You go on home and get your dinner. They can wait until tomorrow," Mr. Alphabet told Grey.

"Oh no, mister. I needs to do it now. It's a full moon tonight, you see."

"Oh yes, I see," replied Mr. Alphabet, who patently obviously did not see but knew that to question was futile. "Off you go then."

Grey sprang up, in Mr. Alphabet's opinion, like a man half his age. How he could estimate this, however, is a mystery since he had absolutely no idea of how old Grey was.

"Good night then, mister. I'll see you in the morning."

Mr. Alphabet, who had turned back to enjoy the novel experience of being able to close the cupboard door completely, called "Good night" over his shoulder but Grey was already out of the house and well out of ear shot.

"Amazing," Mr. Alphabet smiled to himself.

Later that evening, Mr. Alphabet was trying to make himself something tasty for dinner. He was quite fed up with beans on toast or baked potato which seemed to have been his staple diet for the last several months but was not confident enough to experiment with any new dishes. As he was dishing up yet another plate of beans, much to his relief the telephone rang.

"Hello."

"Mr. Alphabet, this is Christine Campbell. I got your message and called as soon as I got back from work. How are you? How's it all going with the restoration project?"

At this Mr. Alphabet laughed, "You make it sound like a..what are those things called...the aristocracy live in them...oh..A..B..C.."

" 'Palace'?" Christine enquired.

"No, no, not quite that grand. D..E.."

" 'Castle', 'stately home'..." Christine sounded impatient. She had forgotten how irritating this problem of Mr. Alphabet could be. 'Come on, girl,' she told herself, 'it's not half as irritating for you as it must be for him.'

"That's it, Christine, 'stately home'," Mr. Alphabet replied gratefully.

"Well, it is pretty grand, isn't it?"

"Big, yes. Grand, no. Anyway, first of all I want to know how you got on with your exams. Am I addressing Sergeant Christine Campbell now."

"You are indeed!" the sergeant replied.

"Oh, well done, my dear. How marvellous! I knew you would have no problems with it."

"I don't know about no problems, Mr. A. I thought I was going to have to wait for old Inspector Irving to die before I would get the chance at promotion. As luck would have it, though, his wife decided that they should move to the seaside before they retired. And no, before you ask, I didn't bribe her."

They both laughed. "But you said that you'd got a problem that I might be able to help with," Christine went on.

"I have. The school's just about ready but now I've got the thorny issue of where to find my staff. In particular, where to find a really good admissions secretary. I was wondering if you knew anyone who might be suitable."

Without a moment's hesitation, Christine replied "Sure do. My Mum. She's been needing a nice little job like that since the doctor she was working for retired. She'd jump at it, I bet you."

Mr. Alphabet was quite taken aback at the speed with which he had been given his answer but there was no arguing with Christine's conviction. "Er, right. I'm not sure that it's going to be either a 'nice' or a 'little' job. I imagine it being quite hard work and of course I will need someone who takes no nonsense from anyone."

"Like I said, my Mum. She won't take any rubbish from anyone and that includes you, Mr. Alphabet!" Christine exclaimed.

Somehow, if Christine were anything like her mother, he did not find this at all hard to believe. "Right, well let's get her up here for an interview. When do you think would be convenient?"

"Tomorrow morning? 9.30?"

Mr. Alphabet got the distinct impression that getting her mother back into work was Christine's latest extra curricular activity. "Fine. What is she doing with herself at the moment if she's not working?" he enquired.

"Oh, not much really. Other than poking her nose into all my business of course!" Christine replied.

"Ah ha, I see."

"What? What do you see?" Christine asked.

"Oh nothing, my dear, nothing at all."

"Some things haven't changed a bit," Christine grumbled under her breath.

"What was that?" Mr. Alphabet enquired.

"Oh nothing, my dear, nothing at all," imitated Christine.

"Very well, I'll see your mother at nine in the morning. By the way, what's her name?"

"Enid. Enid Evans. She goes by her maiden name at work because she didn't want anyone to think that she was Scottish with the surname Campbell."

"Wh..?" began Mr. Alphabet.

"Don't even ask. One of these days, when you've got a spare ten hours, I'll go into the ins and outs of my family history with you. Until then just don't call my Mum, Mrs. Campbell."

"Got it. Bye then, Christine, and thanks so much for your help once again. I hope that now all the exams are over that we can meet up for a dinner some time."

"Love to. Got to fly now. Got a date. And you be sure not to tell my Mum about that too."

"Right you are. Mum's the word!" laughed Mr. Alphabet.

"Ha, ha. Very funny, I don't think. Night night then."

"Goodbye, my dear," said Mr. Alphabet replacing the receiver with a smile.

The next morning, Mr. Alphabet found himself to be curiously nervous about meeting Mrs. Evans. Christine had certainly painted a rather formidable picture of the lady. He was more than a little surprised, then, when the doorbell rang and he saw, framed by the massive doorway to the school, a small, gentle looking lady in her sixties with ice-white hair.

"Mrs. Evans?" he enquired.

"That's correct. Mr. Alphabet?" Mrs. Evans asked, glancing down in a horrified fashion at his feet.

His gaze followed, and he realised, to his embarrassment, that he was still wearing his decrepit carpet slippers with the enormous hole in the left toe. "Oh, I'm so sorry. I was just going to change these, do forgive me."

"Change them? I should think you'd do better to throw them straight in the bin. They look like they've seen better days."

Mr. Alphabet was beginning to realise that this was certainly an example of appearances being deceptive and perhaps Mrs. Evans was going to be exactly what he was looking for.

"Do come in, Mrs. Evans. Let's go through into my temporary study and we can discuss our future possible working relationship."

One and a half hours later, once Mrs. Evans had thoroughly interrogated Mr. Alphabet and finally condescended to take his job, they were taking a tour of the nearly completed school building, when Grey burst in shouting "'Ere, mister. Come quick. You's got to see what's 'appened in the 'ot-'ouse."

"And who might you be?" enquired Mrs. Evans sternly.

"I might ask you that same question. I'm bloomin' fed up with people coming traipsin' in here every five minutes demanding to know who I am. If it's not you, it's that blessed estate agent doing it," Grey grumbled.

Mr. Alphabet considered pointing out to Grey that it was actually more like five years than five minutes since he had met Eddie Eccleston but experience had taught him that this was not only a waste of time but would actually cause a stony silence which had been known to last for some four days and nights in the past.

"I, missis, I am Grey. Gardener here, man and boy, man and boy."

"You will not come marauding all over my school wearing those filthy, dirty wellies," Mrs. Evans shouted.

"Wha….?" Grey was stunned.

"Grey, I'd like you to meet Mrs. Evans our new school secretary. Mrs. Evans, Grey the gardener."

"Humph", Mr. Alphabet's two employees chimed in unison. This was perhaps not going to be a match made in heaven thought Mr. Alphabet.

"Anyway, as I was saying, mister, come and look at what's happened with them there seeds. Quick!" At that Grey was half way out of the door, followed closely by the other two.

On their way down the long garden path, Mr. Alphabet explained to Mrs. Evans about the seeds and the hot house.

"The man is as mad as a March hatter," she said, referring to Grey. "You say he only put the seeds in last night? How does he possibly think that anything…." She did not complete her sentence, however, because they had arrived at the back of the hot house where twenty-six plants, each one just over two feet high, were standing. They were standing on ground that until late the previous evening had been completely empty.

Mr. Alphabet rubbed his eyes. "Someone tell me that I'm not seeing things."

"Well if you are, then so am I, mister," replied Grey.

Chapter H

Mr. Alphabet, Mrs. Evans and Grey spent some forty-five minutes deliberating over the new plants. None of them had ever seen anything quite like it before, not even Mrs. Evans who seemed to feel that she was now a world expert in botany simply because she had spent thirty years standing at the kitchen window watching her husband as he pottered around their tiny back garden.

"I can't be sure," she said, "but it looks a lot like a large fern to me."

" 'Large'?" cried Grey. "If that's what it's done in one day, what on earth's going to happen next. And, incidentally, Clever Clogs, I ain't never seen a fern looking like that. If anything they looks like rubber plants. And giant ones at that." With that he cast a worried glance up to the ornate, and newly restored, roof of the glass house. "Do you want me to rip 'em up now, mister?" he asked Mr. Alphabet.

"I don't think we will, Grey. Let's wait and see how this thing progresses. It really is most interesting. I'd quite like to get an expert in from the botanical gardens to have a look at this."

At that Mrs. Evans, having no time for 'so-called experts', grunted and said, "Well, Mr. Alphabet, if that's all you want with me today, I'll be off home now. All this talking is not getting the baby dressed. I've got lunch to cook and I'll see you at nine o'clock sharp tomorrow morning, as agreed." Mr. Alphabet noticed that this was the second time that Mrs. Evans had mixed up her proverbs but said nothing. He was too busy wondering exactly when they had reached the agreement that Mrs. Evans would be starting the next morning. He found, in fact, that it suited him perfectly and thought that Mrs. Evans seemed to have been able to read his mind.

Grey, watching her stalk away down the path, grumbled something to the effect of "That woman is no better than she ought to be", which to Mr. Alphabet's mind was a rather illogical, nonsensical statement and was not worthy of an answer.

"Well, Grey, I'll leave you to it and come back in about an hour so that we can do our usual tour of the place."

"Right you are, mister," Grey replied, appreciating Mr. Alphabet's ability to know when he really was superfluous to requirements. Little did Grey know, in fact, but Mr. Alphabet was longing to get back inside and get on the telephone to the botanical gardens. Perhaps these seeds, at last, could be a way of tracing who he was and where he had come from.

Walking back towards the main building, he met the postman coming up the path carrying the usual supply of brown envelopes, some with red writing clearly visible through the address window. 'Ugh, more bills and final reminders,' thought Mr. Alphabet to himself. 'Pull yourself together man. This ignoring of the bills has got to stop because pretending that your problems are not there is not really an option and will not make them go away…Maybe tomorrow I'll phone the bank and try to discuss the matter with that nice Mr. Bennett.'

'That nice Mr. Bennett' must, however, have been gifted in the same way as Mrs. Evans, for as Mr. Alphabet was reaching for the telephone directory to look up the number of the botanical gardens, the phone rang.

It was a lengthy conversation between the two men but Mr. Alphabet was at last able to convince the bank manager that his plan was coming to fruition and that there would then be absolutely no cause for concern.

"Fine, Mr. Alphabet. I and the bank respect what you have planned but I have to say that it is now the 26th of May and if there are no deposits rolling in to your account by two months hence, we will have to seriously reconsider your position."

Mr. Alphabet eventually put the phone down with a sigh and wondered exactly what 'reconsidering his position' actually meant. Why couldn't these people speak plainly?

He sat at the bottom of the stairs with his head in his hands for several minutes and was surprised when he finally lifted his head and saw Mrs. Evans standing in front of him with a cup of tea in her hands.

"I thought that you might be needing this," she said and Mr. Alphabet was sure that for the first time he had detected a note of concern in her voice. "I was just getting my coat on and taking a last look around my office when I heard you on the phone."

"That's very kind of you. Please don't let me hold you up any more. I'll see you tomorrow morning."

"What are you talking about man? We've got work to do and if you think that I'm wasting a whole afternoon when we could be getting on with things then you're shouting up the wrong tree."

" 'Barking'," corrected Mr. Alphabet.

"That's charming, that is. I was only trying to help and I get called 'b....'".

"No, no. I was just saying that what you meant to say was 'barking up the wrong tree'." Mr. Alphabet tried, rather unsuccessfully, to smooth over the situation.

"I know what I meant to say and I'll thank you to remember that I *work* at this school and I haven't come here to learn," Mrs. Evans scolded.

"Oh, but I think that we're always learning throughout our life, don't you? It'd be a bit dull otherwise."

"That's as maybe but you can't teach an old fox new tricks," Mrs. Evans replied.

'Dog,' thought Mr. Alphabet. 'You can't teach an old dog new tricks.' If this short exchange of words had told him anything, however, it was that with Mrs. Evans his constant attempts at improving others were not always going to be taken kindly and so he kept his thoughts to himself.

"Did I hear you say that you had been taking a look around your office?" he asked his new secretary, unaware that he had allocated any of the rooms in the school to a specific purpose, apart from the classrooms of course.

"You did hear that, yes. Come on let's go and start sorting it out. We'll need to move things around, naturally."

"Naturally," repeated Mr. Alphabet a little sarcastically.

Mrs. Evans shot him what her husband called one of her 'sideways glances'. At least that is what he called them when she was in ear-shot. 'Death stares' was what he called them when he was one hundred percent certain that she could not hear him.

Mr. Alphabet followed her little bustling figure down the long east corridor to the large corner office with windows on two sides overlooking the area of garden which he and Grey had sown with wildflowers and where he could see one or two poppies and cornflowers just about ready to open. It really was a wonderful sight especially during the summer months.

"Of course, those weeds out there need to be seen to. Some nice rose bushes would be better," Mrs. Evans complained as she turned back from the window.

Mr. Alphabet would have liked to explain why it was important to propagate wild flowers and that they too had their own beauty but he remembered about not teaching an old 'fox' new tricks and simply said, "Actually, I had pencilled this office in as the one which I would be using."

"Oh, well, if it's only pencilled in, you can just rub it out then, can't you?" Mrs. Evans replied, in a matter of fact tone.

Mr. Alphabet realised that he, just like Mr. Bennett from the bank, had not made himself clear and in so doing had managed to deprive himself of a lovely corner office overlooking one of his favourite bits of the garden. He knew, however, that resistance was a waste of time and simply asked Mrs. Evans how she would like the furniture arranged and if there was anything else which she needed in there.

Once the office had been arranged to her liking, they began the lengthy task of working out the admission criteria and policy. Mr. Alphabet had some very specific ideas about these and realised that it was going to take some explaining to his secretary.

"The school will admit children from the age of eleven. Ideally, I would like to begin with just one class of pupils aged eleven but that's not going to satisfy Mr. Bennett and the bank of Barr, Stead & Company. So, I think we'll have to go with five classes each with twenty six pupils. That'll give us…"

"A hundred and thirty," Mrs. Evans said before Mr. Alphabet could finish his sentence.

"My goodness, Mrs. Evans, you really are quick at maths, aren't you?" Mr. Alphabet complimented.

"Oh yes. They used to tease me at school and call me Euclid."

"Why would anyone tease you about being good at something? That doesn't seem to make a lot of sense but I suppose that perhaps the other children were envious?"

"Oh no, Mr. Alphabet. It wasn't the children. It was the teachers," Mrs. Evans said.

"The teachers?" Mr. Alphabet was astonished. "I don't believe it! That is disgraceful! Well, in this school there will be none of that from teachers, children or staff, I can assure you."

"Jolly good. Now, back to the number of classes and that," said Mrs. Evans. Mr. Alphabet could see that Mrs. Evans was going to be invaluable at keeping him in order and organised.

"Right, yes. As I was saying, five classes. The pupils will start at the school when they are thirteen and we will take them through to their national exams. Each pupil's first name and surname must begin with the same letter." Mrs. Evans was looking more and more puzzled but she decided not to interrupt at this point. "What's more there must not be two pupils in the same class who have the same initials as each other. Do you see what I mean?"

"Er, well, no. Not exactly," Mrs. Evans said, rather understating her confusion.

"O.k. In each case there will be one pupil with the initials A.A., one B.B., one C.C., one…."Mr. Alphabet explained.

"I get you, I get you. I don't think we need to go through the whole alphabet, do we? What happens about finding people with X.X., Z.Z., Q.Q, for example?" she asked.

"Well we'll overcome that problem as and when it arises. To coin a phrase, Mrs. Evans, 'where there's a will there's a way.'" Mr. Alphabet smiled.

"I prefer the phrase 'where there's a will there's a huge family argument about money'!" Mrs. Evans laughed. Mr. Alphabet joined in marvelling at both the complexity of the English language and the fact that Mrs. Evans actually appeared to have a sense of humour.

"So, if I've got this right there's going to be this alphabet initial thing in all five classes, right?" Mrs. Evans checked.

"Right."

"All I can say is that you don't like to make life easy for yourself, do you?"

"Life has not been easy, Mrs. Evans, but just because something's difficult it doesn't mean that it isn't worth doing."

"Can I just ask why you're doing it?" Mrs. Evans enquired.

"The alphabet has helped me immensely through my recent difficulties and I somehow feel that it brings me luck."

"O.k. Well it's your school and if you feel that's how you want it then so be it," she said. As she turned away to pick up a notebook from the huge mahogany desk which was now hers, Mr. Alphabet thought that he heard her mumble something like "How on earth we're ever going to manage this, I don't know," but he chose to ignore her and move on with the planning.

"So," she said, turning back to him, notebook at the ready, "we're going to have some kind of entrance exam are we?"

"Indeed we are, but it's not going to be like any other entrance exam," he replied.

"Now, why doesn't that surprise me?" Mrs. Evans exclaimed. "So what is it going to be like then?"

"Well, you know how with the regular exams the children feel under pressure and get sick with the worry of the whole event? Instead of imposing anything on them, we're going to allow students to choose which two subjects they would like to take for the exam and as long as those subjects start with the same letter as their initials, then they may do it."

"Don't you think that you're getting a bit obsessed with this alphabet and initial business?" Mrs. Evans asked.

"Maybe yes, but isn't that better than being obsessed with putting children through a kind of living hell where there is simply pressure on them to succeed at subjects which are imposed upon them?"

"I suppose you're right. Do you also mean to say that those are the only subjects that they will learn at the school, as well?"

"Not at all," Mr. Alphabet reassured her. "They will do all the core subjects but the choice of optional subjects will be left entirely to them."

"Good, I should hope so too. So, how are we going to get people to apply for this school. I mean to say, it's not your usual run of the meal place, is it?"

"No it's not your usual run of the *mill* and the question of getting people to apply has been perplexing me slightly," Mr. Alphabet replied.

"We could just advertise, I suppose, but I don't know how many people are going to take a chance on a new school. How about if you go round to middle and senior schools and talk to some of the teachers? Because you might be as nutty as a fruit tree but I think that people are going to really believe in you."

Mr. Alphabet was a little overwhelmed by Mrs. Evans' praise. "Why, thank you. Do you know that that might not be a bad idea."

"I do have them occasionally you know…despite what Mr. Campbell might say."

For a moment, Mr. Alphabet was a little confused about who Mr. Campbell was but then remembered the business about Mrs. Evans keeping her maiden name and made himself a mental note to ask her about that one day when she was in a more amenable mood. If such a day were ever to arrive was, at that moment, somewhat debatable in Mr. Alphabet's opinion.

The next couple of weeks were very busy ones because he had appointments to see teachers in all the local schools. This was not an easy task because he could only see them during breaktimes and lunch time. One or two he was able to see after school but they were often incredibly busy with the increasing amounts of administration and bureaucracy which were now involved in being a teacher.

"There just aren't enough hours in the day any more to do all the paperwork required. Something has to be put to one side and unfortunately that something seems to be actual teaching," one extremely harassed English teacher told him during his second day of meetings. "I think that I'm just going to have to give it all up because I came into teaching in order to teach, not to fill out forms." She really was very upset and it gave Mr. Alphabet an idea.

"If you had the option, would you stay in teaching and move to a school where the emphasis was on developing the child rather than on destroying the rain forest?" he asked Miss Ellis, the teacher concerned.

"I'd go tomorrow but it's just going to be the same everywhere," she replied.

"That's where you're wrong, my dear." He went on to outline his plan to her and found that by the end of the brief seven minutes which she could spare him, he had the first member of his new teaching staff.

The same thing happened time after time and after four days, he had employed his whole team for the next academic year. That evening he was so excited at his achievement that he rushed in, immediately phoned Mrs. Evans and told her the good news.

"Well, I don't want to pour cold oil on what you've done but the idea was to get children interested in taking the exam because that way you can have money coming in and keep Barr, Stead and Company happy. All you've done is just agree to spend a fortune on salaries for the new teachers. A fortune which you haven't got, I might add." If there was one thing which Mrs. Evans could never be accused of it was mincing her words and Mr. Alphabet put the phone down a little more deflated than when he had picked it up.

The following day, he called Miss Ellis and told her about his difficulties about how to advertise the school. "The problem is," she told him, "all the kids have already taken the entrance exams and got into the schools they wanted to go to, so you're going to be left with the ones who didn't get in to their first choice or even didn't pass at all. Either that, or they're just going to stay where they are and put up with not achieving their best."

"Miss Ellis, I think that we both agree that no child must be written off and far from feeling that I am 'left with these children', I am sure that they are exactly the children who I am looking for."

"I see what you mean," she said and they had soon put together a flyer which was to go out to all schools in the surrounding six counties along with an application form for the forthcoming examination for entry to….to what? Mr. Alphabet realised in all the work and activity that he had not actually thought of a name for the school.

"I'll get back to you on that Miss Ellis," he said.

"Evelyn, please," she said.

"Certainly, Evelyn. I'd like to offer you the same courtesy in return but I'm afraid that I don't know my first name."

Miss Ellis was about to ask what he meant by that when the bell rang to signal the end of break and she quickly ended the call.

"That's another thing which we won't have in my school, the wretched bell," Mr. Alphabet said to himself. It was not, of course, said to himself because he turned to see Grey who had, as usual, entered the room utterly silently, in spite of the hob-nail boots which he was wearing in what can only have been a deliberate snub to Mrs. Evans and her 'rotten parkit floor'.

"So what will you 'ave then, mister," Grey enquired.

"Yet another question I am not at liberty to answer at the moment, Grey. My life seems to be full of unanswered questions," Mr. Alphabet returned with a weary sigh.

Chapter I

Later that afternoon, Mrs. Evans, Grey and Mr. Alphabet were sitting at the table in the vast kitchen having a cup of tea. In spite of being at loggerheads most of the time, Mrs. Evans and Grey had got into the habit of taking their tea together at four o'clock every day. Mr. Alphabet felt that it was perhaps just the opportunity for both of them to sharpen up their skills in arguing and 'putting people in their place'.

This afternoon, however, there were more important issues on the agenda than such things as who knows the best remedy for removing scorch marks from a polished table. The three of them were trying to come up with a suitable name for the school.

"You could just call it what the old place 'as always been called – 'Grauen'," Grey suggested.

"I don't know about that," replied Mr. Alphabet. "I can't figure out why but there just seems something a bit sinister about it."

"I agree with Mr. A," said Mrs. Evans. "It sounds quite horrible to me. Anyway, we need something more catchy, that sounds more like a school. Like 'Greycoats', for example."

"I like that, but I know for a fact that it's already been used. This is the problem, you see, everything will have already been used and we risk mixing ourselves up with another school," Mr. Alphabet said.

"What about if you use something to do with your name? It's not likely that that could be mixed up with anything or anyone else," Mrs. Evans suggested.

"Good idea, Mrs. Evans." Mr. Alphabet was encouraged but they still could not think how to incorporate his name into the name of the school.

"Well," he said after draining his teacup, "if I don't think of something soon, the bank will withdraw their ...oh what's that thing called...A..B... where they give you money...C.."

" 'Charity', mister?" Grey suggested.

"I hardly think Messrs Barr. Stead and Company are in the habit of giving charity to anyone, Grey, do you? No, they give it to you and you have to pay it back with interest. Oh rats...D...E.."

"That'll be a loan, you're talking about it," Mrs. Evans put in.

"That's it. A 'loan'," Mr. Alphabet said in a relieved tone. Grey shot Mrs. Evans an angry look because she knew fully well that this was a game which he and Mr. Alphabet had played for many years and it was no business of hers to butt in like some 'Johnny come lately'.

"Let's not get sidetracked anyway," Mr. Alphabet said, casting Grey a warning look. "If the bank withdraw their loan then all this will be purely academic."

"That's it," cried Mrs. Evans. "Why don't we call it Mr. Alphabet's Academy?"

"'Ow about including something to do with you're A, B, C business 'cos you're going to be 'aving all those peculiar rules about the children in the classes?" Grey proposed.

"I've got it. It's going to be 'Mr. Alphabet's A-Z Academy'. How does that sound? Perfect! You see how good it is when we can all work together?"

"Humph!" Grey and Mrs. Evans mumbled in unison as they stood up scraping their chairs a little too noisily over the flagstones for Mr. Alphabet's liking.

Later that day he called all his new recruits to tell them about the school's new name and that they could start handing out the application forms as soon as possible. As he finished making the final call, he hoped to himself that these men and women were going to be easier to deal with and would get on better than his two present employees.

It was now with excitement that Mr. Alphabet went downstairs to collect the post every morning because he was looking forward to seeing all the application forms come rolling through the door. For the first few days when nothing arrived, he was not unduly concerned because it took more than a moment to make the huge decision of which school to send your children to. When the absence of forms continued, however, he began to worry that this venture really was not going to work and he was starting to formulate in his head the letter which he would send to the bank offering to hand over the school to them as payment of his debts. "Dear Messrs. Barr, Stead and Company, Since you have given me such a short time in which to start repaying my loan and as I am clearly singularly incapable of doing this, you can stick the school up…."

Luckily, his thoughts were interrupted, as usual, by Mrs. Evans bearing a cup of tea. "Still nothing, Mr. A," she asked.

"Nothing at all, Mrs. Evans, I'm afraid. Sadly, I think that we might just have to give up on the whole idea."

"We'll do no such thing. Do you think that's what Edmund Hilary and Sherpa Tensing thought when they were half way up Everest 'Oh, it's actually much bigger than we thought, we'd better just jack the whole idea in'? Or do you think that's what the people thought when they were building the Titanic 'This job really is too big, let's just forget it'. No wait, maybe that's not such a good example." For once, Mrs. Evans had spotted one of her own verbal faux pas. "You know what I mean, anyway. You just hang on, be patient and it'll sort itself out. I'm just off to polish the parquet in the main hall, is there anything you need me to do after that?"

Mr. Alphabet replied in a dejected voice, "No, nothing at all."

"Right you are. Well don't sit there being miserable all day, make yourself useful." As she turned to leave the room, she called over her shoulder, "I suppose that you did tell the Post Office that the building's name had changed didn't you?"

"Oh good heavens, no I didn't. Mrs. Evans, you're a marvel. That'll be it, won't it?"

"I'd say that's every chance of 'being it', yes. It's not exactly easy to deliver mail to an address when you don't even know it exists, is it?"

"Oh I can't believe I was so silly," Mr. Alphabet laughed.

"Can't you?" Mrs Evans questioned in a voice which clearly indicated that she was having no difficulty in believing it at all.

"I'm going to call them up straight away," he said.

"Good idea. Well, I can't stand around here gassing all day, I've got work to do. And remember after you've phoned the Post Office don't keep checking the letter box every five minutes because you know what they say 'a watched boil never pops'."

'I think you'll find that what they say is 'a watched pot never boils', Mr. Alphabet thought to himself but, as ever, did not voice his thought in part because he was trying to dispel from his mind all ideas of boils popping.

69

Mrs. Evans went off to hunt out the floor polisher which was her pride and joy even though floor polishing could not be said to be strictly in the job description of a regular school secretary. This, however, was no regular school and she was no regular school secretary.

The phone call to the Post Office took a matter of minutes and Mr. Alphabet was reassured by the supervisor he spoke to who told him that there was a sack of mail for a 'Mr. Alphabet's A-Z Academy' blocking the hallway outside his office as they spoke.

The following morning, in spite of Mrs. Evans warnings about boils popping, Mr. Alphabet had been waiting in the hallway for forty five minutes when the postman came struggling up the drive, dragging behind him a large grey sack. "This is more post than I normally have to deliver to a whole street at Christmas," he grumbled as he heaved the sack up the front steps and into the hall.

As Mr. Alphabet looked at the sack he felt, in fact, as though it was Christmas and his birthday rolled into one. "Thank you so much for that. Let me give you something for your trouble," he said to the postman. "Wait there a minute, I've got just the thing."

Mr. Alphabet scurried off and the postman waited excitedly thinking that this was sure to be something good. When he returned, Mr. Alphabet was holding a brown paper bag with something inside it. He thrust it into the postman's hands and closed the front door because he simply could not wait to begin going through the contents of the sack.

As the postman walked down the gravel drive he reached inside the bag and pulled out a book entitled 'Coping with Back Strain' by the Italian author, L. Umbago. "Great!" he exclaimed. "I expect he thinks he's really funny."

Back inside the school building, Mr. Alphabet was sitting on the floor opening the first of the letters. Mrs. Evans came in some fifteen minutes later to begin her day's work and found him surrounded by torn envelopes and with a neat pile of application forms next to him. She held her hand out to Mr. Alphabet and offered him what was in it. "I just met the postman at the bottom of the drive. He didn't seem to be very happy and he told me to tell you that if you try to play a joke like that on him again, you will be doing more than 'coping with back strain'. Then he went on to say something about a 'wooden overcoat' but I didn't stay there long enough to listen. He really was a bad-tempered young man." Mrs. Evans suddenly noticed that throughout this exchange, Mr.

Alphabet had not once lifted his head. "Have you been listening to a word I have said?" she asked.

"Sorry what was that? Oh, good morning, Mrs. Evans. What's that you've got there?"

"Oh, never mind," she sighed. He really could be the most exasperating man at times. She put the unwanted book down.

"Have a look at some of these applications. These children are wonderful. They're exactly what I'm looking for." He handed her the ever increasing pile of forms.

"Which ones?"

"All of them," he replied.

"But there's already more than a hundred here and you're not even a tenth of the way through that bag. You can't have them all, surely. You're going to have to do some weeding out."

"Oh, don't say that, Mrs. Evans. One man's weed is another man's flower, as they say."

"Do they say that? I've never heard that. I'll have to remember that one," she said.

"I doubt that you will," Mr. Alphabet muttered under his breath.

"What was that?"she asked.

"Oh, nothing, nothing."

"Well, anyway, whatever you say about water and flour, we're going to have to go through these because there's no way we can have them all here for an exam."

Mr. Alphabet looked downcast, "I know you're right, of course, but where do we even start because they're all so good."

"Why don't you get Miss Ellis to come in and give us a hand because she's used to this exam setting business?"

"Good plan. I'll give her a call right away."

"That's a good idea. It's nine fifteen in the morning. I'm sure that a teacher won't be busy at nine fifteen on a school day!" Mrs. Evans scolded.

"Sarcasm will get you nowhere, Mrs. Evans. Point taken. I'll try to call at lunch time and in the meantime maybe we can go through some more of these."

They moved the bag into Mrs. Evans' office and set to work but were soon disturbed by a tapping at the window which seemed to be growing more and more insistent. Without looking up, Mrs. Evans said, "That'll be that lilac tree. I keep telling Grey that it's too big and he needs to get rid of it before its branches actually break through the window but he never listens to a word I say and you're too soft with him."

Mr. Alphabet had, however, looked up during this diatribe and saw the face of a very distressed Grey at the window. He rushed over and flung the window open.

"Come to the 'ot-'ouse, quick," Grey shouted. Those plants…one of 'em 'as got an enormous flower on it the like of which I've never seen. And another thing…" Before he could go on, Mr. Alphabet and Mrs. Evans were already out of the room and making for the garden.

The three of them rushed down the garden and as they approached they could see through the glass the plants whose tips had been touching the roof of the hot-house for the past week and a half. In amongst them was something which looked like an upside down bell, about two feet high and vivid fuchsia pink.

"My goodness…" began Mr. Alphabet.

He was interrupted by a retching sound from behind him. He turned to see Mrs. Evans bent double, clutching her stomach and trying her utmost not to be sick.

"Are you all right?" he asked her.

She moved back up the garden about twenty feet and called out to him, "All right? Do I look all right? What in James' name is that awful smell? Is that you, Grey? Have you been wearing your socks for a week again, or what?"

Mr. Alphabet turned back to the hot-house and said, "She's right, there really is a terrible smell and it seems to be coming from in there." He pointed straight at the big pink flower.

"Can't smell anything meself, mister," Grey said.

A voice came from way back up the garden, "Why doesn't that surprise me?"

"Now, now, you two. Don't start." Mr. Alphabet inched his way towards the glasshouse, nervous that he might have the same reaction as Mrs. Evans had had to the dreadful stench. "Ooo, it smells like putrefied horse manure and lots of it!" he exclaimed. I need to get in there and see what this is all about but I'm not sure that I can cope with the smell.

"D'you want to borrow my scarf." Grey held out the garment to Mr. Alphabet who was loathe to take it because he was not sure where the worst smell lay. Grey had been wearing this scarf every single day that Mr. Alphabet had known him, whatever the weather or temperature. "It's awfully kind of you to offer, Grey, but do you know what, I've got one of those plasterers masks up in the shed, I'll go and fetch that and wrap a duster round my face." Mr. Alphabet raced up the garden and was back in no time looking like an exotic highwayman ready to rob you of all your cleaning products.

"I'm going in. Wish me luck," he called out, but neither of them did. Mrs. Evans was afraid to open her mouth to say anything at that moment for fear that another wave of nausea might overtake her.

They could see Mr. Alphabet through the glass as he gingerly approached the flower. Although the image was somewhat distorted by the panes, Mrs. Evans thought that it was possibly the most beautiful flower she had ever seen and it quite put Mr. Campbell's begonias to shame. Not that she would ever tell Grey that, of course.

Mr. Alphabet managed to stay in the hot-house for just under four minutes. By the time he emerged he had turned a delicate shade of green and was, just like Mrs. Evans, having difficulty managing to keep his breakfast down.

"That is the strangest, most wonderful, most unpleasant experience I have ever had in my life. What an absolute dichotomy!" he exclaimed.

"I don't know what that means but if it means something's died in there then it's absolutely right," Mrs. Evans said, pinching her nose tightly shut as she spoke.

"That's not what it means but I do see your point. Have you ever heard of a plant smelling like that, Grey?" he asked.

"I don't know what all the fuss is about. I've never understood what people are going on about when they talk about the smell of flowers. I can't never smell nothing."

Under ordinary circumstances, Mr. Alphabet would have felt nauseous hearing Grey's triple negative but on this occasion there was much greater cause for nausea.

"We have to get someone in from the botanical gardens and find out what this is. I meant to ring them weeks ago but I got sidetracked," said Mr. Alphabet.

"I don't call it 'sidetracked' trying to keep the place going and keep us all in jobs," Mrs. Evans put in. "Sometimes there are more important things in life than flowers, you know."

Grey's sole response to this was "Humph!" as he stomped away up the garden.

"It would seem that you and Grey are not quite in agreement on that one," smiled Mr. Alphabet. "I see what you mean but you must admit that this really is very interesting."

"I'm not admitting anything." Mrs Evans seemed to be recovering from her bout of sickness and looking at her watch she added, "I will admit that we have just wasted nearly fifty minutes doing this and we've still got hundreds of envelopes to go through so let's get to it."

"But, I have to call someone at the botanical gardens and get them to come and take a look at this," Mr. Alphabet complained.

"That can wait until tomorrow after we've sorted out all the applications and after you've called Miss Ellis. One more day isn't going to make a lot of difference, is it?"

Mrs. Evans had spoken in her most imperious tone of voice and Mr. Alphabet knew that if he did not compromise, his life would be very difficult for the next few hours. No, probably more likely, the next few weeks.

He started to follow her back up the garden and as he went he glanced over his shoulder. The flower looked magnificent, all two and a half feet of it. He felt sure that it had been a good six inches shorter than that when he first set eyes on it but decided that his frequently unreliable brain must be playing tricks on him.

Chapter J

Mr. Alphabet had managed to get hold of Evelyn Ellis at lunchtime and she had kindly agreed to come up immediately after Poetry Club at school was over. Consequently, when six had chimed from the large clock in the entrance hall and she had still not arrived, Mr. Alphabet started to worry about her. Perhaps she had had an accident. Perhaps she didn't want to work for him any more. Perhaps she was just totally unreliable. His mood shifted by the minute and so he was completely unready to greet a sobbing Evelyn as she came in through the huge oak front doors.

"My dear, whatever's the matter?" Mr. Alphabet asked.

"Oh, I've just been given an absolute ticking off by Mr. Hudson, our headmaster."

"Why?" Mr. Alphabet had dismissed all thoughts of unreliability and fickleness in Miss Ellis and could now no longer imagine this kind and friendly girl doing anything to upset anyone.

Evelyn sniffed and spoke through the tears which were still running down her face, "We're supposed to do mid-half-term bi-monthly statistics on pupil attendance and punctuality and they were due to be on the headmaster's desk by eleven today. Normally, they're due there by eleven fifteen but apparently he had told everyone at a meeting last Thursday evening that he needed them earlier but I wasn't there because I was taking the fourth year on a trip to see the matinee production of Phedra and so I didn't know and I got them in at eleven twenty and I was five minutes late and…" She ran out of breath and began to sob deeply.

There was a noise behind them and Mr. Alphabet turned to see Mrs. Evans scurrying down the corridor carrying a tray of tea and biscuits. She seemed to have an extra sense that could sniff out trouble or distress at a great distance and clearly there is only one remedy – a cup of tea.

"Come along, dear," Mrs. Evans said to Evelyn, "let's go and have this in my office and you'll feel much better."

"Thank you," Evelyn gurgled. She seemed to have used up her supply of tissues and Mr. Alphabet handed her his handkerchief. At this Evelyn began to cry more, "Oh, you're both so kind to me."

"Nonsense, we're just thinking about ourselves. We need you to sort yourself out because we've got a lot of work to do," Mrs. Evans replied in what sounded like a stern manner but the gentle look which both Mr. Alphabet and Evelyn saw in her eyes gave her away a little.

"Of course. Let's go," Evelyn said. Either Mrs. Evans' words or her look seemed to have worked and they all headed to the office.

After the cup of tea and a few biscuits, Evelyn seemed to have regained her composure entirely and threw herself into the sorting of applications with a vengeance. "You seem to have renewed energy," Mr. Alphabet said to her.

"Yes I jolly well have. We're going to show people like Mr. Harry Hudson that there are other ways of running a school, other ways of dealing with pupils, parents and teachers. Ways that don't involve making people feel that they're at the bottom of the pile and that's where they're going to stay."

"Oh yes, there's more than one way to skin a fish, that's what I always say," agreed Mrs. Evans.

Evelyn looked enquiringly at Mr. Alphabet who just shook his head with a wry smile and mouthed 'Don't even ask' to her.

Without lifting her head, Mrs. Evans said, "And what are you two whispering about? Don't you know that it's the ignorantest thing you can do?" Mr. Alphabet and Evelyn had great difficulty containing their amusement at this and both buried their heads back in the forms which they were reading.

Three and a half hours later, when they had opened every envelope in the sack they had three piles of paper in front of them. The first consisted of two letters from companies; one, offering to sell a time-share apartment in Corfu Town and the other, ride-on scooters for the elderly, neither of which Mr. Alphabet considered particularly appropriate for a school. "How after only one week, do these sharks get names and addresses?" He wondered out loud.

The second pile had the twelve application forms which had been rejected because they had clearly been written by parents and the third pile was made up of the remaining thirteen hundred and fifty two forms which had to be kept at all costs.

"This is not looking good, is it?" Mr. Alphabet said dejectedly.

"That's a bit of an understatement," Evelyn replied.

"We're going to have to think of some other way of narrowing these down. And quickly because we've already used up three weeks of the two months which the bank gave us," Mrs. Evans said.

"No. Out of the question. All of these children deserve a chance and we're going to get them all up here to do the exam." Mr. Alphabet was adamant. Mrs. Evans face fell. "Do you mean to tell me that I am going to have two thousand seven hundred and four feet traipsing across my lovely parquet floor?" she complained.

"Firstly, your 'parquet floor' is not yours. Secondly, there are going to be a good deal more feet than that 'traipsing' over it before our time is out here. And thirdly, and most importantly, this school is here for the benefit of the children. It is not about your floor. It is not about you. It is not about me. It is not about Miss Ellis. It is about the children. Do I make myself clear?" Mrs. Evans had never heard Mr. Alphabet speak so firmly. In fact she had never heard anyone speak to *her* so firmly. Once she had recovered from the initial shock, she found that, although she would never admit it, she quite liked it.

"Yes, you make yourself perfectly clear," she replied, trying to sound disgruntled.

"If we are going to set exams for all these pupils, we've got the added problem of having to compile the papers. There must be about a hundred and seventy different subjects which have been requested here. It's not just your usual English and Maths, is it?" Miss Ellis commented.

"No, it's not." Mr. Alphabet looked downcast again.

"Well, it's Friday tomorrow. Why don't we phone up all the other new teachers, get them over here tomorrow evening and we'll just have to get all the exams written over the weekend because we need to be having the children sit them the following weekend," Miss Ellis suggested.

"Do you think they'd do it? It's a lot to ask," said Mr. Alphabet in a concerned voice.

"It's one thirty in the morning and I'm here, aren't I? Believe me, they'll do anything to get out of the situation that we're all in. And if they won't, then they're not going to be right for you and your school, are they?" answered Evelyn.

"I expect you're right. I'll telephone them in the morning and..." Mr. Alphabet began.

"Oh no, you won't. I'll do it. They'll not argue with me," Mrs. Evans interrupted. The other two had no difficulty believing the truth of this.

"Thank you, Mrs. Evans. Well, I think that it's time to turn in." Mr. Alphabet called for a taxi for the ladies and made his weary way up to bed. He got into bed thinking that maybe, just maybe this was actually going to work. He fell asleep before you could say the word 'insomnia'.

Mr. Alphabet need have worried about neither the dedication of his new team nor about Mrs. Evans ability to 'motivate' them. By seven the following evening, all twenty-six teachers were sitting in the large staff room with a vast tray of tea in front of them, courtesy of Mrs. Evans. There were those on the staff who on a Friday evening might have preferred something a little stronger but after a hard week at work, they were frankly grateful for any refreshment on offer.

That entire weekend was spent compiling exams in subjects ranging from algebra and anatomy, to zoology and Zoroastrianism. Questions flew backwards and forwards across the staff room. People were lying on the floor, sitting on the windowsills, pacing the room seeking inspiration. Trays of refreshment came and went almost without anyone noticing. At all hours of the day and night there was someone in the room working.

By three on Sunday afternoon, Mr. Alphabet had left the room only three times and those absences were only for brief visits to the bathroom. He had slept for only fifteen minutes at around midnight on Saturday, had eaten almost nothing and was looking slightly less than his best.

Mrs. Evans came in, put down another tray of tea, took Mr. Alphabet by the hand and led him from the room. Outside in the hallway, she said, "Come on. This is doing nobody any good. If you half kill yourself, you're not going to be much use to teachers, children or Barr, Stead and Company, are you? You need some air. Let's at least go for a walk around the garden. I'm sure that Grey is missing you."

"All right, but only for a few minutes because there's so much left to do." With that they headed off into the garden.

On the beautiful vast lawn at the side of the building they found Grey cutting the lawn with his ride-on lawnmower. Mr. Alphabet smiled when he saw the old gardener charging up and down more like he was practising for a Grand Prix than mowing a lawn which was as flat and green as a snooker table. It was ironic that it had taken about five months to get Grey to accept that he needed to give up the old hand driven machine with which it took about four hours to mow the lawn. He had been insistent that he did not want any 'new-fangled gadgets', that this old lawnmower had served him perfectly well 'man and boy' and that anyway he couldn't drive so what would he want this new thing for? Now, some two months after the mower had been purchased it was almost impossible to get Grey off the thing and it seemed that the lawn needed mowing every day, sometimes twice a day. So it was possible to 'teach an old fox new tricks'.

As he swung the machine back round at the end of the lawn, he noticed Mr. Alphabet and Mrs. Evans and came hurtling over towards them. There was a nervous moment when the two of them felt that the machine might be out of control and they were considering jumping out of the way when Grey shuddered to a halt eight inches from their feet.

The gardener smiled as he saw the look of terror on Mrs. Evans' face, a look which was shortly followed by one of her 'death stares'. Mr. Alphabet thought how much younger Grey looked when he wasn't walking and wondered to himself again about his stick and his ability to move quickly and silently when the need arose.

"Sorry I haven't been out to see you over the past couple of days, Grey, but as you know I've been really busy. How's it all going? How are things in the hot-house? How's our beautiful, malodorous plant?"

"Oh it's gone," Grey replied.

"What do you mean gone? What? The whole plant's gone?" Mr. Alphabet was stunned.

"No, not the 'ole plant but the flower's gone."

"How? Why? When did it go?" Mr. Alphabet asked.

"It went the day after you saw it. I kept going back all day to look at it and it jist kep' on growing. By the time I turned in for the night, it was as tall as the glass-house itself."

"That's ridiculous. That'd make it about twenty feet high. You don't half exaggerate, Grey," Mrs. Evans reproached. "I can't abear tall-tale tellers."

'Can't 'abide' or can't 'bear',' thought Mr. Alphabet to himself but said nothing to that effect.

"I ain't telling tales. It was tall, mind," Grey laughed. "The top of the petals was touching the roof, I tell you."

"O.k. so where is it now? Let's see it." Mrs. Evans was still disbelieving.

"You can't. It's gone"

"Why not? Where's it gone?" This was only adding fuel to her opinion that the gardener was either out of his mind or was a pathological liar.

"I dunno. When I went there first thing the next morning, half expecting to see the roof off of me lovely glasshouse, there it was gone!"

"Well, what had happened? Had it died? Was it lying on the ground? Had it shrivelled up? What?" Mr. Alphabet was getting a trifle exasperated as he always did during these sparring matches between his gardener and secretary.

"No. It'd just gone. No trace of it. Nothing."

"I can't believe that. There must be something," Mrs. Grey said.

"Right, come along with me, missis, and I'll bloomin' show you. Jump on the back," he said indicating a tiny footplate to the rear of the mower.

"You must be joking. I'll walk if it's all the same to you. I value my life too much to get on a machine like that driven by a geriatric boy-racer," Mrs. Evans quipped. Grey, however, heard none of this because he was already revving the engine and bouncing off down the garden.

When they arrived at the hot-house, Grey was obviously already waiting for them. At first, Mrs. Evans was hesitant about entering because, both up her nose and in her throat, she still had the memory of that utterly hideous smell. "Come on, woman. What are you waiting for?" Grey cried out from inside.

Gingerly, she stepped over the threshold onto the elaborate system of walkways which Grey had constructed with old railway sleepers. "Mind you don't stray off the path, missis, 'cos we've never managed to get this floor right in here." For once, Grey seemed genuinely concerned, although Mrs. Evans couldn't be certain whether he was more worried about the effect on his back if he had to haul her from the sludge. She chose, surprisingly, to give him the benefit of the doubt and thanking him, inched along the walkway towards the immense plants at the back of the hot-house.

"Have you noticed anything, Mrs. Evans?" asked Mr. Alphabet.

"Apart from the fact that I'm scared out of my wits, you mean?" She was sure that she heard Grey mumble something about 'needing to have wits to be scared out of them' but she could not spin round and confront him for fear of falling into the green slime which surrounded the walkways.

"No, I meant have you noticed that there's no smell? No stink of horse whatsit. Nothing."

"You're right, Mr. A. It's completely gone." She was still edging forwards, closely followed by Mr. Alphabet and they had now reached the area where the huge waxy-leaved plants were growing.

Grey was right, there was no remnant left of the great pink flower. "I'm sure that we'd see something left of it, if it were still here. But it's true, it's completely disappeared. Where on earth could it have gone? This is a mystery and a half."

"You know there are some flowers that are really expensive? At least that's what Mr. Campbell tells me. So, maybe someone's been and stolen it. It wouldn't surprise me if that Grey hasn't grown something highly illegal and me with a daughter who's a policeman. Oh, this is a tidy situation, this is!"

"Do you not think that you might be jumping to conclusions somewhat? We have no idea what the plant was and now we're going to have to wait for the next one to flower before we call in someone from the botanical gardens. Oh well, I suppose that, logically, that shouldn't be long since there are another twenty-five plants left to flower and they must be going to flower around the same time. I'm sure that when we get the botanists in, they're going to be very interested in it, anyway," Mr. Alphabet said.

"Oh yes, I'm sure they will. Like as not they'll have us all arrested." It seemed that Mrs. Evans was not to be swayed from her belief that Grey had just begun some enormous business involving drugs and forbidden exotic plants.

"Well, let's reserve our judgment for a few days until the next one flowers, shall we?" Mr. Alphabet suggested.

It was, however, to be a lot longer than a few days before the expert from the botanical gardens came to call and when she did, she was, indeed, *very* interested in what she saw.

Chapter K

As Evelyn Ellis had predicted, by the end of the weekend, or rather by the early hours of Monday morning, all of the exam papers were ready. Mr. Alphabet was amazed at what could really be achieved when a team worked well together and once again he went to bed a much more contented man.

A mere four hours later though he was awoken by a hammering on his bedroom door. Although it was already light, he shot up in his bed in terror and called out "Wh…Who is it?" Then he could hear the sound which had been masked by the intense hammering. It was the clinking of teacups. 'Surely not,' he thought to himself, glancing at his bedside clock. 'At five thirty in the morning? Mrs. Evans can't be here already.' The door opened and a familiar little white head poked its way around.

"How are we this morning?" she cried out, cheerily.

"Well, I know how *I* am, Mrs. Evans. And how I am, is very tired and now in shock. What on earth are you doing here at this time in the morning? Have you actually been home at all?"

"Oh yes. Had a good couple of hours sleep, I have." The woman was indefatigable.

"How on earth do you manage to be so lively on so little sleep?" Mr. Alphabet said, taking his first sip of tea to try to revive himself.

"That's one of the advantages of getting older, you see. You need less sleep. Mr. Campbell says that he gets worn out just looking at me. He says I'm up and down like a bobhowler."

"Like a what?"

"Bobhowler. It's one of them, sorry those, big moths. Don't know where it comes from. It's just something Mr. Campbell says. He's full of funny little sayings like that.

I say to him, I say 'Mr. Campbell, I don't know where you get all your funny little sayings from' and he just gives me a bit of an old-fashioned look."

This was all too much for Mr. Alphabet at five-thirty in the morning. All the talk of 'bobhowlers', 'old-fashioned looks' and the irony of Mrs. Evans thinking that other people had funny little sayings set Mr. Alphabet giggling. Unfortunately, he had a mouthful of drink and was forced to rush off to his bathroom to avoid spraying Mrs. Evans with the tea which she had kindly made for him.

When he returned, she said, "Have you pulled yourself together now? Honestly, a man of your age behaving like a child, I don't know." She picked up the tea tray and scuttled off with it, leaving Mr. Alphabet wondering what age exactly he was and whether or not it mattered if adults occasionally behaved like children.

He quickly got dressed and went downstairs to look for her. He searched all the usual places – the kitchen, her office, the cupboard where the floor-polisher was kept, but she was not to be seen. Eventually, he passed the door to the staff room and noticed that it was slightly open. As he peered round he was sure that he could hear talking.

"Mrs. Evans? Are you in there?" There was a shriek and the sound of papers scattering.

"You frightened me half to death," she said. "I was just in here trying to get these exam papers into some sort of order. Everything's all over the place. Your new staff might be hard workers but I don't think that organisation is a word that's in their dictionaries."

Mr. Alphabet raised his eyebrows which, unfortunately for him, did not go unnoticed. "Don't give me that look. These papers have got to be with my brother-in-law at his printing shop by eight thirty this morning." This was the first that Mr. Alphabet had heard about either a brother-in-law or a printer. He suddenly realised that he had not given a thought to how they were going to make the papers legible and accessible to twelve or thirteen year old children. Mrs. Evans, however, had clearly done more than just think about it.

"I know that I've said this before, Mrs. Evans, but you really are a marvel. When did you sort this all out?"

"Oh, I called him when I got home this morning and he said that if we get them to him first thing, he could have them back to us by Wednesday morning. I told him that we need them tomorrow though, just to be on the safe side. You know what people are like, you can't always trust them. And his wife, Mr. Campbell's younger sister is a flighty one."

Quite what relevance his wife had to the printer's ability to get a job done was a little lost on Mr. Alphabet but he decided not to press the point.

"Right, well, I'd better help you to sort the things out." A sudden, rather depressing thought came into his mind. "How much is it going to cost to have all of these professionally printed?" he asked her.

"Oh, you don't need to worry about that. He's going to do them for nothing. He owes me a favour or two, let me tell you, after the fiasco at Mr. Campbell's sixty-fifth birthday," she reassured him. He thought that he was about to be party to a lengthy tale of the said fiasco but it seemed that Mrs. Evans had more pressing things on her mind. "Let's get on then. The best thing we can do is get them into alphabetical order. Do you think you can manage that?" she laughed.

"Oh, it shouldn't be too much trouble. If I get stuck, I'll check with you!"

Having sent the papers off to the printers, Mr. Alphabet and Mrs. Evans spent the rest of that day making an exam timetable and writing to inform all thirteen hundred and fifty two children about when and where their exams would be taking place.

"Who'd have thought that there would be so many children with matching first name and surname initials? This is going to be a logistical nightmare," Mr. Alphabet said.

"Not at all. We just need to be organised and run it like a military operation." This weekend, like the last, was clearly not going to be a problem for Mrs. Evans. Mr. Alphabet, not for the first time, gave thanks for the day that he met this irritating and yet incredibly likeable and efficient woman.

The rest of that week was spent making the school ready so that, as Mrs. Evans said, it would be all 'ship shape and Brighton fashion' for the weekend. While the children were all sitting their one hour exams, there was going to be a chance for the parents to take a tour around the school and grounds. "I'm not having anyone saying that my parquet doesn't shine like a new pen," she said.

"'Pin'", corrected Mr. Alphabet in his head. Quite frankly, he was more worried about the possibility of someone slipping over and being rushed to hospital with a cracked skull, but it would have not been politic to voice this concern to Mrs. Evans.

"All we can hope is that Grey doesn't let us down by producing one of those stinking rotten illegal flowers for the weekend." Mr. Alphabet had hoped that the idea of Grey, the drugs baron, had died down in Mrs. Evans mind, but sadly not yet. "Otherwise, they'll think we've got someone buried in that greenhouse, the stench is so bad."

"I'm sure that everything will be fine, Mrs. Evans. We can only do our best, can't we?"

All over the town that week, there was great excitement as children received the news that they were going to have a chance of getting into the unusual school, in the unusual building with the even more unusual headmaster who, rumour had it, didn't even know his own name.

Some of the children's parents were just curious to go along to the school and see what all the fuss was about. Many, however, were desperate that their offspring should do well in these exams because, if not, they had no idea what they were going to do with them at the start of the next school year which was now only two months away.

One such family was that of Abigail Ayres.

Abigail lived with her mother and father in quite an ordinary looking, medium-sized semi on the outskirts of the town. The house was furnished with quite ordinary looking furniture. They drove an ordinary, average-sized car. Abigail was quite an ordinary looking thirteen year old girl.

All of this drove Abigail's mother, Eleanor, insane. She was not born to be ordinary. She was born for greatness. She wanted more. She wanted more for herself and to achieve this she needed more for Abigail. She pictured herself, twenty years hence, introducing her daughter to friends. "This is my daughter, Abigail. You know Abigail Ayres, the fabulously gifted brain surgeon." "Have you met my daughter, Abigail, she's terribly big in neuro-surgery, you know?" It would all be perfect and they could all move out of this dreary house.

Eleanor had no time for ordinary. Which was a little unfair really since she had never done a thing to raise herself from her own ordinary beginnings and yet expected truly great things from her daughter.

Unfortunately for the girl, Abigail was very ordinary and very happy with it. She loved playing in the park with the ordinary children from the neighbourhood. She loved reading ordinary story books. She loved going to the supermarket with her ordinary Daddy. More times than Abigail could remember, Eleanor had told her "I will not have you being ordinary." She would then, with a jerk of her head, indicate Abigail's father and say "We've got one painfully ordinary person in this family. We don't need another." Abigail often wondered why her father remained hidden behind his newspaper and never spoke up for himself but she was sure that he must have his reasons.

So, most of the things Abigail liked doing had to be done in secret so as not to upset her mother. If she went to the park to play, she would call out to her mother as she left the house, "I'm just off to the library to swap my books in, Mum. See you later." This was quite annoying, of course, because it meant firstly that she had to take her books with her to the park and secondly that she had to cut short her playing time to run to the library and exchange her books. She was certain that if she didn't do it, her mother would notice and then the game would be up. Abigail was always frightened that she would forget and give herself away in some way, but she never did.

On the day that the letter arrived from Mr. Alphabet's A-Z Academy, Abigail was sitting in the bay window of the dining room doing the compulsory twenty minutes of educational reading which her mother imposed on her every morning before school. At least, that's what she appeared to be doing. However, inside the huge book, "The Workings of the Kidney" by Uri Thrar, she had tucked her latest book set in America about the exploits of a group of children turned detectives.

She was engrossed in the book when she spied out of the corner of her eye, the postman coming up the path. She threw down the books, just remembering in time to stuff the little paperback in her blazer pocket, and ran to the door. It was with a mixture of anticipation and dread that she picked up the envelopes and headed down the hall. She was excited about the prospect of trying out for the new school which her teacher, Miss Ellis, had told her was like no other. On the other hand, she was also sure that this would be another exam which she would sit and fail – not fail 'miserably', as her mother had said to her on more than one occasion, but just fail.

She went into the living room where her mother was sitting with the television blaring, doing her usual crossword puzzle. She knew not to disturb her mother when she was concentrating, so she just stood and waited while Eleanor mumbled under her breath "Eight letters 'Trouble for me in writing articles about player'. Why do they have to be so obscure all the time? 'Trouble for me in writing articles about player.'

''Thespian'', thought Abigail who was standing just inside the door. Unlike her mother, one of Abigail's real skills was cryptic crosswords.

Abigail moved the letters from one hand to the other, there was a slight rustle from the envelopes and her mother jumped. "Oh, it's you, creeping Ginny. What have you got there?"

"Letters."

"Get away! I can see that. Who are they from?"

'I'm supposed to have X-ray vision too!' Abigail thought to herself. Without a word she handed the envelopes over and her mother began to tear at the one addressed in Mrs. Evans beautiful script. "I expect it's a letter telling us that you haven't even got as far as the exam at the new school. I don't know why that Miss Ellis made you all fill in the application form in class time. We'd have made a much better job of it if you'd brought it home and I could have helped y...." By now the envelope was open and Mrs. Ayres read " '...exam to be held at two thirty on Saturday 5th June. Please arrive thirty minutes early so that your child may have time to settle before the exam commen.....' blah blah. Oh well, they must be letting everyone sit the exam then." Abigail turned and left the room, not even registering how deflated she felt about her mother's lack of praise for her achievement. This was, after all, how things always were.

On her way to school that morning, she passed by the park and saw her best friend, Robbie Redovitch, gently moving to and fro on the swing with his head hanging so low it was almost touching his chest.

She ran over. "What's up, Robbie?"

"We got the letter from that new school today," Robbie replied.

"Oh no, don't tell me that you haven't passed for the exam."

"No, it's not that. I've got my exam on Sunday morning at ten..." Robbie sniffed and looked back at the ground. Abigail sat on the swing next to him and silently started to push herself backwards. She swung for a few moments until she thought that Robbie had pulled himself together.

"What's wrong then, Rob?" she said quietly.

He was angry now. "Well what's the point? I'm just wasting my time going up there.."

"No, you're not. You'll pass, no trouble," Abigail interrupted. Robbie was just about the cleverest boy she had ever met.

"I'm not worried about that but even if I do, I won't be able to go. Mum and Dad can't afford it." The realisation dawned on Abigail. Robbie lived in a tiny two bedroom flat with his mother and father and two younger brothers. Until his mother had become ill three years ago, she had had a good job as an assistant buyer in Dorrid's, the exclusive department store in town. The family had lived in a much bigger flat and although they were never really well off they were what Mrs. Redovitch used to call 'comfortably off – it's enough for us'. Then, suddenly, she started to get ill. She couldn't get up in the mornings, she couldn't lift anything, going to the supermarket completely wore her out. She kept on trying to go into work but every day she went in, the department manager sent her home. She really was in no fit state to work and when her husband finally persuaded her to go along to the doctor, she was diagnosed as having glandular fever. Dr. Davis told her that it could be months before she was better but unfortunately, the people at Dorrid's could not keep on paying her for months. What had been 'enough' when there were two wages coming in, was no longer nearly sufficient and so the family had had to move into a smaller flat.

"We just haven't got the money for a private school for me," Robbie sighed. "My form teacher, Mr. Levine, said that it'd be just the sort of school for me, as well." At this he began to cry in great gulping sobs.

Abigail stopped her swing and went over to him. Putting her arm round his shoulder, she said, "Come on. Let's both at least go for it and hope that some kind of miracle occurs."

Robbie's face brightened. "You mean, you've got in to the exam, too? That's brill! Well done, girl." He was genuinely delighted for his friend. They had been through a lot together. He perked up. "O.k. It's a deal. We'll give it a go and see what happens."

Chapter L

For the rest of that week, the two met in the park after school and helped each other to study. Their little backs were bent over with the weight of the books they were carrying; Abigail with her books on Anatomy and Acting, Robbie with his on Russian and Radio Electronics. Abigail knew nothing about Robbie's subjects. Russian looked like the hardest language on the planet with all those back-to-front, upside-down letters and its sound like a taped message being played backwards. "You're so clever being able to read and speak this, Robbie," she said, on the second evening when he was reciting a list of verbs. He had written them out phonetically in English script so that Abigail could test him on them.

"There's nothing remotely clever about it. I don't expect I'd be able to do it if Dad wasn't Russian." Neither of them believed that it was only his family interest that made him capable of mastering this difficult language but it made them both feel better to pretend that it was only that. "Right come on then, Kate Winslet, let's hear your Portia."

As part of Abigail's Acting exam, she had had to prepare an audition piece and had decided to go for Portia's 'mercy' speech from 'The Merchant of Venice'. It had taken her ages to decide on it and the only 'advice' that her mother had given her was "Don't bother too much about it. After all, it's only going to be to get you into the school and after that you'll be dropping it so that you can concentrate on studying sciences. If you want to achieve your ambition of being a doctor, you're going to have get down to some serious work pretty sharpish." '*My* ambition?' thought Abigail. 'I think you'll find that's *your* ambition.' Obviously, she kept this to herself and just got on with flicking through her books.

As Robbie listened to his friend reciting her piece, he was, not for the first time, moved by her amazing ability to be completely believable as another person. When the speech came to an end, he said, "You're absolutely going to walk this."

"Yeah, well, the acting bit is not what I'm worried about. It's the rotten old Anatomy that my Mum made me go in for. Who cares where your islets of Langerhans is and what causes narrowing of the arteries? Not me, that's for sure."

"I know but if it keeps your mother off your back, I suppose it's worth it."

Abigail, and her father come to that, seemed to spend their whole lives 'keeping her mother off their backs'. It was a bit tiring at times.

"Well, let's get on with it then. Can you test me on the labelling of cell types? I always get stuck on the nerve cells. Dendrons, dendrites, they get on my nerves! Ha, do you get it?" At this, they fell about laughing which was exactly what they both needed at that minute.

The rest of the week flew by and it was soon Saturday morning. Abigail woke up wishing that her exam was the next day so that she and Robbie could go together or, if it really had to be today, then why couldn't it be in the morning. It was only six o'clock and she'd got another eight and a half hours to wait. As usual for a Saturday morning, she stayed in bed until nearly noon, reading. She knew that really she should be reading a book from the vast pile of anatomy books which her mother had put by the side of her bed 'just as a little reminder'. But all she wanted to do was escape to the old warehouse on the edge of the Hudson River where the boys in her detective book had their hide-out.

She could hear her mother's penetrating nasal voice calling out to her father. "I don't know what she thinks she's doing staying in bed all hours when she's got an exam this afternoon. Sometimes I wonder if she's got something wrong up top. It must come from your side of the family. I'm glad I haven't got your genes." Abigail knew that this was the signal for a long speech about what was wrong with every member of her father's family and in particular with him. She closed her ears to it and immersed herself in her book again.

By the time that Abigail had got up, washed and dressed herself it was half one which was the time that her Dad had told her that they should leave. When she came downstairs, she found her mother sitting in front of the television, still in her dressing gown with the remnants of her breakfast spilt down the front. "Is it nearly time to go, Mum?"

"I'll get ready in a minute, just let me finish this cigarette, will you? You're all rush, rush, rush, you are." Eleanor was in one of those moods where nothing would be right for her. The moods which seemed to be an every day occurrence, in fact. As she watched her mother draw heavily on the cigarette, she wondered about how long it takes the gaseous exchange to be significantly impaired in the lungs of a smoker.

Finally, the Ayres left the house at ten past two, some ten minutes after they were already supposed to be at the school. Her father drove like a demon to get there with Eleanor almost under the dashboard screaming that he should slow down if he didn't want her to have a heart attack. Curiously enough, her scolding seemed to have the opposite effect from the one she was looking for and Abigail felt herself flung against the back seat as they roared away from the lights. For an 'ordinary' man, her father was an extraordinary driver.

At two twenty-eight, they sped up the gravel drive to the school and Abigail had the car door open before her father had drawn to a halt. She ran up the steps clutching a carrier bag. Mr. Alphabet was waiting at the top for her. "Abigail Ayres?"

"Y..yes," she snivelled. "I..I'm so sorry...."

"No need to apologise, my dear, these things happen." He led Abigail into the school and called over his shoulder that her parents should wait in the entrance hall for him. As they walked down the corridor, he told her, "Luckily, we've actually been able to postpone your exam by twenty minutes and Mrs. Evans, our school secretary, has got some orange juice and biscuits waiting for you." They entered a large empty music room with a small stage and large piano at one end and tiered seating at the other. Mrs. Evans was cleaning the blackboard as they came in.

"Right, I'll leave you with Mrs. Evans. Don't worry she doesn't bite, despite appearances to the contrary." He laughed. "You have a little calm down and some refreshment in here and then we'll get the exam under way. I'm just going back to see your parents." With that, he left the room.

Abigail wasn't sure whether she wanted to laugh or cry. She had barely experienced such kindness before and certainly never from a headmaster.

"Come on then, dear, have a nice glass of orange juice and soon you'll be as right as fivepence." Abigail was too full of gratitude to question how 'right' fivepence was and drank down half of the glass of orange juice in one go. Her throat was so dry, she felt sure that she wouldn't be able to utter a word of her speech. She started to panic which made her throat even drier. She was just considering making a run for it when a gentle voice behind her said, "You must be Abigail." The girl turned to see a very tall, slender woman dressed from head to toe, including tights and shoes, in lavender. "I am Daphne Diamond and I'm going to be your drama teacher."

'Drama,' thought Abigail, 'that makes it sound a lot more proper than 'acting''. This thought thrilled her but also filled her with fear. If it was that proper, maybe she wouldn't be able to do it. Maybe she'd flunk this, just like she'd flunked every other exam. What was Robbie talking about? Him and his Kate Winslet!

Abigail's eyes started to fill with tears.

"Come on, dear. Let's just try this together, you and me." Miss Diamond really did have the most soothing voice. As she came closer, Abigail noticed that she even smelt of lavender too. It was lovely. It reminded her of the little trip to Jersey last year when she had gone with her Daddy to visit a lavender farm. Her mother had stayed in the darkened hotel room because she had 'one of her heads'. The appropriateness of this expression never failed to amuse Abigail as she often felt that, when her mother was in a rage, she was like a monster with several heads.

The girl looked around to see if Mrs. Evans was listening but the secretary had slipped silently away.

"Which piece have you chosen?" Miss Diamond enquired.

"Portia's mercy speech. It's from The Merchant of Venice. It's by William Shakespeare."

"I know, dear." Miss Diamond smiled. "It's one of my absolute favourites. For me, you couldn't have chosen a better piece." Abigail was really beginning to feel put at her ease now and she wondered how some people could do this and others so clearly could not.

"You can stand wherever you like. You will have two chances to do it so you can treat the first one like a practice go. Whenever you're ready, you may start."

Abigail looked around the room choosing somewhere to stand. She glanced over at the small stage but decided against it because standing there might look like showing off and that was something which her mother was constantly warning her against. "Can I just say it here?" she asked.

"As I said, you may stand where you wish."

Abigail took a deep breath and began to almost whisper, "The quality of mercy is not strained, it droppeth…." She was overcome by a fit of coughing.

"Have a drink and try again, dear. There's no rush." Miss Diamond handed her a glass of orange juice. Abigail took a small sip, put the glass down and began again. This time she managed to get to the end of the speech with no problems. Miss Diamond was listening intently all the time.

"You have a beautiful voice, Abigail. When you try it the second time, I'd like you firstly to pretend that I'm not here and secondly I'd like you to think about who Portia is and why she is making this speech. She's a lawyer and this is a life or death situation for someone she loves. So now, *you* are a lawyer and this is life and death for someone dear to *you*," the drama teacher advised her. "Just take a couple of minutes to think about it and then began again where and when you want to."

Again, Abigail looked around the room. She saw a small table and chair up the corner behind the piano. She went over, pulled them out and dragged them over to the small stage. She managed to heave them up on to the stage and get them into position. The bag which she had been carrying when she came to the school was on the floor on the piano. She pulled out a large piece of black material and draped it around herself to look like a cloak. Striding over to the desk, she kept thinking 'I must pretend I'm on my own. I'm at home in my bedroom. No-one can see me. No-one can hear me. As she sat behind the desk staring straight ahead at the staged seating, over on her right she could still see Miss Diamond watching her intently. Abigail's nerve started to go again. 'I can't do it. I just can't. she's going to think I'm stupid or, worse, some awful little show-off.' Then she remembered the trick that she always played with her eyes when her mother was telling her off. She could blur them so that she couldn't see anything and then she didn't cry, laugh or show any other kind of emotion. Realising that the minutes were ticking by, she blurred her eyes and got slowly to her feet. 'I am a lawyer and I am going to save this man,' she thought. 'Here goes.'

"The quality of mercy is not strained, It droppeth like the gentle rain from heaven upon the place beneath. It is twice blessed…" she began in a wonderfully calm yet confident contralto voice.

The speech went wonderfully and as she drew to a close, she was shocked to hear the sound of two sets of hands clapping. "Take a bow, dear," Miss Diamond told her. Abigail swung round to the right and there were Miss Diamond and Mr. Alphabet on their feet applauding her.

"That was absolutely marvellous," Mr. Alphabet said. "You should be proud of yourself."

'I am,' thought Abigail. 'I really am.'

***

The anatomy exam did not go quite as well for Abigail but, in fact, the questions were considerably easier than she had thought they were going to be and she only had one or two lapses of memory. All in all, as she descended the stairs at four fifteen to meet up with her parents, she was feeling quietly confident.

Her father shot up form the bench where he had been sitting. "How did you get on, love?" he asked as he put his arm around her and guided her to the huge front door.

"O.k. I think. Where's Mum?"

"She's outside having another cigarette," her father told her.

"How many's that since we've been here?"

"I lost count after six." They both laughed. "So tell me about it."

"Well, I answered most of the questions in the anatomy. One or two I just couldn't re…"

"Never mind that, what about your acting?"

Abigail was surprised. "Oh, it went great. They loved me. The headmaster and the drama teacher clapped me."

Mr. Ayres had to turn his head away as his eyes filled with tears. "Well done, love," he whispered in a voice which seemed a little strange to Abigail.

As they walked down the stone steps together, they saw Eleanor Ayres coming back up the garden towards them. To her horror, Abigail saw her mother drop a cigarette butt in the gravel of the drive and grind it in with her heel.

Mrs. Ayres caught sight of them and Abigail's father dropped the comforting hand from around his daughter's shoulders.

"There you are," called Mrs. Ayres. "What are you two whispering about?"

"Abigail was just telling me how well she did in the exams," her husband told her.

"Well, that's her opinion. The results remain to be seen, don't they?" As usual, Mrs. Ayres had managed, in one sentence, to take away any positive feeling which Abigail might have had about the exams she had just taken.

"Come on now. This is my first Saturday off in ages and I don't want to waste it hanging round this dreary old place. There's an omnibus of 'Riversiders' on telly and it starts in fifteen minutes."

The three of them piled into the car and, strangely, Mrs. Ayres had no concerns about her husband's fiendish driving on the way home.

They arrived home with about thirty seconds to spare before Eleanor's programme started. "Get me a coffee, will you, Ab?" she called as she hurried into the living room.

Abigail went straight to the kitchen, made the coffee and took it in to her mother. The living room was already full of a fug from the cigarette which her mother had lit up.

"Close those curtains, will you, Ab? That awful glare'll give me one of my heads."

Abigail did as she was told, all the while thinking 'I don't suppose that it could be the combination of coffee, cigarettes, lack of exercise and too much television which is causing all these so-called headaches, could it?' A by-product of all this studying of anatomy was that Abigail knew just what foodstuffs, chemicals and behaviours were bad for you.

"If there's nothing else you want then, Mum, I'm going out on my bike to soak up a bit of lovely sunshine." Abigail was unable to hide the note of sarcasm in her voice.

She thought that her mother hadn't even heard because she didn't bother to answer, so engrossed was she in her television programme. As she slammed the front door behind her, however, she heard her mother call out, "And don't you go playing with those dirty, smelly kids from the estate in that rotten old council park."

Abigail pulled her bike out of the garage and headed straight for the 'rotten old park'. As she set off, she noticed that just like normal her father seemed to have vanished. Perhaps he was in his shed. That seemed to be the place he went to escape.

When she got to the park, Abigail saw Robbie waiting for her on the swings. It was the exact spot that she knew he would be.

He came running over to her. "Well?"

"Well what?" she teased.

"Oh come on, Beeg," he said addressing her in the pet name that he had invented and which only he was allowed to use. He had long ago decided that her name was really 'A beagle' and 'Beeg' for short. "How did it go?"

Abigail was unable to contain her excitement any longer. "They loved me, Rob. D'you know, I think I might just have passed."

Robbie threw his arms around her, ignoring the fact that the gang of hard boys from the estate had just entered the park. "You see, what did I tell you about Kate Winslet?" he laughed.

Abigail felt ashamed at the earlier thoughts she had had about Robbie's confidence in her. "Never mind that, all we've got to do is get you in as well and then we're sorted," she said.

His face fell and he pulled back from her. "That might not be so easy. I've got something to tell you. Mum and Dad are thinking about moving away to live by the seaside because it's cheaper and they think that it might be better for Mum's health."

Robbie was barely holding back his tears.

Abigail turned away and thought, 'Why, in my life, can happiness never last for more than about five minutes?'

This was a blow, indeed.

Chapter M

On the Sunday morning, Mr. Alphabet woke early. The previous day had been hectic, to say the least and yet he was not at all tired. Quite the reverse, in fact. He felt energised and motivated by all the wonderful children he had seen yesterday. At the back of his mind, of course, was the worry that he was going to have to turn away a huge percentage of them because there simply was not room in the school for them.

He was standing, gazing out of the window of his tiny little office which, actually, he had grown to love, in spite of it not being his first choice. In walked Mrs. Evans with the pile of that day's exam papers. "You might have your back to me but I can still see that you've got that dreamy look on your face. We haven't got time for that now. We've got to get all these set out in their right places. The first children will be arriving at nine and we can't afford to have any confusion. This needs to run like a well-watered machine."

'Oiled,' thought Mr. Alphabet. 'A well-oiled machine.'

"Your staff are here already and they've started marking yesterday's papers. I've had a look at one or two of the marks and it's really peculiar because some of the children seem to be brilliant in one of their chosen subjects and pretty poor in the other one. I can't understand the point of choosing a subject if you're going to be rubbish at it," Mrs. Evans complained. "I would go for something that was easy for me, if I had the choice."

"That is the point, don't you see?"

"No, I don't see at all. Sometimes you don't half talk in a roundabout way. 'Mr. Riddle-Me-Ree' you should have called yourself, not Mr. Alphabet." This was the first reference which Mrs. Evans had made to the curious manner in which he came by his name.

"I don't think that all of the children have chosen *both* of their subjects at all. Probably most of them have, at best, selected one. The chances are that fifty percent of the subjects are what the parents or teachers think that the children should be doing rather than what they themselves want to do."

Mrs. Evans was beginning to understand. "O.k. so that's why you said that only one of the two subjects would be important because that way the parents might ease up a bit on the little ones and let them choose their second subjects. You're not just a pretty face, are you?" For once, she seemed impressed with her employer.

"Thank you for that, Mrs. Evans! You're right on both counts! And that's why we made one of the two exams easier for each child. Take the little girl I saw yesterday afternoon. Abigail, was it? Her acting was a dream but I'm sure that if she'd had an equally difficult exam in anatomy, she wouldn't have managed it. She's just not interested, you see, but talking to her parents – or rather being talked at by her mother - I realised that *she*, the mother, wants the child to be a doctor."

"Well, that's just daft. You can't make a child do something just because *you* want them to."

"You can, in fact, and people do. All the time. That, my dear Mrs. Evans, is what this school is here to help with."

"Ooo, I'm having a headlight moment," said Mrs. Evans.

"Sit down. Put your head between your legs." Mr. Alphabet rushed over to her.

"Why?"

"Well, if you're feeling light-headed, it'll help."

"No, not light-headed. Headlight. It's when you suddenly cotton on to what someone's been talking about for ages. I saw it on daytime telly once. 'A headlight moment' the girl on the show called it. I thought an educated man, like yourself, would know all about that." She shook her head, smiled and went off to the staffroom to see how the marking was progressing.

"Light bulb," said Mr. Alphabet when she was out of earshot. "A light bulb moment." This time it was his turn to smile.

At nine fifteen, the whole Redovitch family, mother, father and three boys, came walking up the path to the school. They had set out at eight from their flat and walked all the way to the school. Mrs. Redovitch was shattered and could barely take another step. She was almost being carried up the steps by her husband and eldest son. Robbie was looking very flushed both with the exertion of helping his mother and with nerves about the forthcoming exam.

Mr. Alphabet watched the family's slow progression from the window of the classroom where he was adjudicating the first exams of the day. He wanted to rush downstairs and help but knew that he couldn't leave the room until the exam was over at nine-thirty.

When he finally got downstairs, he found Mrs. Redovitch drinking a cup of tea in the hallway. Robbie stood next to her with his hand on her shoulder.

"Good morning, I am Mr. Alphabet. And you are?"

Robbie's mother opened her mouth to speak but her voice came out in such a tiny whisper that Mr. Alphabet could not work out a word she said. "Sorry, I didn't catch that."

"She said her name is Mrs. Redovitch and I'm Robbie." The boy's voice sounded almost impolite.

"Ah yes, Robbie Redovitch. Russian and Radio Electronics, isn't it?"

Robbie was impressed. There were children crawling all over this school and still the headmaster knew what everyone was doing. "That's right, yes. I'm only doing Russian because my Dad speaks it and thinks that I should too." As he was saying these words, Mrs. Evans came along the corridor to collect Mrs. Redovitch's empty teacup. She smiled at Mr. Alphabet as she heard the boy's words. It was true, her boss was 'more than just a pretty face'.

"Anyway, I'm not going to be able to come to this school because my Mum and Dad have got no money and on top of that they've got to move out of town 'cos my Mum's sick."

"The nice gentleman doesn't need to know all our business, Robbie," his mother admonished.

"Not at all, Mrs. Redovitch. I'm glad to know as much as possible about my future pupils. And, Robbie, there might be something that we can do about your problems if you pass the exam." Mr. Alphabet had no idea what that something was to be but he felt sure that he would be able to come up with a solution of some kind. "Let me show you to the room where your first exam will be. Meanwhile would you and the rest of your family like to take a look around the school grounds, Mrs. Redovitch?"

"I'd love to, Mr. Alphabet, but I'm really not sure that I could walk another step."

"No problem, I have the perfect solution. You just sit there for a couple of minutes and I'll be right back." The family wondered what on earth Mr. Alphabet was going to do.

Soon, they could hear a chugging sound outside the big front doors. "What on earth's that?" said Robbie's mother. Robbie ran to the top of the steps and saw Grey sitting on his ride-on lawn-mower in the driveway.

"You the lad with the poorly Ma?" he asked.

Robbie said that he was and Grey told him that her taxi had arrived. They all helped Mrs. Redovitch down the steps and onto the small seat at the back of the tractor. As soon as she was settled, Grey set off. He was obviously under strict instructions to take it at a very gently pace because Robbie's father and little brothers had no problem in keeping up.

Back inside the school, Robbie was settling down to his first exam. The time seemed to fly by and Robbie had no problem with the exam at all.

Soon both exams were over and he was heading back down to find his parents. He met Mr. Alphabet as he turned the corner of the upstairs corridor. "How did it go, Robbie?"

"Fine, thanks. No problems."

"You don't look very pleased about it."

"Whether I've done well or not doesn't make any difference because I'm still not going to be able to come to your school, am I?" Robbie realised he sounded terribly ungracious and added, "But thank you very much, sir, for at least giving me the chance."

Mr. Alphabet was touched. This family was certainly having an undeservedly rough time. He was going to have to come up with a plan for them and any others like them. He was, however, at a loss as to what exactly that plan could be.

"Let's see, shall we. Like I said, if you've done well enough, we should be able to come up with something to help you." This was said with a great deal more confidence than Mr. Alphabet actually felt.

"Thanks again. I'd better go and find my Mum. She must be shattered by now and we've got to walk home."

"Oh, don't worry about that Robbie. I've called a taxi for you all."

"No, no, you can't. We can't afford it. You don't understand…" The boy was really terrified.

"I understand perfectly. Don't worry, the school is paying for it."

"Wow, thanks. That's brilliant."

Mr. Alphabet was touched by Robbie's gratitude. "Run along then and enjoy the rest of your day. I really hope to be seeing you again very soon."

"Me too, sir. Me too. Bye." He was off, skidding along Mrs. Evans freshly polished parquet, obviously keen to enjoy the novel experience of a taxi ride home.

'Right,' thought Mr. Alphabet, 'now, what are we going to do about that boy?'

"What was that about the school paying for a taxi ride? Where do you think you're going to get the money for that?" Mrs. Evans was standing behind Mr. Alphabet.

"Oh, don't worry, Mrs. Evans, I'll find it somehow. I'll take it out of your wages if I have to." He smiled at her to show that this really was only a joke. "Seriously, though, I've got a more pressing problem at the moment and I'm sure you'll be able to help me with it."

"Go on, then, but make it quick because the next lot of children will be arriving any minute."

"Well, here it is. Unless I'm gravely mistaken, that boy there is going to do really well in both his exams because he is just a very bright boy. However…."

"I'm listening." Mrs. Evans could tell that something was coming that she really wasn't going to like.

"His family have got no money and they're not even staying in the area because his mother's ill and they need to move away and…."

"And?"

"And I'm really sorry but I've promised that I will help him if he passes the exam but I haven't got the foggiest idea how."

"Easy, Scholarship. If he's as good as you say he is, then he'll deserve a scholarship." Mrs. Evans seemed, contrary to expectation, completely unfazed by the problem.

"But the school can't afford to have non-fee paying pupils, surely?" Mr. Alphabet enquired.

"Well that's where you're wrong, you see, because when I was calculating out the fees, I thought 'that man's as soft as cheese, there's sure to be some kids he's going to want to help out'. And lo and behold, here we are."

"Mrs. Evans, you never cease to amaze me. That's wonderful."

"Hold your whatsits there. There are only two scholarships in each year otherwise you'll be wending your non-fee-paying way to the bank and handing over the keys."

Mr. Alphabet's face fell but he knew that what his secretary said was true. "O.k. I promise. Two is better than none. Well, that's the problem of little Robbie Redovitch sorted." Mr. Alphabet was delighted because he had really taken to the boy, to the whole family, in fact.

"Is it? Aren't you forgetting something?" the secretary asked him.

"I don't think so, no."

Mrs. Evans was exasperated. "If his folks move away, where do you suppose the little mite's going to live? If it was only him, we could find room for him somewhere, but you can bet your bottom doo-dah that there are going to be a good many children wanting to come here whose families live miles and miles away."

Mr. Alphabet's face fell again. "Oh no, you're right, Mrs. Evans. Now what are we going to do?"

"We? We? You're the one who promised the boy the earth."

"I didn't promise him the earth, I just promised to help him get to a school where I'm sure he'll thrive and where he's going to encounter no criticism about where he comes from or where he lives."

"I know, I know. All I'm saying is that you've got to be careful because it could happen over and over again." Mrs. Evans was right, of course. "But that being said, now that you *have* promised, we'd better just get on and do something about it. Once these exams are over and marked, we'll all get our thinking caps on and try to come up with something. Maybe he could board with one of the other families during the week or something. Anyway, until we know the results of the exams, it's all hypercritical, isn't it?."

"No it's not, it's all hypothetical." Fortunately for Mr. Alphabet, Mrs. Evans had buried her head back in her accounts book and didn't hear his rather 'hypercritical' comment.

Once again, the new staff worked all night and by Thursday morning, the acceptance letters had arrived on the doorsteps of all one hundred and thirty new pupils.

It was a typical English June morning. Rainy, grey, cold and generally not designed to fill you with the joy of being alive. Abigail was miserable. She was miserable because it was Thursday and there was the after school Science Club which her mother had signed her up for. She was miserable because her best friend was moving away. She was miserable because she was sure that she was going to have failed the exam for the Academy and her mother was going to be livid. She was miserable because she was miserable.

As the house door banged, Abigail looked out of her bedroom window surprised to see her mother standing on the drive taking the letters from the postman. Eleanor Ayres stuffed all the envelopes into her bag and climbed into the car for the two minute drive to the pharmacy where she worked and where today she was doing an especially early shift.

Abigail was sure that today was the day that the results would be coming from the school and now she would have to wait until she got home at seven fifteen this evening to find out how she'd done. 'Oh no,' she thought, 'Two of Mum's soaps are on this evening, so I'm not going to be able to ask until eight o'clock. What's the point in worrying about it, anyway? There's no way I've got in.' With this thought, her mood plummeted to new depths of misery. She picked up her school bag and headed off via the park.

On her way through the park, she looked everywhere for Robbie but he was nowhere to be seen. This was not like him, especially not on such a momentous day. Maybe he had turned his back on her as well or maybe his family had upped and moved over night or maybe he was ill.

Abigail wanted to speak to him so much. She wanted to find out whether he had got into the school. Why couldn't he have been here like normal? It must be something she'd said.

The truth of the matter was that Robbie was at Hope House Hospital with his Dad and brothers. He'd been there since ten the previous evening when his mother was taken critically ill and rushed in.

No thoughts of the Academy or Abigail or his future came to mind. Without his Mum there would be no future.

Chapter N

That Thursday was the longest Abigail had ever known which is really saying something because she had always hated Thursdays, they were always her least favourite day of the week. This one seemed to go on and on for ever. In one way, she wanted to know as soon as possible what her results were, but in another way, she was absolutely dreading what her mother was going to say when she had failed.

She ran all the way home from Science Club, that evening, thinking how much she disliked Mr. Stallet, the science teacher and how little she cared about the colour of potassium permanganate. When she crept through the front door at just after seven, she tried to detect the atmosphere in the house. She dared not go into the living room where her Mum was glued to the T.V., so she stood in the hall sniffing the air like a dog trying to decide whether the smell it was picking up was fear or sausage. Usually, she could pick something up but today there was nothing which was surprising because she felt sure that her Mum must have opened the letter and be mentally chewing over the contents and over how she could take revenge on her ungrateful, intellectually inadequate daughter.

Her next option was to head into the kitchen and see what Mum had left her for dinner. Even in here, though, there was not Eleanor's standard demonstration of displeasure with Abigail which was the already plated up meal of liver and mushrooms, congealing in their gravy on the stove top. Abigail hated liver and she hated mushrooms even more, which is why she was given that when she was 'naughty'.

Abigail simply could not understand why there was no evidence of her mother's disappointment but that is because she didn't know at that time that her mother hadn't even opened the envelope from the school yet, having stuffed it into her capacious handbag that morning and then forgotten all about it.

There was nothing for it but to wait until eight when there was a brief half hour gap between the programmes which her mother simply *had* to watch.

Abigail opened the fridge and took out the bowl of limp salad which was in there. As she closed the door, she spotted, on the top shelf, a packet of liver which was four days beyond its sell-by date. Her mother was obviously ready to give her the bad news.

The girl watched every second of every minute tick round on the large kitchen clock as she munched her way through the salad.

At eight she heard the familiar synthesised drum introduction to the closing music of 'Riversiders' and her heart leapt up, blocking her throat.

"Ab? Are you there?"

Right this was it. "In the kitchen, Mum."

"Come in here a minute, will you?"

Abigail, naturally, did as she was told but when she got into the living room, her mother had nothing in her hand apart from the obligatory cigarette.

"There you are. Pass me that remote." She pointed to the remote which was on top of the telly some six feet away from her.

Abigail, marvelling again at her mother's infinite capacity for laziness, picked up the controls and handed them to Eleanor. Then she stood and waited. And waited. And waited.

Having found a suitable piece of rubbish on television to watch, Mrs. Ayres turned to her daughter and said, "What are you standing there for? Haven't you got homework to do?"

"Er…I was just wondering…er.." Abigail began.

"Spit it out, girl. You're interrupting my programme. I've been waiting all day to see this."

"Er…have you opened my envelope?"

"What envelope?" Eleanor asked.

'*Which* envelope' thought Abigail. "The envelope from the school."

"Firstly, I think you'll find that that envelope is not, in fact, yours. It was addressed to me and your father. And secondly, no I haven't. Quite honestly I'd tried to put it from my mind because I didn't want to be disappointed again so I haven't bothered to check it," her mother lied. "Well I suppose if you really want to find out, we'd better have a look. Fetch my bag, it's in the hall."

'Just behind the front door where you always leave it so that I can trip over it, spill the contents all over the floor and get into trouble,' Abigail said to herself as she went down the hall to pick up the bag.

She gave her mother the bag and waited the customary ten minutes for her to find what she was looking for among all the paraphernalia of combs, receipts, keys, lipsticks and cigarette packets, empty and half-full.

"Here it is. Now let's see....'We are pleased to inform you that...'" Mrs. Ayres read on. When she had finished, she turned the letter over and over, scrutinised the envelope and then went back to re-read the letter. "There must be some sort of mistake."

Abigail was turning herself inside out with anticipation but knew that she dare not ask her mother what the news was.

"It says here that you've got in, but that can't be right. You've never got in anywhere." Abigail's smile was as wide as her whole face. Her mother threw the letter to the ground and picked up the cigarette which was burning away in the ashtray. "All I can say is, that the school can't be much cop if they let in the likes of you." She turned back to watch the scene unfolding in the hospital accident and emergency department on the television.

Meanwhile in the real life accident and emergency of Hope House Hospital, there had, for Robbie, been more drama than he could reasonably handle over the past day. For twenty-two hours now, they had all been sitting on the hard plastic chairs or pacing up and down the hospital corridors trying to keep sane. Still no bed could be found for his mother.

The doctors had told his father that they were sure that Mrs. Redovitch had got a blood clot on her lung but that they could not be sure until they had done a proper chest X-ray. Unfortunately two of the three X-ray machines in the hospital were out of action and so the backlog of patients waiting had built up. In the meantime, she was not to be moved or to get out of bed because any jolt might cause the clot to move with potentially fatal consequences. Robbie's Dad had no idea that his son, who had been listening to all of this from just outside the door to the doctor's small office, was now utterly terrified.

The doctor went on to tell Mr. Redovitch that, as a precautionary measure, they had to wire the patient up to a drip and a heart monitor and the nurses were under instruction to come and check on her every twenty minutes.

All of this care and attention should have reassured Robbie. It, in fact, had the reverse effect and as the hours wore on, he became more and more distressed.

Abigail, of course, knew none of this and, although it was by now eight-thirty, she crept out of the house in search of him. She need not have worried about anyone hearing her leaving the house because her mother was engrossed in her programme and her father was, she assumed, making his long way home from work.

Running into the park, she could see at once that Robbie wasn't there. Five or six boys her age, in red nylon football shirts, were trying to set light to a plastic rubbish bin. As they saw her, they stopped what they were doing and formed a menacing semi-circle. "Look, lads. It's little Miss Ayres-and-Graces. Let's have some fun, shall we." The arc started to move towards her and without a moment's thought she turned and fled.

"Don't worry, lads, we've got plenty of time. We'll have some fun with her when we all go up to George Davis in September," the ring-leader told them, mentioning the local senior school which had the reputation of being little more than a juvenile reform centre – without the reform.

Abigail, in spite of her fear, smiled to herself. 'That's what you think.'

She had a great deal of difficulty getting to sleep that night so excited was she about her news. There were only two people in the world she wanted to talk to about her wonderful news. Robbie and her Daddy.

She listened out for her father to come home but ten o'clock chimed and then eleven and still no sound of the key in the door. Unable to contain herself any longer, she tiptoed downstairs and found her mother glued to the television screen again. This time it was not a rubbish programme which she was fixated on but a rubbish computer game which Abigail, had she ever been interested in them in the first place, would have grown out of long ago.

At a suitable point in the game, the girl asked "Mum, where's Daddy?"

Without looking at her but still managing to convey her glare through the side of her head, Mrs. Ayres replied, "Your *father* is working late I believe. There's some reorganisation going on at work and they've asked him to help out. Like the lemon that he is, he's agreed to do it. I don't know why he doesn't just stand up to them and say no. They're always putting upon him."

Abigail believed that there was only one person he truly needed to stand up to and that being 'put upon' at work was really the least of his worries.

Disappointedly, she climbed up to bed unable to find anyone to share in her delight. She didn't know when or if she would next see Robbie. She was sure that she wouldn't see her father until after work the following night and then only if he wasn't working late again. He seemed to work late more often lately which Abigail could understand completely because getting home late for her was the only benefit of all the after school clubs which her mother had enrolled her in. Less time in the house, less time to be told off – simple mathematical equation.

She climbed into bed again feeling a little lonely when she heard a soft padding on the landing. The door inched open a little wider and in crept Britt Pollitt, the lovely tabby stray which Abigail, to her mother's disgust, had adopted.

"Guess what, Britt, I'm going to a great new school and I'm going to do great there and everything's going to be great." The cat looked up at her with what Abigail thought was an expression of admiration. They curled up together on the bed and both were soon fast asleep.

The following morning, Abigail left for school as usual and was just passing the bus stop in the High Street when her father stepped from the shop doorway where he had been waiting.

"Oh, Daddy, you made me jump. I thought I heard you leave about an hour and a half ago?"

"I did, love, but I've been waiting here for you to come by. Good job you didn't go through the park as usual on your way in," he laughed, revealing that he knew Abigail's secret playing place. His daughter looked horrified. "Don't worry, you know I won't tell your mother. Anyway, why I was waiting is, she told me that you got into the school and I just wanted to say well done. I…I…" There was so much he wanted to tell his daughter but the words failed him.

Abigail rescued him. "Thanks a lot, Daddy. I'm really chuffed too. It's going to be so exciting. I hope the people there'll be nice. I'm a bit scared that I won't know anyone."

"Ah yes, that's what else I meant to tell you. Your little chum, the Redovitch boy, his mother's in the hospital. I expect you haven't seen him about much in the last couple of days." It seemed that her father knew more about her life than she had given him credit for. "I thought it was funny when I didn't see Raman, his father, at work the other day because he's always there regular as clockwork. Never takes a day of. The guys in the packing department where he works told me what had happened. Shame. He's a nice bod, actually."

"That explained it" Abigail was momentarily relieved until the realisation of what her father had said truly hit home. "Is she o.k. I mean, it's not really serious, is it?"

"From what they said, it could be looking a bit dodgy," her father replied. Now Abigail was really worried because in her father's vocabulary, 'a bit dodgy' translated as 'catastrophic' or 'at death's door' in this case.

"Oh poor Rob."

Mr. Ayres looked at his watch. "Oh blimey, I'd better get going or I'm going to be late. They said I could come in a bit late today because of working so long yesterday but you know how long that rotten old bus can take to get into town, don't you? Still, it's cheaper than the train and that's what counts." He looked up the road and saw the big yellow and blue bus coming towards him. "See you later, love, hopefully. As long as there's no more overtime that needs doing."

"Bye, Daddy. And thanks a lot," but her father didn't hear because he was already unhappily jostling his way onto the bus with all the other commuters.

Abigail watched the bus as it disappeared on its long journey into town and realised that there was going to be yet another advantage to going to the Academy. She would get to travel in with her father almost every morning.

She looked at her own watch and realised that if she didn't get a move on, she too would be late. She wanted to have a bit of time with her classmates before lessons began because she was dying to find out who else had been accepted at the school.

Unfortunately, perhaps because she was tired from staying up too late the previous evening, the walk to school seemed to take longer than ever. She arrived just as the hated bell was ringing to signal the beginning of assembly.

She had to wait until break to talk about the Academy exams with everyone in her class. It seemed that the three people she liked most of all in her class had all got places and there was a great deal of both celebration and speculation about what it was going to be like. Miss Ellis had painted a very interesting picture of life at the new school and for the first time ever, the children thought that it might actually be nice to go back after the wonderful long summer break.

Just before the end of playtime, Sally Sturgeon came over and joined the happy group of Abigail and her friends. "What you all talking about?"

One of the boys in the group looked downcast and mumbled, "The Academy results."

"Don't suppose any of you losers got in, did you?" Without giving them a moment to answer, she went on, "Well, what do you expect? I'm going, natch."

Abigail's stomach turned over as, it would seem, did those of her friends. "You got in?" said Govinder Gohil, sounding utterly shocked. "What did you take in your exams?" He found it difficult to imagine that there would be any subject at all in which Sally could pass an exam.

"What d'you think? Sewing and Stage Management." It was true that, out of school, Sally was always dressed beautifully. She was very tall for her age and quite well-built, in that kind of hockey-playing way. Her clothes were always the height of fashion and most of what she wore, she had made herself. "It's not only you, Govinder 'Genius' Gohil, who can pass an exam, you know." Sally rolled her grey school socks down, her skirt up and was ready to face the rest of the world.

As she watched Sally walk away, Abigail said glumly, "Can you believe that? 'Stage Management'! You know what that means, don't you?"

"It means the organisation involved in running a theatre from managing the actors to…"

"No, no Gov. I mean, you know what it means for me. If I'm doing Acting and she's doing so-called 'Stage-Management' then I'm never going to be able to get away from her, am I?"

The other two looked pityingly at Abigail. "Just when you think it can't get any worse.." said Gov.

"Yeah, you go and slip over in a pile of your own vomit!" Abigail interrupted causing, as usual, mass hilarity.

Chapter O

It was another two days before Abigail saw Robbie again. She was not the only one who had been needing to speak to him in that time. Almost every hour, Mr. Alphabet had been calling the Redovitch's home number. He wanted to speak to Robbie's parents about the plan which he and Mrs. Evans had formulated to provide the boy with a place at the school.

Inside the main school, there were three extremely large halls. Two on the ground floor and one, right in the centre of the building on the first floor. This was the one which, until two days ago had had no specific use allocated to it. The others had been individually designated as the main assembly hall and the gymnasium.

On Wednesday evening over dinner, wracking her brains about the problem of the Redovitch boy, Mrs. Evans had had a flash of inspiration. "Upstairs!" she cried out.

Mr. Campbell looked the most shocked she had ever known him. He took off his bifocals, stared at her and said "What? Now?"

"Eh? What are you talking about?" Now they were both as confused as each other.

"You said 'upstairs' and I'm asking if you want me to go now or can I at least finish my stew first."

She made no attempt to hide the exasperation in her face. "Not you, silly. The Redovitch boy." Mr. Campbell then realised she was talking about the wretched school again and dejectedly went back to his beef and potato stew. "We could make that upstairs hall into somewhere for him to sleep, along with the others from out of town." Mrs. Evans continued expounding her idea for the next few minutes during which Mr. Campbell concentrated on eating his delicious dinner. His concentration was broken by the words "…..don't you agree?"

He suddenly realised that he hadn't heard a word she'd been saying. "What? What was that?"

"Either you are going mutton or you're not listening to me, as per usual. Oh never mind, I'm going to go and phone Mr. Alphabet."

Mr. Alphabet was in his little office trying to do the daily crossword in the newspaper. He never bothered with the cryptic one because, for him, the whole point of doing them was not to show off his intelligence to anyone but rather to expand his vocabulary to what he imagined it must have been before the accident.

"Nine letters. 'Place of safety, usually in a church.'" He was so deep in reverie that the telephone ringing startled him. He picked up the receiver, dropping the newspaper at the same time. "Sanctuary!" he exclaimed.

"What's that? Sorry, I think I've got the wrong number." Mrs. Evans began to put the phone down when she heard a voice calling her.

"Mrs. Evans, Mrs. Evans, It's me, Mr. Alphabet. You have got the right number, I was doing a crossword and I had just worked out the answer to one of the clues when you rang."

"Haven't I told you that we need to start answering the phone with the name of the school?" the voice at the other end admonished. "Anyway, never mind. I've got the answer."

"Oh yes?"

"The upstairs hall," Mrs. Evans told him.

Mr. Alphabet had been looking at the next clue in his crossword puzzle and wondered how the upstairs hall could possibly be the answer. His mind quickly cleared and he soon realised what his secretary was talking about. "That's right, we haven't really thought about what to do with that space, have we? It'd make a perfect…now what are those places called? A..B…C…D…D, yes that's it. Dormitory. Especially because it's got the dividing doors in the middle so we can have girls at one end and boys at the other. How many children do we need to accommodate as boarders, Mrs. Evans?"

"About one whole class full, so that's twenty-six."

"I don't see that being a problem, do you? Great idea. And we've got a couple of months to kit it out, so we should be able to get it all done. Thanks for that, Mrs. Evans. I'd better let you get back to your evening with your husband."

"Oh, you needn't worry about him, Mr. A. When you've been married as long as we have, you make your own entertainment."

As he put down the receiver, Mr. Alphabet felt sure that he could hear a door slamming in the background.

Mr. Alphabet finally managed to get hold of Raman Redovitch on Saturday afternoon. "Mr. Redovitch, I've been trying to get hold of you for several days."

"I have been up at ze hospital. My vife is unvell," Raman replied.

"I'm so sorry to hear that." Mr. Alphabet was concerned having seen how poorly the lady looked the previous weekend.

"Do not vorry. She is getting better now. Alzo, ve probably von't have her home for at least anozer veek. Anyway, you did not call to discuss viz me my problems. Vot can I do for you?"

"Did you get our letter saying that we would like to offer Robbie a place at the school?"

"I have opened no mail at all, I am afraid. But I am sorry to tell you that…"

"Robbie's exam results were in the top three percent of all candidates and, therefore, we would like to offer him a full boarding scholarship. Robbie will be accommodated in the school from Monday to Friday and there will be no tuition fees to pay. Of course, I understand that you have probably had many offers like this from schools wanting to admit Robbie. He really is a bright boy. I am sure that you will need to think about it, so why don't we say that you give me a call on Monday afternoon. Is that too soon?"

"No, no. zat vill be fine." Raman greatly appreciated Mr. Alphabet's diplomacy in making no mention of the family's difficult financial circumstances.

When the phone rang first thing on Monday morning, Mr. Alphabet was sure that it would be Robbie's father. "Hello…er..Mr.Alphabet's A to Z Academy." This time he had remembered to answer it according to Mrs. Evans instructions.

"Hello Mr. A, is my Mum there?" It was Christine Campbell.

"Christine! How are you?" He was always pleased to hear from her.

"Great, thanks. You?"

"Oh, you know, rushed off my feet. But I must say, your mother has been an absolute gift. I don't know what I'd have done without her. Thank you so much for recommending her."

"No prob. Actually it's done me the biggest favour because it's got her off my back!" They laughed.

"Well, I don't want to keep you hanging on because I'm sure that you're busy. I know she's here somewhere. I'll see if I can find her, hold on."

"Actually, d'you know what, don't worry. Just give her the message that we'll pick her up at five thirty this afternoon, will you?"

"Will do. Does this mean that I'll get to see you, too?"

"Only for five minutes, I'm afraid. We're going out for a family dinner. Fate worse than death if you ask me but unfortunately no-one *did* ask me. Anyway, see you later."

Mr. Alphabet was looking forward to it.

About an hour later, Mr. Alphabet found Mrs. Evans in her office rifling through catalogues from various companies selling linen and towels.

"If I order these now, we probably won't have to pay until we've had at least some of the deposits in from the parents."

"Good. Good. We're really getting straight, aren't we?"

"*We* are, yes!" the secretary answered.

As he left the room, Mr. Alphabet remembered why he had been looking for Mrs. Evans in the first place. "By the way, I forgot. I took a call from Christine earlier. She said she'll pick you up at about half five."

"Ooo, good. I'm going to meet her new chap for the first time this evening. She's courting, you know? A nice inspector from her station. Stephen, his name is. Stephen Spencer. We're all going out for dinner so I'll be able to find out all about him."

"Ah, that explains it…"began Mr. Alphabet but stopped himself short, thinking that it might not be politic to give away any of Christine's misgivings about the upcoming family dinner.

"Explains what?" asked Mrs. Evans.

"Er..that explains..that explains why you're getting a lift home this evening." He managed to wriggle his way out of the nasty situation but the look on his secretary's face told him that his wriggling had not been entirely successful. "I'm sure that you'll have a lovely evening. Well, I really must get on now," he said backing out of the office door. "I need to go and have a word with Grey and see how he's getting on with the watering. This dry weather is playing havoc with the garden and if they introduce a hosepipe ban, I can't imagine what on earth we're going to do."

"Well, we'll cross that boat when we come to it, shall we?" Mrs. Evans advised him.

' 'Bridge'', thought Mr. Alphabet. 'We'll cross that bridge when we come to it.'

"Before you go, Mr. A, that Mr. Redovitch called to say that he'd like to accept your offer. Didn't sound too grateful about it, I must say!"

"I think that he's possibly got a little more on his plate at the moment than worrying about hurting our feelings, don't you, Mrs. Evans." Mr. Alphabet was barely able to veil his sarcasm. "Anyway, I'm delighted for the boy. And he'll be an asset to the school, I'm sure."

———————————————

At exactly five- thirty that evening, Inspector Spencer's car rolled gently up the school drive. Mr. Alphabet went out to greet the couple.

"Afternoon, sir," said Spencer. Christine's been telling me all about you on the way over here. You're the gentleman who was in that nasty car accident about five years ago, aren't you? I hope you don't mind me mentioning it?"

"Not at all, Inspector. You remember it, then, do you?"

"It's not something one could forget in a hurry. I was a sergeant on the case at the time." He turned to look at the school building. "So this is your place, is it? Beautiful. And a really stunning garden as well, from what I saw coming up the drive."

"Would you like to take a look around it?"

"Love to." The police inspector did not need to be asked twice.

"Don't be too long, Steve. You know that Mum's booked that table at the Skwitz for six-thirty and we've still got to pick Dad up," Christine warned.

"The Skwitz. My, my. Your mother really is pushing the boat out. Or as she'd probably say 'pushing the bridge out'!" Mr. Alphabet and Christine laughed but, as yet, Stephen was not in on the joke. "Don't worry, Inspector, give it about half an hour and you'll know exactly why we're laughing. Anyway, let's get on with that tour of my lovely garden. I don't know if you're interested in exotic plants but Grey, my gardener, has grown some wonderful, unusual specimens in our hot-house."

"Oh, yes, I'd love to take a look at those." He followed Mr. Alphabet down the garden.

"Here's Grey now," Mr. Alphabet said as they entered the hot-house, which, at this time of year, was really living up to its name. "He's amazingly green fingered, you know. I found some seeds a while back which must have been sitting around since about the time of the accident. Grey just stuck them in the ground and hey presto, that patch of what looks like jungle at the back there, that's them."

"Seeds!" exclaimed Inspector Spencer.

"I know you'd never believe it, would you?" Mr. Alphabet agreed.

"No, no. You misunderstand me. I have been trying to think what it was that was niggling me since I first turned in through the gates and noticed how lovely your garden was. When we were first investigating your case, we found a packet of seeds in with your money and I thought that they might give us a clue to who you were so

I had a quick look to see if I could find out about them," Spencer stated, playing down the hours he had spent poring over the botany books in the basement of the police station.

Mr. Alphabet was excited by this. "Did you discover anything?"

"Nothing at all, I'm afraid." This did not unduly disappoint Mr. Alphabet since he had, over the intervening years, grown accustomed to the mystery surrounding him.

"Well, they really have turned out beautifully."

Mr. Alphabet was about to tell his new friend about the amazing flower which one of the plants had produced but they both heard a voice calling from the top of the garden.

"Come on you two, we're going to be late!" It was Mrs. Evans. As they emerged from the greenhouse, she shouted, "And you, Mr. A., had better get your glad rags on if you're coming with us."

This was the first Mr. Alphabet knew about it but he was more than happy to accept. It had been many a long month since he had eaten out and five years since he had set foot inside the hotel which had been his luxurious home for a short time.

He raced back up the garden and a mere ten minutes later they were all piling into Inspector Spencer's lovely new car.

The meal at the Skwitz was, as ever, delicious and the conversation between the little party of five was energetic. One of the main topics of conversation was, of course, Mr. Alphabet's new school and he was more than happy to talk about it, both because it was his pet subject and also because while he and Mrs. Evans were in full flow about the school, she had no opportunity to cross question Stephen. Mr. Alphabet was convinced that she was heading towards asking the old-fashioned question about Stephen's intentions towards her daughter. He was also convinced that, should such a question arise, Christine would simply die on the spot. So, he kept the conversation well and truly centred on the school and all its associated problems.

He told Stephen about why it had suddenly become such a rush to get the students into the school and about how the bank had given him an ultimatum.

"I spent every last penny I had on the place. It's not cheap, you know setting up a school."

"You mean the whole one million three hundred thousand has gone," asked the Inspector.

"Well remembered, Inspector. You're just fifty thousand pounds out. I had one and a quarter million," Mr. Alphabet corrected him.

"No, no. I remember quite distinctly because it was such a lot of money. Something like that I'd never forget."

Christine was confused because over the time that she had really got to know Spencer, she had come to realise that he had a phenomenal memory, so much so that she had never known him to forget anything. The mix-up over the money was quite confusing then.

"When Irving handed that money over to me there was only one point two five million." Christine was trying to retrace her steps from some five years ago which was not an easy task. "I'm sure Irving wouldn't have had anything to do with it. He might be obnoxious but he's not dishonest. So who…?" As she said it, the realisation dawned on both police officers.

"Ibbotson," they chorused.

Spencer was annoyed. "Now we know why he skipped off like that without working his notice. What a slimer!"

"What? You mean to say, that he's got fifty thousand pounds of my money?" asked Mr. Alphabet. "We could do with that right now, couldn't we Mrs. Evans?"

"I'll say. I'm a bit lost with all this though. Can you explain it to me again?" She had not been listening because she had been busy making sure that Mr. Campbell didn't spill any of his dinner down his front and that he was using the right knife and fork and that he didn't eat with his mouth open. She was not going to be shown up in a place like this.

It took quite some time for Mrs. Evans to get to grips with what had gone on and as they were leaving the restaurant, Spencer told Mr. Alphabet, "I hope that this is not going to be too uncomfortable for you, sir, but in the light of these latest developments,

I'm going to have to reopen the investigation." Then turning to smile at Christine he said, "And I thought that the most exciting thing that would happen this evening would be getting trapped in the crossfire between you and your Mum."

As they crossed the lobby on their way out of the hotel, a voice called out, "Mr. Alphabet, isn't it?" There were, as yet, still very few people who really knew him so Mr. Alphabet was quite shocked to hear his name being called. "I don't expect you remember me." The young man speaking was standing behind the high marble reception desk.

"Oh yes. You were here when I had that brief stay here, weren't you? It's Daz, isn't it?" Obviously the young man had made an impression on him.

"Er..Darren, that's right sir." Mr. Alphabet noticed that, at least with regard to his name, Darren must have matured considerably in the last five years.

"And what are you doing here now, Darren? If I remember correctly you were going to do a book-keeping course?"

Darren was pleased at how much Mr. Alphabet remembered. "I did that, sir. Then I started doing accountancy and passed my first two years, no problem."

"I'm sensing a 'but' coming."

Darren's voice dropped to a whisper. "The thing is, sir, that they've got the idea into their heads that I'm only fit for reception work and so every promotion and every job that comes up in the accounts department, they just overlook me and leave me stuck here. Also the longer you go on with the exams I've been doing, the more expensive they are and the more work you have to put in. There's just not enough hours in the day to put in the overtime here to pay for the exams *and* find the time to study. So I've just had to jack the night school in." Suddenly his voice got much louder and more business like. "Right well, I'm glad you enjoyed your meal, sir, and we look forward to seeing you again soon."

The snooty chief receptionist from five years ago was scurrying across the lobby and Mr. Alphabet, noticing this, was quick to take the cue. "Indeed, I will call you about the matter we were discussing and I look forward to seeing *you* again soon." Darren was grateful to Mr. Alphabet for going along with his charade but felt that there was almost more to his words than mere play acting.

Chapter P

It was a happy relaxed summer for Robbie and Abigail. They spent hours talking and chatting in the park until late in the evening. Their chats were interspersed with mad dashes under the disused pavilion to avoid the frequent heavy downpours. Abigail's mother, luckily, seemed to have turned her focus away from the girl and her searchlights were currently trained on her husband. He had made the fatal mistake of telling her that his supervisor at work had handed in his notice. She felt that this was an opportunity too good to miss especially because if he got a pay rise, she could get the new car she'd had her eye on.

It was a positive summer for the Redovitch family. Mrs. Redovitch's recovery seemed to have been speeded up by the easing of worry about Robbie's future and the plans were well under way for their move to the little house which Raman had found for them in a quiet seaside town.

It was an industrious summer for Mr. Alphabet, Mrs. Evans and all the new teachers at the Academy. They bought hundreds of text books and exercise books; they bought beds, bedding and assorted items necessary for the boarders; they bought a new leather chair for Mrs. Evans office because she was insistent that the small swivel chair she had was not fitting for someone 'in her position'. All of this was bought with the money which the parents had given as deposits for their school fees. Money which Mr. Alphabet delayed paying into the bank until three twenty-nine on Friday the twenty-fourth of July. This was the last banking minute before the two month deadline given to him by Messrs Barr, Stead and Company and he was keen to make a point.

It was a challenging summer for Darren Darby. He worked out his month's notice at The Skwitz much to the chief receptionist's disgust because, as he told Darren, there was a great career in the hotel trade ahead of him. Darren, however, felt that since this career had not shown any signs of materialising in the last seven years, in spite of all the efforts that he had made, then it was unlikely to suddenly start now. His first month as Bursar at Mr. Alphabet's A-Z Academy was certainly different from standing behind the reception desk greeting the, mostly, ungrateful rich.

It was a rewarding summer for Grey. The vast quantities of rain which had fallen in July meant that there was no shortage of water and, more importantly, it meant that the grass everywhere was growing like fury. There was ample opportunity to get out his favourite toy, the lawn-mower.

It was an interesting summer for Sergeant Campbell and Inspector Spencer. They had one or two great leads to follow in the hunt for Ibbotson, the man formerly known as Inspector.

The first week of September arrived and there was great excitement mixed with trepidation among all those involved with the school. Timetables were set, classes allocated, parquet polished, lawns mown. All that remained was to fill the place up with children and start the year.

On the evening before the first day of school, Abigail was ironing her new school blouse. She loved the crisp whiteness of it and it was so satisfying to see those sharp creases disappear.

"I don't know what you're doing that for. No-one's going to be bothering to look at you. And anyway that shirt's brand new. Cost a rotten fortune too that whole get-up. *And* I expect you'll have grown out of it in five minutes." All of this came as quite a shock for Abigail because Eleanor had hardly addressed a word to her in the past couple of months.

"It's just for something to do, really." Abigail spoke nonchalantly. It was vital that her mother didn't find out how excited she was about going to her new school or how important it was to her. She remembered Robbie's words when they had been discussing her problem one day in the park. "Never give her anything she can use against you," he had advised and she knew that she must stick to this policy.

"Well, if you're that desperate for something to do, you can at least help a bit round the house instead of running off to play with whoever it is." This was a bit rich since the only thing which her mother did around the house was a little bit of cooking, and that not often. "Try not to think about yourself all the time, Abigail Ayres. Just like your father, you are. I'm the only one in the family who ever considers anyone else's feelings." Mrs. Ayres' eyes filled up with tears but Abigail did not see them because she was already applying her trick of blurring her eyes and pretending she was somewhere else. Anywhere else.

Suddenly, realising that the tears were not working, Mrs. Ayres was no longer upset but was now shouting which brought Abigail back from her other world. "Look at you. Don't hear a word I say. Gormless, you are. Just like your father." The shouting had brought on an enormous coughing fit and when she had regained her composure, Mrs. Ayres said, "I'm not going to stand around here and waste my breath.". She flounced off to the living room and Abigail could hear the sound of the computer game booting up and a match being struck.

"I wonder what 'gorm' is, if I haven't got any!" Abigail laughed to Britt Pollitt as she picked him up, interrupting his game with the cord for the iron.

She heard the sound of a key in the front door and ran down the hall to greet her father. "What kind of mood's your mother in?" was the first thing that he quietly said to her.

"Hello, Daddy. Not too great, is how I'd put it."

"Hello, Abi. Sorry about that. How rude of me." He looked so sad. This was not the news that he had been wanting to hear but it *was* the news which he'd been expecting.

"No, no. Don't worry about it," she whispered. "I'm not really sure what's kicked the tantrum off this time."

"Oh, I know exactly…"

"What are you two whispering about out there?" Eleanor shouted from the living room.

"I'll tell you in a minute," her father told her conspiratorially. He raised his voice. "Nothing, love. I was just asking Abi, if she's ready for tomorrow." He walked into the living room and addressed his wife, "How are you getting on?" There was no answer. "I'll just go and get changed then and have my dinner, shall I?" Still no answer. Anthony Ayres, knowing not to push his wife when she was in this mood, left the room.

Over dinner, he told Abigail that they'd got a new supervisor at work and that, in fact, he hadn't even tried for the job. "I can't do it, Abi. I don't want the responsibility. Life's stressful enough, without that. But your Mum's not very pleased because she really wanted that new car."

'There's nothing stopping her getting up of her own behind and going for promotion herself,' Abigail thought.

"Never mind, eh. When you're a famous actress taking Hollywood by storm, you can take me away from all this, can't you?" Her Dad knew exactly the right things to say.

The next morning, Abigail and her Dad were up at the crack of dawn and on their way to the bus stop even before Eleanor had thought about stirring from her bed.

It was great to be travelling into town with her Daddy. He got off at the same stop as her even though it was a long way from his work. "You don't need to go all the way to school with me, Daddy. I'll be fine." Abigail said as they ambled gently the last few hundred metres to the school.

"I'll just make sure you're all right and then head off. And you needn't think you're getting this treatment all the time," he laughed, ruffling her chestnutty brown hair.

Robbie must have been looking out of the dormitory window waiting for her to walk up the drive because by the time she and her father reached the great stone steps to the main entrance, Robbie was racing across the hall.

"I'm guessing that you're Robbie, Raman's boy," Mr. Ayres said.

"I am, yes."

"How's it going, Rob? What was the dorm like? What are the other kids like?" Abigail was full of questions.

Robbie sniffed and hung his head. "All right, I suppose."

Anthony Ayres put a comforting hand on Robbie's shoulder. "Come on, young man. It'll be fine once you're settled in, you'll see. And maybe, one of the evenings you can come out to dinner with us." Robbie and Abigail gave each other a look which did not go unnoticed by Mr. Ayres. "It'd be just the three of us. Maybe we could go out for a pizza. What do you think?"

"That'd be fab," said Robbie, already beginning to brighten.

"It's a deal then. Now, I must get off. Have a good day you two and good luck."

"Thanks," they chimed and, turning, made their way into the school. Mrs. Evans was waiting for them inside the entrance hall.

"Did I see you running and skidding on my parquet floor a minute ago, my lad?" Without waiting for an answer, she continued, "There'll be none of that in this school. A bit of decency and decoration is what we want."

The children looked puzzled until Govinder Gohil, who had been scrutinising the notice board, came over and said, "I think she might mean a bit of decency and decorum." The three of them laughed and Mrs. Evans called over to them, "There'll be no laughing at people. Don't you know it's one of the ignorantest things you can do." This was not helping the children to control their giggles at all. "If you look on that noticeboard, you'll see which form you're in and there's a map showing you how to get to your classrooms….Let's hope you're not all in the same form because it looks to me like there'll be no work done."

Govinder whispered to the others, "I don't know what she's getting so upetty about. She's not even a teacher, she's only a secretary."

Robbie, who had already had a run in with her the previous night, gave them a word of warning. "She might only be the secretary but she seems to think she's the sergeant in charge of an army boot camp. Watch her!"

All of a sudden, there was the sound of an Albinoni Oboe Concerto coming through the air. "That's the bell," Robbie told them.

"Wow!" Gov exclaimed. "This school really is going to be different."

"Come on, you two, we'd better get to classes because I've got off to a bad enough start as it is and I don't want to get into any more bother if I can help it." Robbie started walking quickly towards his classroom and Govinder and Abigail headed off together to the classroom for Form B.

Entering the classroom, Abigail was delighted to see that her form teacher for this year was going to be Miss Ellis. They had always got on very well in the junior school and Abigail was glad to see a familiar face. She was also glad to see that another familiar face, that of Sally Sturgeon, was noticeably absent from among the twenty-five other children in her class.

"Right, class." Miss Ellis was standing at the front of the classroom on the raised platform where her desk was. "We need quickly to take the register and get down to the Main Hall for morning assembly." It was a job which did not take too long and they were soon all filing down the long back corridor of the school.

When everyone was gathered in the Hall, Mr. Alphabet emerged from his small office at the side and climbed onto the platform.

"Good morning, school." His confident tone belied his nervousness and excitement. There was silence in the Hall. "I said, Good Morning, School."

The pupils had not realised that he was waiting for a response this not being the usual run of things in a morning assembly where they were used simply to being lectured at. A few of them called back hesitantly. "Good morning, sir."

"Well, maybe that'll get better as time goes on. In the meantime, there are a few things which I wanted to say. Firstly, a hearty welcome to the school. You all have the advantage over me because there's only one of me and one hundred and thirty of you but I hope to have learnt all your names fairly soon. If I struggle with them, please help me out by just giving me your initial. Secondly, and very importantly, I have to tell you that you may go anywhere in the school building and grounds, including my office, the staffroom, the kitchens, etc. But, and I can't stress this strongly enough, the hot house at the bottom of the garden is absolutely and categorically out of bounds. Any child found entering the place will be asked to leave the school permanently for their own safety. This may seem harsh but let me reassure you," he went on, noticing all the glum little faces staring up at him, "this *is* only for your safety. Some places in our lives, just like some people, are more dangerous than others. On that subject, and thirdly, bullying will not be tolerated in this school. That includes bullying from pupil to pupil, from pupil to teacher, from teacher to pupil and from teacher to teacher." The children looked at each other, stunned. They had never heard of such a thing as one teacher bullying another. "Any incidence of this must be reported immediately so that appropriate action may be taken. Fourthly and finally, this school is about enjoyment. If, at any time, you find that you are taking subjects which you don't like or which don't get the best out of you, then you must come and see me immediately. My door is always open and I am always ready to listen to whatever you might have to say on any matter." Mr. Alphabet was ready to draw his speech to a close and leave the podium when he noticed Mrs. Evans glowering at him. With a sigh, he muttered, "One more thing, there is to be no running, sliding or skidding in the corridors. I would ask you please to be careful because they can be very slippery because Mrs. Evans frequently applies…Oh what's that stuff called…A..B..C..Comes in a tin, makes wood shine…D…E.."

"Polish," came a hesitant voice from Form D.

"No, no. Good try though. F…G…Is that it G?"

"Grease?" suggested another helpful pupil.

"Thanks but no. H..I.."

"Wax, sir?"

"That's it, well done. Wax. What's your name, lad?"

"Govinder Gohil, sir."

"Well done, Govinder. One form point for you." Govinder was very pleased with himself and, looking down the row, winked at Abigail. It looked like their form was going to be doing pretty well, if this was anything to go by.

The first couple of weeks flew by fairly uneventfully for the new pupils at the school. Their only concern was finding their way around the vast building. By the end of the third week, Abigail and Govinder were down to getting slightly lost three times a day and hopelessly lost only once daily. This was a major improvement on their previous weeks' records.

They were laughing about their orientation problem one day outside the language lab after double French. "You'd think that you of all people, would be able to find your way around, Gov. After all your special subject is Geography!" They sniggered. "Anyway, where are you off to now, cos I've got double drama? Hurrah!"

"Ugh! Lucky you! Double Games for me. Rotten old cricket. That stupid games teacher at our old school. Why did he have to put me down to take the exam in rotten old cricket? Just because he's seen India play Pakistan on the telly, he thinks anyone who has even a vague connection with the sub-continent must be interested in the stupid sport. Frankly, I'd rather have all my toe-nails ripped out than have to play a whole game of rotten old cricket. Still, never mind. It's just got to be done."

"No it hasn't. Why don't you go and see Mr. A about it. I bet he'd let you drop it if you told him what you've just told me," Abigail suggested.

"Let's see, eh? Maybe I'll grow into my racial stereotype and come to love it!"

"I doubt it, Gov. Anyway, I'd better get a move on 'cos I don't want to be late for Miss Diamond." Abigail hurried away looking like a power-walker as she tried to restrain herself from running along the corridor.

She turned the corner and headed up the small spiral staircase which led directly to the music room. The walls were brick, the floor was stone, there was no handrail and

Abigail was just thinking that, if Mr. Alphabet wanted to talk about safety, he could begin by having a look at these stairs. As she neared the top, she realised that a figure was blocking her exit from the staircase.

It was Sally Sturgeon.

"Abigail Ayres, I've been hoping to catch you on your own." Other than her mother's, she had never heard a voice more full of menace. "I want a word with you."

Chapter Q

Abigail couldn't believe her bad luck as she inched her way up the stairs. She had managed to avoid having any direct contact at all with Sally since they started at the school but it looked like she might well be going to have some pretty close physical contact right now. Sally had had the reputation at their old school of being quite aggressive. She wasn't the most gifted speaker but it was said that her fighting skills made up for it. None of Abigail's circle had ever actually witnessed one of these fights but, Abigail thought, 'You don't need to put your hand in the fire to know that it's hot.'

Abigail was wishing and wishing that someone would appear to rescue her but it looked like her luck had run out this time.

"Anyone'd think you were avoiding me, Abigail Ayres." Sally grinned at her through parted lips, revealing a set of teeth not dissimilar to those of Abigail's least favourite creature on earth, the shark. 'I wonder if she bites too,' Abigail thought to herself. "I've been trying to have a word with you for days." The bigger girl was backing away from the top of stairs now so that Abigail could get out onto the landing. "Have you been given any projects to do before the end of term?" This was not quite what Abigail had been expecting but she thought that maybe she was going to force her to do some homework for her or something.

"Er.. w..ell," she stammered. "The only thing I've got so far is the Christmas production which you know about anyway because you're going to be stage managing it, aren't you?"

"Oh yeah. No I meant anything else."

"No, no, I haven't." Abigail was more and more curious. What on earth could the Sturgeon want?

"Well, you see..I was wondering…" This time it was the taller girl's turn to sound nervous. "I've got to make this outfit for the Fashion Show at the end of term….and all we've been given for the title is 'Living Doll'…and…I…."

"Oh, Sally, I can't sew at all. You must remember last year with Miss Taylor how it took me a whole year to make a wrap-around skirt that was just sewing a waistband on to a piece of material. I am useless at it." Both girls laughed, Abigail with nerves and Sally because she found it genuinely funny.

"Almighty! I wouldn't want you to sew it for me, you nutter! I don't want to be thrown out in my first term here, do I?" She laughed again. "No. What it is, is…I was wondering…" For an extremely confident girl she was sounding extremely frightened, in Abigail's opinion. "Well, I know what I want to make but I can't model the outfit on me. I mean look at me, I look about as much like a doll as Pamela Anderson looks like someone who hasn't had surgery. But you, you're tiny. You'd look great in what I'm going to make. So, I was wondering if you'd be my model." Abigail was so stunned that she nearly fell backwards down the stairs and only just managed to stop herself by putting her hands out. Unfortunately the exposed brickwork of the staircase wall grazed her hand and she cried out.

With her hand in her mouth trying to stop it from bleeding, Abigail stared at Sally.

"Look, forget it right. I knew I should never have asked. I mean why would little Miss Ayres-and-Graces help the likes of me?" She turned to walk away.

Abigail took her hands from her mouth and said quietly, "I'd be delighted to….One thing though," now she had her eyes trained fixedly on Sally, "if you ever call me that name again I might be forced to stick your outfit right up where the sun don't shine!" Sally looked surprised, to say the least. "Is it a deal?"

"Deal!" She offered Abigail her hand and they shook on it. Unfortunately, Abigail shook with the hand which had just been wounded and she cried out again.

"Ow, that really hurt!"

Just then, the two girls heard a rustling coming round the bend in the corridor towards them. It was Mr. Alphabet. "What's going on here? Is there some kind of trouble?"

"No, sir," the girls said in unison. He examined both of their faces closely to see if he could detect any deceit. "Well, you both run along to your drama class now. And if I hear that there's been any intimidation or fighting," he looked from one girl to the other, "you will both have to answer to me."

"Yes, sir." Sally hung her head dejectedly. As they hurried towards the music room, she said, "People always think I'm up to something even when I'm not. So I might just as well be, mightn't I?"

"This time you've definitely done nothing wrong, Sal, and I'll vouch for you." These were words that she never thought she'd be uttering.

The days, weeks and months of the first term flew by. By the second half of the term, around fifty percent of the pupils had changed one of their special subjects to something that they might actually want to do. Govinder Gohil's subjects were now Geography and German, both of which he was excellent at.

In spite of saying that Abigail would be finding her own way to school after the first day, Anthony Ayres could not resist spending those extra few minutes alone with his lovely daughter. She would tell him, on their journeys into school, about what she was doing, about her friends and teachers, about the school lunches which were a little better than in her last school but still not great. Mr. Ayres knew that Abigail was loving the place and he felt that it was really bringing her out of herself because until that point she had been a lot like him, very loving and caring but more than a little introverted.

It was a surprise then, one drizzly Tuesday morning, shortly before Hallowe'en, when Mr. Alphabet met Abigail and her father on the school steps. "I was wondering, Mr. Ayres, if you could spare a few moments for a little chat." Abigail was crestfallen. She tried to think over what she might have done to cause displeasure. It must be the supposed bullying incident. That was the only thing she could come up with.

Both men noticed the look on the little girl's face and, before she was able to withdraw into herself completely, Mr. Alphabet said, "Don't be scared, my dear. It's really nothing to worry about. I'd like you to be in on the discussion too. Shall we go to my office?"

The three of them squeezed into Mr. Alphabet's tiny study but far from feeling at all cramped, it felt cosy and homely.

"Right," the headmaster began when they had all taken their seats. "I just wanted to speak to you both about Abigail's special subjects." Abigail was worried. Surely she wasn't going to have to give up drama?

Mr. Alphabet continued, "As you know her acting ability is beyond question and there is no doubt that she will, and will want to, continue with that. The problem really is anatomy. When I say 'problem', it's not really a problem because your daughter, Mr. Ayres is a very hard-working pupil and she is obtaining more than satisfactory grades in the subject. No, the problem is that she is not getting the best out of anatomy and anatomy is not getting the best out of her." This came as no surprise to Anthony Ayres because he, of course, knew that this subject had not been Abigail's personal choice. "How would you feel about changing from anatomy Abigail?" Mr. Alphabet asked.

"Yeah, great, but...." Abigail looked at her father.

Mr. Ayres told the head, anxiously, "It's obviously something I'm going to need to discuss with my wife, Mr. Alphabet. Can I get back to you?"

"Of course you may. I would, of course have asked you and your wife together but we don't very often see her at the school and I didn't really want to make a big deal of it and call a formal meeting. I tell you what, why don't you think about it over half term and let me know at the start of the second half?" Mr. Alphabet had anticipated this problem and was not overly hopeful that the situation could be resolved.

"Thank you, we will. A...and I just wanted to say thank you for everything you're doing for Abi."

"My pleasure, that's what we're here for."

As he watched them leave his office together, Mr. Alphabet thought how lovely it was to see a parent who quite evidently cared so much for their children and how depressing at the same time that both that parent and the child lived most of their lives in fear.

To lighten his mood, Mr. Alphabet thought that he would take a stroll around the garden. Grey really had done the most amazing things with it over the past five years. He had clearly developed renewed interest and pride in the place after years of neglect. Even at this time of the year, with all the leaves on the ground, various shades of yellow, orange and copper, the garden had a sculptural beauty about it.

He found Grey in the avenue of copper beech, forking dead leaves into the small trailer attached to the back of the lawn-mower. The gardener's little dog was bouncing about barking, thinking that it was a great game to run through the piles of leaves which his master had carefully raked together. "Roo-ah, Frizzy," Mr. Alphabet heard the old man say to the dog.

Frizzy seemed such an odd name for a dog whose coat was quite clearly smooth. Maybe it was Grey's idea of a joke. Frequently, though, Mr. Alphabet couldn't even be quite certain that it *was* Frizzy. He often thought that he could hear a 't' in the middle there somewhere.

"Morning, Grey, how are you?"

"Fair to middlin', mister." This was Grey's stock response.

"I'd like to take a look around the hot-house with you, if you don't mind."

"Right you are, mister. I'll just put the dog in the house. Don't want 'im falling into that slime, do we?...Komm, Fritzi." There it was, there was that 't'.

They met up again in the glass-house and Mr. Alphabet was amazed to see how well everything was still doing. "Have we put any heat in here, Grey? It feels incredibly warm and I'm sure that some of these plants should be dying back a bit. I mean to say, it's going to be November next week."

"No, no heat, sir. No money for that, not with that young Darren Darby looking after your accounts. I'm surprised he even gives you any money for pens and paper." Mr. Alphabet could see in the old man's face a touch of admiration for Darren's frugality.

"Why is it so warm in here, then?"

"It's coming up from the mud there. Dunno' what exactly it is. In all the seventy years I've known it, this place 'as always 'ad something about it that's a bit of a mystery. All those fellas coming down 'ere and never coming back and leaving no trace behind, I mean that's not normal, now, is it?"

Mr. Alphabet had to agree that this was indeed 'not normal' but he tried not to think about it any further and so changed the subject.

"Those plants at the back there still seem to be doing really well. And to think that you just put them in as seeds." The strange plants to which he was referring had had the most unusual growth pattern that Grey had ever seen. In just over one day after being planted, they had grown so much that they were almost touching the roof of the hot-house. They had then never grown another centimetre. "Have we had another flower on any of them, by the way?" his boss enquired.

"Not a one. Maybe the rest of 'em's all duffers. I ain't got time to be pulling 'em up now, though."

"I don't suggest that you do. They look interesting enough as they are anyway....I must get on and call the botanical gardens one of these days." Mr. Alphabet knew that this was unlikely in the near future because he had his work cut out running the school and a few plants in the old glasshouse were the least of his problems.

"Well, I'd better get back into school and get on with things. Thanks for your time, Grey. You can go and get Frizzy out again now….By the way, is it 'Frizzy' or 'Fritzi'?"

"It's 'Fritzi', mister."

"That's most unusual. How did he come by a name like that?"

"It's not unusual everywhere, mister," Grey corrected the headmaster. "Anyway, all my dogs, all my life have been called the same thing.

Mr. Alphabet made his way back up to the school building wondering what Grey meant about the name not being unusual everywhere.

Anthony Ayres had spent the rest of that week and until the Friday of the half-term week which followed, wondering how on earth and when he was going to discuss the issue of Abigail's special subject with his wife.

This was not going to be easy on several counts. Firstly, and most obviously, she was going to go mad about Abigail changing from Eleanor's chosen subject of anatomy. Secondly, she was going to want to know why the head had chosen to speak to him and not Eleanor herself about it because up to now, any and all decisions about Abigail's life had been her mother's sole responsibility. Thirdly, she was going to want to know how it was that Mr. Ayres happened to be at the school anyway and she would then find out about him walking their daughter to school, which, in itself, would drive her insane. Fourthly…he stopped worrying at fourthly because he was making himself feel sick.

He had decided that the subject must be broached while Abigail was out of the house. Unfortunately, every evening during half-term, Abigail had been up in her room reading and learning her words for the Christmas play. There never seemed to be a good opportunity for him to begin the conversation.

As luck would have it, for him if not for Abigail, there was an under twelves' party at the local golf club on the Friday evening and Eleanor had told Abigail that she was to go. This did not go down at all well with the girl because, to begin with, she disliked the children of the people who were members of the club. She had nothing in common with them at all and they all seemed to look down their noses at her. The next problem for her was that because her father, much to her mother's disgust, was not a member, Abigail had to go as someone else's guest. That 'someone else' was possibly the most obnoxious boy she had ever met in her life and the thought of spending ten minutes with him was a complete nightmare to her. Never mind the prospect of a whole evening as his guest. On top of which, she knew that her mother had only befriended *his* mother so that they could be invited to such naff events as this one.

The final insult came when her mother told her that it was a fancy dress party for Hallowe'en. How could her mother do this to her?

Abigail never minded dressing up for a proper play but dressing up to ponce about at a stupid party? No way!

She tried to reason with her mother that it'd be easier all round if she didn't go because everyone there would be dressed to the nines in costumes hired, at an exorbitant rate, from Engel and Bowman and they couldn't really afford it, what with the school fees and everything. However, 'reason' and 'her mother' were not words which sat happily in the same sentence.

"I'm not having any of those stuck-ups thinking that we can't afford a fancy outfit for you. I'll ask your Uncle Eddie if he'd like to pay for your costume. After all, it is your first important party and you never know what useful contacts you might make there."

'Useful contacts?' thought Abigail. 'I'm thirteen years old, for goodness sake! What do I need with useful contacts?'

"It's a good job we've got good genes on my side of the family. People who know how to get on and make a decent living for themselves. Not like your father." She went on, "Your Uncle Eddie has made a name for himself and his estate agency business in this town and he's well known for his sharp brain."

Abigail knew that he was actually more 'well known' for his sharp business practices than his sharp brain.

She conceded defeat and at six forty-five on the Friday evening there was an ugly lime-green goblin standing in the hallway of the Ayres ordinary suburban semi waiting for its lift. This was the only costume which Engel and Bowman had had left by the time Eddie Eccleston had bowed under the pressure from his overbearing sister and agreed to pay for his niece's outfit.

As Abigail was leaving the house, she was surprised to see her father arriving home early from work.

He addressed her quietly. "Just thought I ought to warn you, old girl, I'm going to speak to your mother about the 'Anatomy Issue' this evening, while you're out."

The evening, which had not even begun yet, was already one of the worst she could remember. Surely it couldn't get any worse?

Chapter R

On entering the house at nine-forty after a dull, embarrassing evening, Abigail found that it could get and, in fact, had got worse. Much worse. She could hear her mother screaming from the living room as soon as her Dad opened the front door to her.

She heard the voice screech from the living room. "Is that you, you cheeky madam? You'd better get in here now. We need to have words." Abigail knew that this meant her mother was going to have words and Abigail was going to listen.

Abigail and her father exchanged sympathetic glances and the girl went down the hall.

Unusually, her mother was standing. The room was full of smoke and, looking at the overflowing ashtray, Abigail realised that this must have been a very difficult evening. The computer game on the television was on pause.

Her mother was doing that sucking in her cheeks face which she did when she was really angry. She actually always looked a bit comical to Abigail when she did this, but now was not the time for a little snigger.

"Right, my lady. Let's get this straight. You *are* going to be a doctor. You *are* going to carry on with anatomy. You are *not* going to listen to anyone who tells you otherwise. That includes your idiot father. Do I make myself clear?"

"Yes, Mum," mumbled the girl.

"Good. We're going to put all this nonsense behind us and get on with our original plan." All this 'we' and 'us' Abigail felt must refer to the royal 'we'. "Are we in agreement?"

"Mmm."

"Stop mumbling. You're just like your father. He never opens his mouth when he speaks."

'Too frightened, I expect.' Abigail was well aware of the hold which the woman had over her father.

"Again, are we in agreement?"

"Yes, Mum." Abigail could barely speak through the lump in her throat.

"Right, now, go upstairs, get that ridiculous looking costume off. I don't know what you think you look like, making a show of me like that." That was a bit rich considering that Abigail had never wanted to dress up in the rotten thing anyway. "If you see your idiot father on your way upstairs, tell him to get in here now. I haven't finished with him. Not by a long way."

Abigail left the room but was summoned back by the nasal squeal of her mother. "Oh, I was nearly forgetting. There's one other thing I need to tell you....*I'll* be taking you to school of a morning now."

The tears could be held back no longer and Abigail ran from the room clutching her green goblin head in her hand.

Luckily she didn't bump into her Dad on the way upstairs because seeing him now might have been too painful. She lay on her bed and sobbed and sobbed and sobbed.

She was still sobbing when, an hour later, Britt wandered into the room, leapt on her bed and put his little pink nose against hers. "Don't worry, Britt, I'll get over it. Maybe being a doctor won't be so bad after all." She wasn't doing a very good job of convincing herself and an even less good job of convincing the cat who turned his bottom towards and started cleaning his face.

Watching him, Abigail began to drift off to sleep and woke in the middle of the night to find that she was still sporting her green tights and tunic.

———————

As promised, on the first day back after the half-term break, Eleanor took Abigail to school in the new car which she had bought anyway, disregarding the fact that Anthony hadn't got promotion, hadn't had a pay rise and had told her that just now they couldn't really afford a new car.

This was not the best journey into school which Abigail had ever had. Her mother was not a great driver. There was always the possibility the she would forget to brake and plough straight over a roundabout or plough into a tree which she would swear had not been there on the previous day. So, it was hair-raising.

Yet more hair-raising was the cross-questioning which Abigail had to undergo for the entirety of the journey. Torquemada and the Spanish Inquisition could have learned one or two things from Mrs. Ayres. By the time Abigail arrived at school, she was exhausted from fending off her mother's interrogation. The problem was that she really did not want to lie but there was so much that she knew she couldn't tell her mother because there would be at least one, if not several, explosions. She had to use all her skills of economy with the truth, therefore to wheedle her way around the issues.

As luck would have it, it was not possible to drive up to the front of the school during the school day because Mr. Alphabet felt that it was too dangerous. So, her mother stopped outside the school gates having mounted the kerb unceremoniously.

Abigail thanked her mother and couldn't get out of the car quickly enough. Why exactly she had thanked her mother, she didn't know because she'd have been far happier making her own way to school.

Robbie and Govinder were kneeling on the floor by the school steps, picking things up. "Gov's just tipped his whole bag upside down….Hey, where's your Dad, Abi?" They had got used to seeing the pair arriving every morning, Mr. Ayres carrying Abigail's heavy school bag.

Abigail told them about her awful weekend and about the drive into school this morning. "She kept on saying 'I hope you're not wasting your time on stupid drama. Why does anyone want to do drama, anyway? Ridiculous waste of time. It won't get you anywhere. No-one's interested in drama or the people who do it.' I thought it'd never end."

"Take no notice, Abi." Robbie advised her. "Oh, I take it your parents won't be coming to the Christmas play, then?"

"I hadn't thought about that. Oh no. And Daddy was so looking forward to seeing me in it."

"Maybe he'll be able to come on his own," suggested Robbie.

"Yeah right! And maybe I'll be able to take on Mike Tyson and become champion heavy weight boxer of the world," said Gov. Looking at his slender frame, the other two realised that even this was probably more likely than Mr. Ayres being let out on his own.

Their discussion about Abigail was interrupted by the sound of a car crunching up the gravel drive. The three children looked round to see who was breaking Mr. Alphabet's rule and were surprised to see a large police car coming towards them.

Mr. Alphabet strode down the stone steps, climbed into the police car and was driven away.

That day the school was alive with gossip at what could possibly have happened to Mr. Alphabet. Teachers were pumped for information but had none to give. Teachers checked with each other to see if anyone had clues. No-one did. There was a great deal of speculation, all of which was tinged with worry because the thought of Mr. Alphabet being in some kind of trouble and the school being forced to close was really too much for almost everyone.

After lunch, Govinder, Abigail and Robbie were sitting together in Robbie's dorm going over and over the past few days to see if they could come up with anything. Mrs. Evans passed by the open dorm door on her way to check the linen cupboard and Govinder noticed that she had a more than usually self-important look on her face. "She knows something, I'd swear."

"Probably, yeah," agreed Robbie. "But if you think you're getting any information out of her, you must be joking. She's as tight as a drum, that one. Anyway, we'd better get out of here because she's not keen on people being in here during the day."

"What does she think you're going to do? The days of apple pie beds have gone." Govinder had read a lot of Enid Blyton to his younger sisters.

"Who knows what goes on in that woman's mind? I wish we could think of a way of getting the information out of her though because if this school closes down, I'll have to go to the local one out where we live. That, let me tell you, is a fate worse than death," Robbie told them.

"I thought you liked it where your folks live?" Gov was surprised by Robbie's strong reaction.

"Oh, I do. The town's great and Mum's doing really well down there. Dad's got a much better job than he had up here. So from that point of view, no problem. But the school is just awful. Boring subjects taught in a boring way. Sometimes at the weekends I hang out with one or two lads who go there and they tell me how bad and strict it is."

"You see, this is the thing. We've been really spoilt here." Abigail was always able to recognise and appreciate a good thing when she saw one. "Anyway, instead of worrying what might happen, let's think of a way of finding out what Mrs. E. knows for a start."

At the same time as the three friends were poring over this problem, Grey was also chewing over the same dilemma. He had seen Mr. Alphabet go off in the police car that morning and he had no idea why but what he did know was that that 'rotten old busy-body' would know all about it. He said as much to Miss Ellis when she came out to the rugby pitch where he was putting down some fresh white lines.

"I'll be blowed, miss, if I'm going to *that* woman for anything. She won't give anything away, anyway, she won't. Wouldn't give a blind man a light, that one!"

Evelyn Ellis realised what a mistake she had made asking Grey about Mrs. Evans. Over the past few weeks, she had been so engrossed in the start of the new school year that she had clean forgotten some of the spats she had witnessed between Mr. Alphabet's two oldest employees.

She knew that she needed to back out of this corner pretty quickly before Grey's mood deteriorated further. "Well, perhaps Mr. Grey, if you happen to find out any information from *any* source you will let me know. Like you, we are all worried for Mr. Alphabet's welfare."

"More like worried about your jobs. How d'you think I feel, miss? This is my home too."

"I think that we shouldn't jump to too many pessimistic conclusions, don't you?" Evelyn was backing away now. "Have a good afternoon anyway, Grey. Must fly!"

" 'Have a good afternoon. Must fly!' The only person flying round here is that old busy body, Evans, on her broomstick!" Evelyn heard none of this because she was already dashing back into the school to begin the afternoon's lessons.

Grey deliberately didn't go up to the school kitchen for his tea as usual that day. With Mr. Alphabet absent, it wouldn't be so enjoyable anyway and he didn't want to give that 'busy body' the opportunity of talking to him, knowing all the time that she knew something he didn't.

He was astonished, later that afternoon then, to hear a tapping on the outside of the greenhouse glass. He jumped so much that he nearly fell off the walkway into the deadly mud. Having regained his balance, with a look of ferocity on his face, he looked up to see Mrs. Evans peering in through the glass at him.

Fritzi dashed out of the hot house and stood growling in front of the alarmed secretary. "Get that stupid mutt away from me," she shouted.

"That ain't no mutt. And he's got more intelligence in one paw than you've got in your whole body. Over here Fritzi, there's a good boy." He reached into the pocket of his decrepit looking trousers and pulled out a small piece of salami which the dog quickly took from his hand. Grey spoke to the dog but Mrs. Evans couldn't understand a word of what he said.

"I don't know why you can't just talk to the animal in plain straightforward English, like the rest of us do."

Grey didn't bother to answer.

"Anyway, I haven't come here to talk about your dog. I thought that you might have had the decency to come and enquire about where Mr. A's got to." Mrs. Evans was at her most sanctimonious.

"Ooo, you mean to tell us that you know. Now, there's a surprise. And I suppose it doesn't matter that you've waited about eight hours to come and tell us. And me worried sick."

"If you were that worried, you'd have come and asked yourself."

"No I wouldn't. Anyway, where is he? What's happened to him?" Grey couldn't help himself.

"My Christine and her young man, Inspector Spencer, have discovered some missing money which rightfully should belong to our Mr. Alphabet." Govinder, Abigail and Robbie had been following Mrs. Evans since the end of lessons and were now hiding behind the large run of laurels at the side of the hot house. They looked at each other knowingly. 'My Christine and her young man', that explains the smug looks.

Mrs. Evans went on, "They've taken him off to Scotland to interview the ne'er do well who pinched the money."

"Well, is it much money 'cos it seems like an awful long way to go to me? And he's always saying how much there is to do here so I think he should have a good reason for going."

"He's got fifty thousand good reasons!" Mrs. Evans was now, more than ever, full of her own self-importance.

"You mean to tell me that it's fifty thousand quid he's lost?" Mrs. Evans nodded. The children stared at each other. Fifty thousand!

"Himmel!" Grey was not thinking clearly. "I mean, Heavens. That's a bit bloomin' careless, isn't it, losing fifty thousand big ones?"

"You might think you're funny but I don't and if you're going to take everything as a joke then I'm not going to bother telling you how it happened and that's that!" She stalked away from him and there was a rustling outside the greenhouse as the three children raced back up the garden to give the news to everyone else.

Mrs. Evans had been discussing their windfall earlier in the day with Darren Darby, the Bursar. "Well, Mrs. E., fifty thou'd ease the old burden a bit, I must say. We're just about at break even at the mo. This school seems to run away with money."

Mrs. Evans looked intently at Darren, who blushed thinking that one of the constant drains on school funds was his own accountancy course which Mr. Alphabet had agreed to pay for. "It's what all decent employers do Darren. It's called Staff Development. But I wouldn't expect you to recognise it because there didn't seem to be much evidence of it at The Skwitz," Mr. Alphabet had said.

Darren had had the feeling that, though Mrs. Evans had never mentioned it, she had not been one hundred percent in agreement with this. He was sure that now was the moment that she was going to reveal her displeasure.

Mrs. Evans, however, was too delighted at the prospect of all the extra money to even think about using the opportunity. "Imagine all the things we can do with it. We could get some more equipment for the gym, Another machine for the computer room – that big one up the corner's never been right since Wendy Williams in Form E spilt her pop all over it."

"Pop's not one of the things that computers take kindly to, Mrs. E.!" Darren laughed. "I don't think that we should get too excited though. We haven't seen the money yet, have we?" With his cautious manner, Darren was ideally suited to a career in accountancy.

"No, of course, you're right, Darren. Never count your chickens before they're cooked, that's what I always say."

"Hatched," came a voice from the doorway.

141

Darren and Mrs. Evans looked up to see Mr. Alphabet standing dolefully before them. "What was that?"

"Never count your chickens before they're hatched, Mrs. Evans." Mr. Alphabet was too demoralised to worry about having his pedantry pointed out by Mrs. Evans. "I'm afraid that it looks like our chickens are never going to hatch."

"Whyever not?" the secretary asked. "My Christine and her Stephen found that rogue who stole it didn't they?"

"They did indeed. But I think we were both guilty of the same thing you and I. My vision had been so clouded by the thought of getting my hands on the money that I didn't even stop to ask about it. Christine and Stephen *had* managed to track down Ibbotson and they took me to see him. He's been charged and he's out on bail, so we went to visit him at his home." Mr. Alphabet's expression darkened yet further. "Oh, it was terrible. He lives in a huge high rise. Thankfully only on the eighth floor because we had to walk up, the lift being out of order. The whole place stank – of pee and rubbish and babies' nappies."

Mrs. Evans looked like she might be about to heave.

"Sorry, Enid, I was forgetting how tickle-stomached you are. Anyway, suffice it to say, it was the worst place I have ever stepped into in my life…I think."

Mrs. Evans had regained her composure and was back on form. "It'll just be a front to make you feel sorry for him. He's probably got another luxury apartment somewhere…or maybe he's turned into one of those awful money-grabbing Rackman landlords. That'll be it. That was probably just one of the flats he lets out and he'd borrowed it for the day to trick you."

"If it were a flat that he lets out, which it's not, then his tenants would have nowhere to sleep, nothing to sit on and no food to eat."

"How do you mean?"

"Ibbotson hasn't got a penny to his name. He's had to sell everything he's got. Every household item, every last stick of furniture, everything. Stephen's checked it all out and it's absolutely true."

"Where's the fifty thou then, Mr. A?" Darren put in.

"Gone, Darren. Along with every other penny he might have had."

"Gone where? This is ridiculous. The police must have overlooked something." Darren and Mr. Alphabet were amused to note that now that Mrs. Evans was calling into question the efficiency of the force, they were no longer 'my Christine and her young man'.

"I really don't think so, Mrs. Evans. The problem, which no-one knew at the time of course, is that Ibbotson has had a gambling problem for years. Maybe fifteen years. In that time he has consistently run up massive debts. So you can imagine that when he saw my bag of money, the temptation was enormous. A temptation only made greater by the possibility, or rather likelihood, that I was in a coma and never going to wake up."

"Don't say that." Mr. Alphabet thought that he saw one of those rare glimmers of tenderness on his secretary's face, but it was gone in a flash. "Anyway, he shouldn't have taken your money to get himself out of debt. It's wrong."

"Of course it's wrong, Mrs. Evans. But he wasn't taking it to get out of debt. He was taking it to leave town, go somewhere that nobody knows him and start his life all over again. Without the gambling, this time."

"So what went wrong then, Mr. A?"

"What went wrong, Darren, is that gambling is an illness. There's no choice involved. Like anything else, you can't just move away and think you've left your problem behind you. Your problem goes where you go."

"What a lot of rubbish. He just wanted to pull himself together and get on with it. No will-power that's what it is." Mrs. Evans had no time for sympathy in these matters, which made Mr. Alphabet angry.

"Do you not think that he tried? Do you think that people like living with an addiction like that? No, they don't Mrs. Evans. They really don't."

"All right, all right. Keep your wig on!" the secretary was shocked at how irate she had made Mr. Alphabet.

"So what happened, Mr. A? Did the mob he owed money to down here, did they catch up with him?" Darren watched a lot of gangster films.

"Nothing so dramatic, I'm afraid, Darren. No, in one way, the man was very lucky because he did manage to leave his debts behind. But, he told us that gradually, gradually, bit by bit he went back to gambling." Mrs. Evans loud sniff of disgust was ignored by her employer and he went on, "Firstly it was just a little flutter on the Grand National." "No harm in that. Everyone does it," Darren said.

"No harm in it at all if you're not a gambling addict but for Ibbotson it was the beginning of the slippery slope. Then it went to a bet on the horses every day, maybe two. Then he was spending all his days off in the bookies. I don't need to bore you with all the details but suffice it to say, he started going to casinos and that was the end for him. And that's how come we found him living in that filthy dirty place."

"So what happens to him now?" Darren asked.

"Now I suppose that he'll be convicted and sent to prison. He'll be viewed in a worse light than other people stealing the same amount of money because he abused a position of trust and power. The judge will, no doubt, want to make an example of him."

"Ooo, how horrible, ending up in prison." This was one of Darren's worst nightmares, based largely again on his film viewing.

"D'you know, if I had to choose between that rotten flat and prison, I think I'd opt for the stretch inside. It might have a double benefit for him because he will probably also be put on a rehab plan. Then maybe he really will be able to start a new life when he comes out."

"Humph!" Mrs. Evans was not convinced. "Once a bad 'un, always a bad 'un. A tiger never changes its spots, that's what I always say."

The other two laughed and for once Mr. Alphabet was grateful to Mrs. Evans for lightening the mood with her verbal stumbling.

Chapter S

Abigail managed to convince Mr. Alphabet over the next few weeks that actually she really liked Anatomy and that she was quite happy to carry on with it. Naturally, he believed this about as much as he believed that parking wardens really were nice people, just misunderstood.

The term wore on and the whole school was preoccupied with the various events planned for the run up to Christmas. Abigail had a bit of a job on her hands trying to rehearse her lines for the play without her mother hearing her. "What on earth do you keep talking to yourself for, girl?" her mother said to her one day when she was pacing up and down at the bottom of the garden where she thought she'd be safe. "And don't you know it's December and freezing cold. Well, I suppose it's your business if you want to freeze to death. But don't come running to me when you're dead of pneumonia." Abigail laughed at the prospect of being able to run when you were already six feet under. Logic was not her mother's strong point.

Eleanor continued to get the washing down from the line. As she was taking the last peg from a large bed sheet, a huge gust of wind came and blew the rotary drier round and round. Eleanor, not used to moving at speed, found herself completely entangled in the still damp laundry, like some ghostly Houdini. She shouted to Abigail for help but no help came. The more she struggled, the more tangled up she became. Abigail stood and watched, almost convulsed with silent hysterics. She was thinking that if this laughter didn't stop soon, there'd be more underclothes to go in the dirty laundry basket! So, as her mother looked as though she was just about to free herself, Abigail legged it down the garden and over the small fence at the back of her Dad's shed.

She knelt at the other side trying to relieve the stitch in her side. Once the pain had subsided, she peeped through the slats in the fence and saw her mother finally extricate herself from the sheets with a face as red as a beetroot. There was washing everywhere, half hanging off the line, lying all over the lawn but best of all her mother was standing there with a large pair of her off white knickers on her head, covering her eyes and one of her Dad's threadbare brown weekend socks stuck right across her face.

"Now that's what I call putting a sock in it!" Abigail bent over again and opened her mouth as wide as possible to let the laugh out without making a sound.

From then on, Abigail decided that she'd better stick to reciting her part at school or in the park. The problem was when to do it. It was just tricky trying to fit everything in.

The day after the Wind-Sock-Incident, she met Sally Sturgeon on the way into school. "Can we have another fitting for the outfit, Abi?" Sally asked. "Only I've made one or two changes and I just need to see if they work." This was a regular event which happened at least once a week and so it didn't come as much of a surprise to Abigail.

"I've got to give it to you, girl, you aren't half putting the hours in on this show."

"Yeah, well, I don't want any of those stuck-ups thinking I can't be just as good as them," Sally replied. Abigail had no idea which 'stuck-ups' the girl could be talking about but hadn't got the time or the inclination to question her.

"O.k. Well, anyway, what time do you want to do it?"

""We've got that play rehearsal just before lunchtime. What about doing it straight after that?"

"O.k., no prob. Gotta' getting going now. Anatomy first thing. Whoop-de-doo, I don't think! Another test as well! Joy unbounded!"

Sally commiserated with Abigail and the smaller girl dashed off.

When they met up again later, Sally carefully removed her creation from inside the suit carrier which she had been hugging close to her pretty much all day. Sally read a lot of serious fashion magazines and she knew that it was a competitive world out there where everything had to be kept secret until the last minute. So she'd decided that this was good enough opportunity to practice her skills in subterfuge and concealment.

The dress she pulled out of the cover was simply the most stunning creation that Abigail had ever seen. It was a kind of dusty pink colour with the colour graduating upwards from the hem to the neckline so that the top of the dress was almost white. It was longer at the back than the front and as Abigail put it on and started parading up and down she felt that the material moved just like liquid.

"Cor, Sal, this is fantastic." Glancing down at the bodice, Abigail asked, " How long did it take you to sew all these sequins on? It's so artistic."

Sally didn't look up from the back of the dress which she was repinning and readjusting all the time. "'Spose it's o.k, really. Didn't take too long, 'spose." Sally was obviously bursting with delight at the compliments which she had just received but, from experience, Abigail knew that she would never admit it.

Sally came round to the front of the dress. "Oh no!" she cried.

"What, what? What have I done?" Abigail's instinctive reaction to someone else's displeasure came out before she could stop herself.

"It's not what you've done, it's me?" Sally seemed heartbroken yet irritated at the same time.

"What? It seems perfect to me." Abigail tried to reassure her.

"Go over to the side of the stage and have a look in that mirror."

Abigail did as she was told. As she approached the mirror she could see the problem. The dress fitted perfectly round the waist and hips. It couldn't have looked better, in fact. But around the top it was sagging and bagging everywhere.

"Oh blimey, Sal, what's happened?"

Sally explained her mistake. "When we were given the title of the project I thought and thought and thought what I could do. What doll I could use. I didn't want to do one of those naff things that you see in museums. You know the ones, all faded lace and starey china face? Ugh, give me the creeps those." Abigail was glad that this option had been ruled out immediately. "Then I thought about doing something a bit different so I was going to do a cabbage patch doll." Abigail's face was a picture of horror and Sal quickly said, "But that wouldn't have suited your look at all." The back-handed compliment was well received.

"So, I thought, there's nothing for it, I'll have to do a Barbie. It's a bit obvious to choose that but it was the only way I was really going to be able to show off how good I am."

'This girl's a real contradiction,' thought Abigail. 'One minute she can't take a compliment or any nice thing being said to her. Next minute, she's bragging about how fantastic she is.'

147

"Well, what's the problem with Barbie, then?" Abigail asked.

"The problem with Barbie is that she's too well endowed up top, if you know what I mean!" Sally told her.

Abigail looked down at her own still flat chest and could see straight away what the girl was talking about. "I'm really sorry, Sal."

"Hey, it's not your fault. You look great. It's me. I'd got so involved with the Barbie idea that I wasn't thinking straight."

"Maybe you can get someone else to model it for you. There's that girl Yolanda. She seems quite…you know…"

Abigail was interrupted. "Nope, no-one else is going to model my stuff, except you." She dropped her voice. "You've been nicer to me than anyone ever. You're the only person who's ever believed I can be any good at anything and so if it's not you, it's nobody. You're my best friend. Actually, if I'm honest, you're my only friend."

Abigail was completely floored by this short speech. If anyone had told her at the start of term that she would be friends with Sally Sturgeon, she'd have told them they'd taken leave of their senses. "Er..well..thanks, Sal. But that doesn't really solve your problem, does it?" The girls sat on the edge of the stage staring out into the main hall as if seeking inspiration.

Abigail was still wearing the beautiful dress, unwilling to take it off in case this was the last time she ever wore it and the last time she ever felt this glamorous. Suddenly she noticed the small orange racquets which were used for indoor games in the main hall when the weather was too bad to go outside. "Hold on a minute, Sal. I think I've got it." She ran over to where the racquets were piled up and dug through the other equipment which was with them.

"Whatcha doing?" Sally called over. Abigail had her back to her friend so it was impossible to see what was going on but when she turned round, the large bodice of the dress was fitting perfectly.

Sally leapt down from the stage. "How've you done that? What's in there?"

"Ta-na," cried Abigail pulling two large softballs from out of the top of her dress.

Both girls snorted with laughter. The noise was so loud that it disturbed Mr. Alphabet in his office next to the hall.

"Quick get back behind the curtain and get that frock off," hissed Sally.

"Why? It doesn't matter if he sees it?" Abigail whispered back.

"Yes it does, dummo. The opposition have spies everywhere." This paranoia was a bit much for Abigail but she was unable to pass comment. She was currently involved in a struggle with the dress and all the pins still inside it. It was proving a little difficult to get it off over her head without piercing herself full of more holes than a tattooed man in Camden.

Having convinced Mr. Alphabet that there was no cause for concern and that the two girls were just having a laugh together, Abigail ran off in search of Robbie and Gov to tell them all about her new 'falsies'. She hunted everywhere – the dorm, the classrooms, even the gym in case they had lost their mind and suddenly bizarrely got into exercise. But neither of them was to be found anywhere. She was sure that they couldn't be outside in this weather. True enough, it wasn't actually raining but the wind and the cold were biting. It being her last option, she put on her winter duffle and long woolly scarf which her Grandma Ayres had knitted for her, and set off into the school grounds.

Eventually, she found the two boys hiding behind the laurels close to the hot-house. The same place they had hidden when they had been eavesdropping on Grey and Mrs. Evans.

"What you doing?" she asked, loudly.

"Shhhhhhhh," they hissed in unison.

"Why? What's up?"

"We're listening to Grey," Robbie whispered back.

All this time Govinder was still and silent in concentration.

"What for?" asked Abigail. "Who's he with?"

"The dog."

"The dog?" In her astonishment, her voice really was too loud.

"Who's that? Who's out there?" Grey started making for the door of the hothouse, closely followed by Fritzi. He reached the laurels in time to see three grey duffel coated figures with their hoods up making for the main school building at top speed.

"If I catches you down 'ere again, I shall tell Mr. Alphabet. You know it's out of bounds down 'ere. You won't 'alf be in trouble." He stood shouting after them for about five minutes but the children missed most of it because they were already inside the cloakroom, hurriedly removing their coats and making for a classroom.

When they had all recovered their breath and their composure, Abigail said," Are you both mad? A) you know we're not allowed near that place, B) it's the middle of winter and you'll catch your death and C) – which actually should have been A, by the way – what on earth are you doing listening to a man talking to his dog. What d'you think he's doing? Giving away state secrets to the dog? Is the dog an enemy agent?"

"You might not be far off there. Not about the dog being an enemy agent. That's just plain ridiculous. But there are definitely some secrets there and I'm sure that Grey's not all he's cracked up to be." Gov seemed excited.

"Well, what is he then?"

"Don't tell me I've lost my mind again but I think he's German. Not only that, I think he's a really posh German."

"Are you...?" Abigail began but was cut off by Govinder.

"I just asked you not to say that! And anyway I'm not. We've been studying the different accents and dialects in German. How people speak from different countries and different regions. And I'd say that he's got a very Hanoverian accent – they're the posh ones."

"That's a bit unlikely for a gardener, isn't it?"

"Don't be such a rotten snob, Abi." Robbie admonished his friend.

"Sorry. Touch of my mother coming through there!"

Her friends smiled and Gov continued, "You might even be a bit right in your snobbishness, actually, little Miss Ayres-and-Graces." This earned him a swift punch to the upper arm which he was sure would bruise later. "Ow, that hurt!"

"What Gov is trying to tell you, Abi, is that from the little bits he's overheard, it's probably true that Grey has lived here for a very long time but..."

"But what, for heaven's sake?"

"But he wasn't always the gardener."

Abigail looked puzzled and turned to Gov.

Gov couldn't help her out much further, however. "It's just a feeling I've got from the way he's talking. He seems to know a lot more about this place than you might think but I haven't really pieced it together yet."

"Let me get this straight. You got all these hunches from a conversation which he had...with his *dog*?" The disbelief was evident in her voice.

"Well, sort of."

"And what did the dog say back?" Abigail laughed.

"Look, if you're just going to make a big joke out of this then you can forget I ever told you." Govinder looked as though he was about to launch into one of his mega-sulks.

"Sorry, sorry. I promise I won't laugh about it again. It's just…well, you must admit it's kind of hard to believe."

"I know it is. If only we had more evidence."

"Yes but he's hardly going to tell his whole life story to the dog, is he?" Robbie put in.

"And besides," Abigail couldn't help herself, "the dog's probably heard it all before….All right, all right," the boy's glares had not gone unnoticed, "sorry, o.k.?" She was interrupted by the door opening and the rest of Form B filing in to begin the afternoon's lessons. "Seriously though," she whispered, "we're just going to have to get our heads together and come up with a plan to find out Grey's secret."

Chapter T

As well as the Christmas play, the fashion show and what seemed like a million other things, there was also to be an end of term party for the whole school. Every teacher, pupil and member of staff was to be invited, along with a select list of others who would appear by invitation only. The party planner was, inevitably, Mrs. Evans.

One icy December morning, Mr. Alphabet met his secretary in the entrance hall as she was making her way into the school. "My, my Mrs. Evans, you look like Nanouk of the North," he laughed admiring her get-up of thick woven scarf, huge leather gloves and puffed coat which seemed to reach to the floor. "Did you not bother to get dressed this morning?"

"What?" she snapped. Mr. Alphabet's 'little jokes' as she liked to call them, were just about the last thing she was ready for this morning.

"You look like you're wrapped in a duvet!"

"What's a duvet?"

In some matters, Mrs. Evans was even more stuck in the past than Mr. Alphabet himself. "Continental quilt?" he tried. Still Mrs. Evans was puzzled. "Oh, there's an old word for it…now, what is it?....A..B..It's the name of a wretched duck. C"

"A duck? Mallard?" Mrs. Evans tried to help but she had never been as good at 'the game' as Grey.

"No, no. ..D…E..Yes! E! Eiderdown. That's it!"

"Well, why didn't you say eiderdown in the first place. 'Duvay' indeed! You and your new-fangled foreign words!"

Mr. Alphabet didn't bother to point out to her that 'eider' sounded about as English as 'duvet' and that there was every chance of it having been a 'new-fangled foreign' word once.

"Don't just stand there anyway, man. At least give me a hand with all these folders," she said indicating the ten or so lever arch files which she had somehow managed to balance under each arm.

"What in the world have you got here, Mrs. Evans?"

"They're the party folders." Mr. Alphabet was filled with a sense of doom. It was great to have someone as organised as Mrs. Evans around but he felt that the party didn't really need to be organised along the lines of the invasion of a small oil-producing country.

"Don't you think that we'd be better to go with the flow a bit more, Mrs. Evans?"

"You know where going with the flow gets you, don't you?"

"I don't, no." But Mr. Alphabet felt sure that his secretary was about to enlighten him.

"It gets you washed out to sea, that's where it gets you!" Mrs. Evans snuffled and snorted. "You see, you're not the only one who can make 'little jokes'!"

"I do indeed see." Mr. Alphabet was having slightly more trouble than his employee in seeing the clearly abundant hilarity in this comment.

"No doubt you know best, then, on the party front."

"No doubt!" she repeated vehemently.

"So what exactly is in these folders?" He had already given up the idea of trying to sway her away from such an extravagantly organised evening.

"Oh you know, caterer's info, stuff about equipment hire, guest lists, invitations and acceptances." She looked very pleased with herself.

"You'll have had plenty of practice by the time Christine comes to tie the knot, won't you?" Mr. Alphabet regretted these words even before he had finished getting them out.

"What do you mean?" Mrs. Evans asked excitedly. "Do you think she and Stephen will be getting hitched soon? Ooo, how marvellous! What a day that'll be! I must speak to Mr. Campbell about it…."

"No, no. You misunderstand me, Enid." Mr. Alphabet quickly tried to rectify his mistake. "I simply meant that when and if that happy day arrives, then you'll be ready for it."

"There'll be no 'if' about it if I've got anything to do with it."

153

Mr. Alphabet did not find this hard to believe but not wishing to excite Mrs. Evans further, he quickly changed the subject back to the impending party.

"Do we really need to run to the expense of caterers? Couldn't we just ask everyone to bring something?"

"What and have forty dozen sausage rolls and no nice cakes for those that like cake?" Mr. Alphabet knew that Mrs. Evans was referring to herself with this last comment because her penchant for a 'nibble of a biscuit' with her tea had not gone unnoticed.

"I'm sure you could arrange it so that that wouldn't happen. How about drawing up a list of what's needed and getting everyone to sign up for something? Some of the children could even make their contributions in their cookery lessons. And maybe the boarders could do theirs in the school kitchens…" He noticed Mrs. Evans horrified look. "..under your express supervision, of course."

Knowing his secretary quite well by now and knowing that she was not terribly keen on adopting someone else's ideas, Mr. Alphabet realised that he needed to leave her with this thought. "I'll just pop these folders in your office. Then I really must press on. Lots to do. I've got to start going through the end-of-term reports, for a start."

Lessons that same day began for all of the children with a double period of one of their special subjects. Abigail ran off to spend another hour and twenty minutes as the Covent Garden flower seller, Eliza Doolittle. Rehearsals for the play were going well and Miss Diamond was especially pleased with Abigail's enthusiasm as well as her talent. "This looks like being one of the best productions I've ever been involved in," Daphne told her class that morning. "I'm very proud of all of you." Abigail felt that every word Miss Diamond said, was addressed directly to her. She just had that way of making you feel really special and important.

At break-time, Abigail was dying to tell her friends about how well everything was going and what a success it was all going to be. This was not just from a need to blow her own trumpet but also because each child acting in the play was responsible for selling ten tickets each. Abigail was practising her public relations skills, something she hadn't realised was involved in acting!

She soon spotted Govinder and Robbie huddled together in the corridor near the little school shop. She knew from the way they were standing, that they were plotting something. Creeping up on tip-toes, she managed to get about a foot away from them before saying, in an exact reproduction of Mrs. Evans voice, "Don't you two boys know it's one of the ignorantest things you can do, whispering?"

The boys nearly jumped out of their skins as they turned around and saw that it was only their friend standing in front of them. "I almost wish you'd never discovered how good you are at imitating people, Ayres!" Robbie shouted, half seriously.

Abigail, naturally enough, was convulsed with laughter. Since she had unearthed this hidden talent for mimicry, the opportunity for playing benign little tricks on people was endless.

When she had gathered herself together, she asked, "What are you up to again, anyway, you two?"

"There've been developments on the German front," Robbie told her.

"You make it sound like you're just about to announce that Poland has been invaded again," Govinder quipped.

"What *are* you about to announce then?" Abigail asked Robbie.

It was Govinder who replied, however. "I was waiting for my German lesson to start this morning and we waited and waited but no Miss Grueber." At the mention of the young German teacher's name, Robbie and Govinder both became starry eyed.

With raised eyebrows, Abigail tutted and said, "What are you boys like? You're obsessed with that woman!"

"I can't imagine why, can you, Gov? What is it that does it for you? Is it the lively blue eyes or the long blonde hair or the perfect figure or the..."

"All right, all right. I get the picture," Abigail laughed. "Why was she late, anyway? Getting her roots done or something?"

"Miaow! Saucer of milk for the cat up the corner, please!...She wasn't late. She didn't turn up at all. She's got flu or something. Mr. A came in after about ten minutes and told us. He said that it doesn't look like she'll be back before the end of term."

"Oh no! What will you boys do without her?"

"Shut up, Ayres!"

"Is that all you had to tell me on the 'German front'? I thought it was going to be something to do with Grey. If you can't come up with something better than your heartthrob having flu then I'm off to do something more interesting, like revise anatomy." This was a low shot and nearly meant that she missed out on what the boys had really been plotting.

They needed her help, however. "There must be a way that we can use this missing German teacher business to help get to the bottom of the mystery of Grey," Robbie said.

"Well, Gov, has she given you any work to be going on with? Maybe you could ask Grey for help with that?"

"Yes, she has left us some stuff to do but it's dead easy, so I don't need help with it."

"Can you not just pretend, for once, to be dumb and ask Grey to help you?" Abigail asked.

Both boys were in agreement on this, however. "Certainly not!" they cried in unison. It was clearly against some 'Clever boy's code of ethics' to act daft and ask for assistance when you really didn't need it. Abigail was at a loss to understand this because she spent most of her life pretending. Pretending to be happy. Pretending to be busy. Pretending to like liver.

"And another thing, Abi, how are we supposed to ask a man for help in a language which 'officially' none of us know he speaks? Tricky, eh?"

"There must *be* a way. We just haven't thought of it yet." Abigail said.

Just then came the sound of 'The Birdie Song' signifying the end of break. "Who on earth chose that? No-one in their right mind would actually like that rubbish, would they?"

Mr. Alphabet had been insistent, when he was setting up the rules for the school, that one of the last things he wanted was the sound of a normal school bell to be breaking into the children's thoughts every forty minutes at least. Or indeed, breaking into his own thoughts. He had an absolute horror of the sound. A horror for which he, as yet, had found no rational explanation.

His solution to the problem was to allow a different child every day to choose the sound or song which they would like to be the 'bell'. The results had been varied and interesting to say the least. They ranged from the Adagietto from Mahler's 5th Symphony, chosen by one of the more serious music students, to..well, to 'The 'Birdie Song', chosen by...Abigail Ayres. Mr. Alphabet had had his doubts about the latter choice but rules were rules.

Abigail had no doubts at all. She knew how much it would annoy her friends but was convinced that they needed to lighten up a little and was under the misguided impression that this might help.

Returning to the dilemma of how to involve Grey in the 'absent German teacher' problem, Abigail said, "Leave it with me. I'm not sure what the answer is exactly but I'm sure it'll come to me, if I sleep on it."

"I hope it does," Robbie said, "because it's less than two weeks until the end of term. You'd better get your skates on and come up with an idea. After all, if anyone is experienced in being sneaky and plotting, it has to be you!" He was referring to Abigail's constant manoeuvrings around her mother.

"Ha!" Abigail laughed mirthlessly, "I suppose you're right. I'll see you first thing before lessons tomorrow and we'll see what I've managed to come up with." Reverting to Mrs. Evans's voice, she said, "Strike while the iron's plugged in, that's what I always say."

Mr. Alphabet, who happened to be passing at that precise moment and seeing the three friends giggling, realised that he was not alone in finding Mrs. Evans's mixed sayings more than a little amusing.

That afternoon the 'real' Mrs. Evans had quite a lot on. She hurried into Mr. Alphabet's office five minutes after 'The Birdie Song' had sounded the start of afternoon lessons. "Which bright spark chose that ridiculous noise for the bell?" Mr. Alphabet was not about to tell her that it was the bright spark who he had found, earlier in the day, doing a carbon copy of Mrs. Evans voice, down to the slight Welsh lilt which she would swear on her life that she had never even had. Instead of giving Abigail's game away, he just mumbled something unintelligible under his breath. "Can't make out a word you're saying. But, what's more to the point, which bright spark let the children choose their own bell anyway? Whoever heard the like?"

"I think that I must be the bright spark to whom you are referring, Enid. Was there something you wanted?" Mr. Alphabet was more than usually short with his secretary both because he knew that given half the chance she would be off into a diatribe against his 'barmy bell idea', as she called it, and also because he was really trying to get through examining the children's reports prior to writing his own comments on them.

"No need to get shirty. I just thought I ought to let you have a look at the list of party food I've prepared for the children, you being the boss and all. But pardon me if you're too busy for such renal tasks." She turned and began to bustle out of his tiny office under a cloud of umbrage and extra-firm-hold hairspray.

"No, no, Enid, come back. Of course I'll have a look at them." The error she had made was one he really could not let her get away with. "Can I just say that the word I think you were looking for was 'menial', 'menial tasks' not 'renal tasks'?"

"Menial, renal, it's about the same, isn't it?"

"Not quite no. 'Renal' has got to do with your kidneys so 'renal tasks' would really be the filtering of waste products into the bladder, which probably, and hopefully, has little to do with the production of party food." Mr. Alphabet had tried to maintain his composure through this little lecture but, unfortunately, lost it at this moment and was richly rewarded for his sniggering by four sheets of paper, containing the food list, flying across his desk and the back of Mrs. Evans heading for the door.

"Ignorantest man I've ever met," was the last thing he heard her say that afternoon as she scooped up her 'duvet' coat and stormed out of the school an hour and a half early.

Mr. Alphabet contritely picked up the sheets, glanced over them and finding that they were, as anticipated, perfect resolved to pin them to the notice board in the corridor just before home time. Mrs. Evans had thought of everything and everybody. There was something for those 'vegetablians', as she called them, who didn't eat meat and fish. There was something for the rich and something for the poor to prepare. There was something for those who liked savoury and something for the more sweet-toothed guests, like Mrs. Evans herself.

'She must have spent all day over this.' Five minutes before the end of afternoon lessons, Mr. Alphabet, standing in the entrance hall with a handful of drawing pins felt guilty for making fun of her but as soon as he remembered the 'renal' comment, he was double up with laughter once more.

"Are you all right, sir?" came a voice behind him. It was Abigail Ayres.

Quickly gathering himself together, Mr. Alphabet assured her that he was absolutely fine. "But are *you* o.k., Abigail? Lessons haven't finished yet, so what are you doing down here. You're not sick, are you?"

"Not exactly, sir. I've got to leave a bit early because my Mum's taking me to the orthodontist." Abigail did not look particularly impressed at the thought of this visit but Mr. Alphabet could not be sure whether it was the prospect of the dentist or Abigail's mother which was most daunting for the girl.

"Ah yes, of course. I remember signing your pass now. Nothing really wrong with your teeth, though, is there?" he enquired.

"Oh no, but Mum thinks…" Abigail stopped. She might have had a very difficult relationship with her mother but she didn't feel that it was always necessary to share this with the whole adult world, least of all her headmaster. "…Mum thinks it's a good idea to be on the safe side. You know how it is?"

"Oh, yes, Abigail, I know exactly how it is," he replied and she was sure that he did, indeed, know. "As you're here, anyway," he said, changing the subject for both their sakes, "you can have first pick of what you'd like to cook for the Christmas party. Have a look at this list." He showed her the sheets. "Is there anything particular you like cooking?"

Abigail loved cooking anything and everything. Well, everything that wasn't liver or mushrooms. "Erm…." She was nervous, though, because she hadn't told her mother that there was going to be a party at school for fear that her mother might muscle in on it and wangle herself an invite. The problem was that you could never rely on her mother's mood – she could either be the absolute life and soul or she could be pretty awful. The 'pretty awful' was the most common state of affairs and it usually involved her mother sitting well away from everyone else, with a big plate of unhealthy beige food in front of her, spilling most of it down her front, complaining that there was nowhere to smoke and telling Abigail and her father, if he was unfortunate enough to be present, that they were an embarrassment, that they said the wrong things, they showed her up and that she didn't know why she bothered going anywhere with them.

All in all, then, it was by far the easiest thing to do to keep quiet about such parties and hope that she never found out.

Mr. Alphabet, blessed with more than his fair share of intuition, realised that Abigail was in a quandary. "Do you know something, the boarders are going to be making their contributions together in the school kitchen? Why don't you join them and cook yours there too? It'd be company for Robbie, wouldn't it?" The headmaster always managed to make it sound like you were doing someone else a favour rather than wriggling yourself out of a nasty hole.

"Oh, yes, that's a great idea. Put me down for two trays of flapjacks and the sticky honey chocolate cake," she said happily.

At least for that, Abigail would get into Mrs. Evans good books, thought Mr. Alphabet, which might come in handy if she ever finds out about the wicked impressions. He smiled to himself as the girl ran to the car, waiting at the bottom of the school drive.

Chapter U

All the way to the orthodontist, Abigail was pretty quiet. She was turning over in her mind how she and her friends could make use of the missing German teacher to get more information out of Grey. Luckily, her mother didn't notice the girl's silence at all because she was too busy telling her how she'd been to the local frozen food shop where they had a promotion on ready-made Chinese meals. "Five for the price of three! Can you believe it? Lucky really that these shops have started doing offers like that because with the money your father gives me every month, I can barely make ends meet." This little gem managed to work its way through into Abigail's consciousness. 'Maybe if you didn't spend a third of your housekeeping on cigarettes and the other two thirds on food which gets wasted then ends meeting wouldn't be such a problem,' thought Abigail.

She soon slipped back into her own thoughts and they had arrived, parked and entered the waiting room without her even noticing.

"Miss Abigail Ayres?" called the receptionist. "Abigail Ayres, please?"

"Come on, Dilly Day-Dream, what are you waiting for?" Eleanor Ayres was already on her feet.

"Are you coming in with me?" Abigail was downcast.

"Certainly, I am. I'm not having them miss something. Can't be trusted these people." This earned Eleanor a look of utter disdain from the already disapproving receptionist. Abigail tried a meek little smile on the woman but she had buried her head back in the appointments book. 'Great! Another place where I have to feel embarrassed every time I visit,' thought Abigail. 'Oh well, maybe they'll say I'm fine and don't need to come again.'

Which is exactly what the orthodontist did say. But what did he know? He'd only trained for six years at university and had nineteen years of on-the-job experience so how would he know anything about teeth? Eleanor soon put him straight and before Abigail knew it she was being fitted for a brace. A brace which would be ready in a weeks' time – the day before the first performance of Pygmalion.

'That's just what I need – Victorian flower-seller's costume with a mouth like a Bond villain! Marvellous!'

Her mother ushered her out of the surgery and towards the car for the two minute drive home. "Actually, Mum, er… I think I'll walk…er…because…" an idea came to her, "I've got an anatomy test tomorrow and I need to look some things up in the library. Loads of things actually. It's going to be quite a big test."

"Oh, right. I *had* thought you might help me write the Christmas cards. I wish you'd told me sooner about this test. You leave everything to the last minute and then I have to change all my plans." Her mother had never changed her plans for anyone at any time, in fact.

"S..Sorry, Mum. It's just.."

"Oh don't bother to explain yourself. You just carry on keeping everything to yourself. Just like your father, you are, secretive." Eleanor then gave a mock laugh. "I don't know, anyone'd think I was some sort of ogre, or something."

Abigail was glad she wasn't eating at that moment. She felt that she might well have choked. Not that Eleanor would have heard because she was already in the car, starting the engine.

True to her word, strangely enough, Abigail headed off to the library. It was not in front of the Anatomy section which she sat because there was, in fact, no test looming. The end of term test had been and gone and Abigail had managed to do well enough in it so as not to alert the attention of her teacher and Mr. Alphabet. At least there'd be no ructions at home because of that, she had thought.

She sat for a couple of hours in the darkened library under a bright reading lamp and completely lost track of time because she was so absorbed in her pile of books on Stagecraft. It was a shock to her, then, when she heard a voice behind her. "We're closing now, miss. Will you be all right to get home? It's very dark, you know."

"Oh no! What time is it?" she asked the librarian.

"It's seven forty-five, dear."

Abigail was downcast because the whole point of coming to the library in the first place had been so that she could meet her Daddy off the bus from work and tell him about the play next week. Unbelievably, she hadn't been able to snatch a moment on her own with him for weeks without her mother calling out "What are you two whispering about?". Honestly, the woman must have ears like an elephant. Why not? She'd got a stomach like one!

"Seven forty-five?" She had only planned to stay in there until quarter past which would give her enough time to get to the bus stop at the end of the road for half past which was the time her Dad usually arrived there. "Oh, oh, I've got to go." Abigail stood up knocking half of the piles of books flying. She bent to pick them up. "Sorry, sorry. My Mum's always telling me I'm so clumsy. I'm really s.."

The librarian could see how flustered Abigail was. "Don't worry, my dear. I'll do that. You run along. We don't want your Mum to worry about you, do we?"

'No danger of that!' thought the girl. She gave the woman a grateful smile and ran out of the door and down the High Street. She saw one of the large double deckers from town just pulling away from the bus stop and to her surprise she saw her father standing at the stop.

Running up to him, she called out "Daddy, Daddy, what are you doing getting off here. It's another half a mile home."

Her father looked guiltily at her. "Oh hello Abi. I like the walk you know. It clears my mind a bit."

"But aren't you really tired?"

"I am a bit actually. Had a dreadful journey back as well. Had to wait forty minutes for a bus to come that wasn't rammed full….Anyway, what are you doing out here at this time of night?" They started to make their slow way home.

"I've been to the library..I was hoping I'd catch you actually."

"Oh, no trouble is there?" Mr. Ayres and his daughter were always on the look out for trouble.

"No, it's nothing like that. It's just, well, I've been wanting to tell you for ages but..well, there's this play at school…"

"Yes. Go on."

"And well, I'm sort of in it."

"Good for you," her father replied. "What's the play?"

"It's Pygmalion by George Bernard Shaw. Do you know it?"

Abigail's father smiled. "I know it, love. So have you got many lines?"

"Quite a few, yes."

"So what part are you playing?"

"I..well, I'm sort of playing, well, Eliza Doolittle."

Her father stopped and looked her. "But that's the biggie. That's the main part. Oh my, oh my. You clever old thing." He gave her a little hug.

"When is it?"

"That's just it. It's next week. Three nights, Thursday, Friday and Saturday."

Her father looked worried.

"What? What's the matter? Don't you think I should do it? What?" Abigail too was worried now.

"No, it's not that. And of course I think you should do it. You're my star…" That was why Abigail loved her Dad so much. "It's just that on Friday, your mother's invited those awful people from the golf club round so I've had to ask to leave work early. Not ideal two weeks before Christmas when we're so busy but I suppose she didn't think of that."

"I suppose she didn't, no." So much for Eleanor accusing everyone else in the house of being selfish.

"Anyway, they've let me go early but have said that I have to make up the extra time on Saturday. So that means the only day left for me to come and see it is Thursday."

Abigail immediately saw the problem here. "But, that's the day I've got to go and have my brace fitted and…"

"Brace? What's all this about a brace? You don't need a brace surely?"

"Apparently I do! So, Mum's taking me and I've got to tell her that I'm needed back at school for some reason. If you go up there too, she might see you."

"I'll just have to make sure that she doesn't then, won't I?"

That week was spent in plotting, secrecy and excitement. Plotting and secrecy for the Ayres, father and daughter. Plotting and secrecy for the three friends, Abigail, Robbie and Govinder. Excitement for all involved in the school. There was so much going on that it was difficult to know which thing to be most excited about first.

163

Mrs. Evans spent hours checking and re-checking lists for the party. Sally Sturgeon pored for hours over the final touches for the Living Doll outfit. Abigail recited her lines over and over to Robbie. She knew them back to front and Robbie could probably, by now, have played the entire part of Eliza Doolittle himself – in Russian!

The friends, in between all the serious activity they were involved in, had still not managed to come up with a sensible way of getting Grey's secret out of him. Govinder had tried, a couple of times, to hang casually around the part of the garden where Grey was working. Abigail had told him to take his German book with him and act as if he was really struggling with some knotty word order problem or something. She thought that this might make Grey take pity on him. She had not, however, taken into account that Govinder was not quite as gifted in the acting department as she was and that Grey was neither sympathetic nor daft enough to be taken in by a boy lurking about the garden in the middle of December pretending to have trouble with his homework. All that Gov got for his pains was to be chased away with the words "Out of my garden now and if I sees you near that 'ot-'ouse you'll need to be going to 'ospital to 'ave that book removed from where I'm going to put it!"

In the end, they decided to give up on it and concentrate on more important things. After all, it's not as though it was really a pressing issue. They had got another few years before leaving the school to find out about Grey's dark past.

For Anthony Ayres, the problem of how to get to see Abigail's 'Eliza' was proving a little more difficult to resolve. It was already Wednesday evening and he had still come up with nothing suitable. The tricky thing was that he did not like lying to anyone, least of all his wife. This was not just out of fear of being found out, although that was obviously a consideration. He knew that Abigail had devised an ingenious manner of covering up her need to be present at the play and it involved no actual fibs, just a bit of economy with the truth. He recalled overhearing the conversation on Tuesday evening.

Abigail had handed her mother a note from Mr. Alphabet written on official headed notepaper. "What's this? Not in trouble again, are you?" her mother scowled. Abigail said nothing. Her mother began to read the note. "Play? What's this about a play? I hope you haven't been wasting your time on stupid plays, my girl." Looking back at the note, she said "It just says here your 'presence will be needed'. What's that supposed to mean? Why do these people always have to beat about the bush?"

"Well, maybe he means that they'll need the presence of someone who knows about First Aid. You know I'm doing that First Aid course and I suppose that all sorts might happen in a play, what with all that scenery and everything and…" Abigail forced herself to stop, realising that adding more to her story was only going to make it seem less and less believable.

Amazingly, Eleanor Ayres seemed to be taken in by this explanation. "Oh well, I suppose that's o.k. It might be good practice for you."

'It *will* be good practice for me. Just not the kind of practice you're expecting!' thought Abigail. The girl tried to give nothing away in her expression, however, as she handed her mother a pen to sign the form. She had almost stopped breathing with fear that Eleanor might change her mind.

"Wait a minute!" This was it. This was what Abigail had been expecting. "Friday? We've got people coming to dinner on Friday. You know that! I told you weeks ago." Abigail *did* know but not because her mother had told her. This was a usual trick of Eleanor's to spring things on her husband and daughter at the last minute so that she could scream at them when they said they knew nothing about it and had made other arrangements. "Oh well, I just suppose I'll have to manage all on my own, as usual. I've asked your father to come home early but I don't suppose he will. He's never here when we need him, is he?"

Abigail, unsurprisingly, chose to ignore this question. "So is it o.k. then? Can I be there at the play?" She chose her words very carefully.

"All right, all right. Give me that pen." Mrs. Ayres snatched the pen, hurriedly signed the paper and thrust it back at her grateful daughter. "Make me a coffee now, will you? I'm gasping."

'Gasping…and paralysed, presumably,' thought Abigail sarcastically. Luckily her mother did not notice the smirk on Abigail's face as she left the room because, had she, the game would have been up.

Since Abigail's conversation with her father about the play, every time they had passed in the hall, on the stairs or on the landing, she had raised her eyebrows at him in enquiry. Sadly, each time, he had shaken his head. Still no plans. Still no solution.

So it was that Thursday morning dawned and Abigail, naturally enough, unable to sleep, had heard her father go downstairs very early to have his breakfast. She tiptoed down after him, although quite why, she had no idea because she could hear her mother snoring fit to wake the dead and felt sure that Eleanor would be unlikely to hear if a bomb went off.

As she gently pushed open the door to the kitchen, she saw her father with his head in the fridge getting out the stuff for his sandwiches. He jumped when he felt her presence behind him. "Oh, Abi, you gave me such a start."

"Sorry, Daddy. I just wanted to ask you..."

"I know. I know what you're going to ask. Have I sorted anything out for this evening? Well, no. Not exactly." Seeing his daughter's face, he said, "Don't worry, I've got a cunning plan that cannot possibly fail." They both giggled quietly at this.

"I'll be there. Come what may."

"What's the plan then?" she asked him.

"To be honest, I think it might be better if you don't know. I'm not very pleased with what I'm about to do but needs must..."

Abigail was really puzzled now. What on earth could he be going to do? Murder her mother? Drug her? What? Abigail's vivid imagination was running away with her.

Looking up at the clock, Anthony Ayres said, "I must go now, love. I'll see you later." With that, he hurried out of the kitchen. As he went, he picked up his sandwiches and a large raw baking potato, much to Abigail's surprise.

He glanced back and saw the expression on his daughter's face. "Don't worry love," he said, brandishing the potato. "All part of the plan!"

Chapter V

That morning at school seemed to go on for ever for Abigail. It was not helped by the double lesson of Anatomy which she had to endure before lunch. She didn't think that she was ever going to get to grips with this tarsal and metatarsal business in the foot. Or was it the hand?

Finally, lunchtime arrived and Abigail rushed straight to the Main Hall for the last dress rehearsal of Pygmalion. "You're early, Abigail. Have you eaten your lunch already?" the drama teacher asked her as she arrived.

"Not exactly, Miss Diamond," the girl replied sheepishly.

"What you mean is, you've had nothing at all to eat. Am I right?" Daphne Diamond did not need to wait for Abigail's answer. "I know you're nervous, my dear, but you really must eat. You know that it helps concentration and energy. Without those you're not going to be much of an Eliza, are you?"

"I know. I promise I'll get something later." Miss Diamond looked sceptical but decided not to press the matter at that moment.

Gradually, the others arrived and the rehearsal got under way.

At all of the other rehearsals Abigail had been the only actor who reliably knew their words and their stage position. She was always right on cue. She always knew which props to use and when. *She* was the one to prompt the others if they needed a little help. In fact, it seemed as though she knew every line of the play and every stage direction.

Until today, that is. It was just as if someone had locked up the part of her brain labelled S for Shaw or P for Pygmalion. Not only had they locked it up, but they had thrown away the key. And buried the key under ten tonnes of horse manure!

As she tried to dredge up her words and failed, Abigail looked around despairingly at the others. No-one could help her. She had forgotten everything. This was it. The play would just have to be called off.

Daphne Diamond tried to continue with the rehearsal and only decided to draw an end to the torture after ninety minutes. Every minute of that ninety, Abigail wished that the ground would swallow her up.

She now had a mere four hours before she was going to publicly humiliate herself. Perhaps she could just run away. Or pretend that she had suddenly gone mute. Or….

Abigail began to cry. There was nothing that she could do. She sat in the wings and sobbed. She soaked her own hankie and then worked her way through the packet of tissues which Miss Diamond had given her. Nothing could stop her tears, it seemed.

She heard Mr. Alphabet's voice calling from the door near to his office. "Abigail Ayres? Abigail, are you in here?"

'What does he want now?' Abigail was not feeling her usual charitable self.

"I believe you have a dental appointment," the headmaster continued. "Could you make your way to the front entrance, please?"

'I've got to pull myself together,' she thought as she ran off to the lavatories. As she walked towards the wash basins the monstrous face that greeted her was not exactly a pretty sight. She almost didn't recognise herself. Her face was swollen. She could barely see her eyes. Her cheeks were red and blotchy.

What on earth was she going to tell her mother? Normally, First Aiders didn't get quite so emotionally involved in the production of a play!

She did her best to calm her face down with cold water but was still not looking too great as she rushed to the entrance hall. She had her head down with her hair hanging over her face and so did not notice her parent waiting for her until she had nearly collided with…..him!

"What are you doing here, Daddy?" she asked. "Where's Mum?"

"Well, I had a phone call at work about an hour ago. It was your mother. She said that apparently there's something wrong with the car. She got it to go once but it stalled and now it won't start again. I said I'd have a look at it for her when I get home." Her father had his head turned away during this little speech but Abigail didn't notice because she was busy trying to hide her tear-stains. "So Mum asked me to collect you and take you to the orthodontist because she didn't feel up to the walk and the bus journey."

'Oh, and she's usually so keen on exercise as well!' Abigail thought, tongue in cheek.

"I said that I'd bring you back to school and wait until the play's over to walk you back home." Anthony Ayres was sounding please with himself now. "Didn't go down too well, but at least I'll be able to see my little rising star in her first performance."

Abigail's father had expected the girl to be pleased at this news but she said nothing. She simply walked along by his side, seemingly very interested in either her shoe laces or the gravel on the school drive.

"Everything all right, love," her father enquired.

In answer, Abigail just shook her head. She knew that it was hopeless to try to speak because it would only make her cry all the more. This day just could not get any worse. Why was her father so reliable? Why, just for once, couldn't he have let her down and not managed to appear at the school as promised? Now, she was going to let *him* down and give him the most embarrassing evening of his life.

Abigail quickly corrected herself on this last point, however, because she knew that, having lived with her mother for more than twenty years, he had had many much more embarrassing evenings.

All the way to the dentist's, Abigail was silent. She was alternating between trying to remember Eliza's lines and trying to think of a way of leaving the country with no money and no passport.

Mr. Ayres knew better than to try and draw his daughter out of herself when she was feeling like this. He filled the silence with prattle about his work and the crazy people he encountered daily. This was a distraction which suited them both and Abigail soon found herself sitting in the dentist's chair waiting for the industrial equipment to be cemented into her mouth.

It was, for once, then a pleasant surprise when the orthodontist produced a flimsy little piece of plastic held together by elastic bands.

"You can take this out whenever you like, Abigail, so don't worry too much about it. If you want, you can just wear it at night. See how you get on." At last some good news.

Mr. Ayres looked at his watch as they left the surgery. Five forty. "We'd better hurry, love. That first act's not going to be much good without you in it, now, is it?"

"Think it might be better actually," Abigail said sullenly.

"What d'you mean by that?"

Abigail, through sniffles, told her father about the disastrous rehearsal and about how upset Miss Diamond had been with her and about how she was going to let everyone down, most of all him.

"Don't you know what they say? A rubbish dress rehearsal means a perfect performance."

"Do they?"

"Yes, of course. I thought everyone knew that," he teased. Then more seriously, "Listen, Abi, the fact that you've even been brave enough to put yourself up for the part goes a long way in my book and if you have the courage to put just one foot on that stage tonight, then I'll be the proudest Dad there ever was."

Abigail was a little cheered by this but couldn't work out how her heart managed to have defied all laws of anatomy and ended up somewhere around her molars.

Abigail and her father arrived back at the Academy to find preparations for the play well under way. It seemed that everyone in the school was in some way involved with the production.

Darren Darby was setting up his table and money box by the main entrance. He was in charge of selling tickets and programmes. In advance ticket sales, they had already made four hundred pounds. "Four hundred and two pounds fifty, actually!" he excitedly told the Ayres as they walked through the main doors. "You see, Abigail, people'll pay a fortune to see you." This did not help Abigail's nerves one bit.

"Where's the money? You haven't spent it yet, have you?"

"No. Why?"

"Oh, no reason. Just wondering, that's all…" Abigail was glad that the money was in tact because it would make it so much easier to give everyone their refunds. Her thoughts were interrupted.

"Oy! Ayres!" It was Sally Sturgeon. "Get a shift on. We've got to get you dressed and made up and everything." As well as stage managing the event, Sally, naturally enough, was responsible for the whole cast's costumes, which was no mean task since Abigail alone had four changes during the course of the play. Thankfully Sally's abilities with regard to dress were a little more advanced than her knowledge of politeness and etiquette! "We've got to get you dirtied up. I've dug up some choice bits of mud from the garden…at least I think they're mud." She laughed.

Both Abigail and her father looked quite horrified at this prospect. "Just kidding, mate. We've got proper brown make-up stuff to make you look filthy."

Mrs. Evans happened to be passing through the hall on her way to the kitchen. "Yes, and it cost an arm and a leg too. So you two girls be careful how you use it."

Was everyone ever going to shut up about how much the play cost and how much was riding on it? "Come on then, Sal, let's get it over with." This was not the level of enthusiasm that the others might have expected from their star performer but they were all too busy with their own jobs to really notice that something was amiss.

"Yes, we'd all better get on," agreed Mrs. Evans. "I've got to go and check on the half-time refreshments."

"It's not a football match, Mrs. Evans," Darren joked. "You make it sound like we'll all be sucking on half an orange at the interval."

"Humph!" The secretary gave him a look that was more like someone sucking on half a lemon than half an orange. "You lot might have time for larking about but some of us have got work to do." She scuttled away making it clear that she was far from amused.

"Sometimes that woman has got a face like a bulldog chewing a wasp!" Sally exclaimed.

This was exactly what Abigail needed. She burst out laughing. "Oh Sal, you're priceless. She might have heard you."

Sally flicked her hair from her shoulder. "Don't care. It's the truth and the truth never hurt anyone."

"I wouldn't be so sure about that young lady," Mr. Alphabet said from behind her.

Sally turned the colour of raspberry jam.

"Sometimes it's better to be cautious with your honesty."

"I…I'm really sorry, sir. I was just…" Her eyes were filling with tears.

Mr. Alphabet knew that Sally's life was full of people telling her off and she had, despite all evidence to the contrary, developed great sensitivity to it. So, to make her feel a bit better he lowered his voice to a whisper and said to her, "Actually, bulldogs are quite big so I think if we're to get the simile exactly right, it would be better to think of one of those little pug dogs!" He winked at her and strode away.

Sally brightened. "Come on then, Ayres. Say goodbye to Daddy and let's get this show on the road."

Abigail turned and gave her father a hug. "You're going to be great, love. And remember what I said..whatever happens, I'll be prouder of you than you'll ever know."

"Thanks, Daddy. I'll see you at the end then. Will you be o.k. on your own?"

"I think I'll manage, love. You concentrate on yourself. I'm going to have a look round the old place. Haven't seen it properly."

"Okey doke." Abigail and Sally ran off to the classroom at the back of the main hall which had been designated as the girl's dressing room.

As soon as Sally entered the room, a couple of dozen voices went out to her. "Sal, help me with this….", "Sal, I can't get this blouse right…", "Sal…", "Sal…".

Sally was beaming. 'She loves it,' thought Abigail. She was right. Being needed really brought out the best in her friend.

"You go and help them, Sal. I'll be fine with my costume and you can come back and do my make-up when you've finished."

In what seemed like no time at all, they heard a boy's voice outside the classroom calling, "Five minutes, everyone. Five minutes, please."

This was their cue to make their way around to Mr. Alphabet's and Mrs. Evans's offices where they were to wait until they were needed on stage. The wings of the school stage were only quite small and it seemed like they had a cast of hundreds. The children were not exactly delighted at having to be in the headmaster's office because it also was pretty small and even though almost everyone liked him, he was still the headmaster after all. Nevertheless, to a boy, or girl, they all tried to cram into his office. No way was anyone setting foot in the school secretary's enormous domain. They knew that if there was so much as a paper out of place or if the pile on the carpet was rubbed the wrong way, then their life would not be worth living.

Abigail had trailed behind them all on her way to the front of the school and consequently, by the time that she got there, there was no room for her in Mr. Alphabet's office. Especially not, since she was carrying the huge basket of dried flowers which Sally had managed to pick up in a charity shop. From a distance they looked quite effective but close up they were very dusty indeed and the dust was beginning to irritate Abigail's nose.

She stood alone in the middle of Mrs. Evans's huge office, gazing out of the window into the darkness. She could feel the panic rising. All her attempts to calm herself down had failed and she now felt surer than ever that this evening was going to be the disaster to end all disasters.

As her mind drifted further and further away she was suddenly very frightened to see what looked like the figure of a man outside the window. It was coming closer. She turned to look towards the connecting door into Mr. Alphabet's office but the others had closed it firmly to so that none of them might accidentally step across onto the precious cream carpet.

She slowly turned her head back towards the window and saw that the face of the man was now pressed up against it and he had his finger over his mouth indicating that she should stay quiet.

Relief ran through her as she managed to piece together the shadowy features and make out the face of Grey.

He was beckoning her over to the window and even though she knew him, she was still reluctant to go to him because there was something a little weird about the man, something which made her feel a bit uneasy. It didn't look as if he was going to give up, however and so, finally she went behind Mrs. Evans's big highly-polished desk and opened the window.

"Evenin', miss. I got something for you." Abigail was puzzled. What on earth could he possibly have for her? "I knows it's not much but I thought it might be a bit of a help."

Abigail then saw what it was he had been holding in one of his hands as he raised it and, with a grunt, passed through the window the most enormous basket of spring flowers she had ever seen. The girl was overwhelmed by the man's generosity and regretted the slightly unpleasant thoughts which she had just been having about him.

"Not much, Grey? These are amazing. Where did you buy these?"

"Buy?" Grey was indignant. "I didn't buy 'em. I'm a gardener. What would I be doing buying flowers?" This was more like the Grey she knew. "I grew 'em in me 'ot-'ouse."

"But, it's the middle of winter. That's amazing!"

"Oh aye, miss. It's amazing what you can do if you really want to." He gave her a peculiarly knowing look, pushed the window shut and shuffled back off down the garden.

Abigail stood stunned, contemplating what had just happened and inhaling the wonderful scent of the flowers. There were daffodils, crocuses, snowdrops and many more the like of which Abigail had never seen.

She was brought out of her stupor by the sound of shuffling and banging in the next room. Someone, too, was calling her name. "Miss Ayres, Miss Ayres. On stage now, please."

'Miss Ayres'. She liked the way it sounded. 'I could get used to that'

Abigail opened the connecting door to the headmaster's office and saw Daphne Diamond standing there. "You look marvellous, Abigail. Where did you get those wonderful flowers from? Sally really has come up trumps, hasn't she?" Abigail just smiled at Miss Diamond. For some reason, she didn't feel it was right to tell her teacher who had given her the flowers. She wanted it to be her own secret for the moment.

"I've got a good feeling about this. I think you're going to be great."

Abigail glanced back over her shoulder through the window in Mrs. Evans's office and could just make out the figure of Grey standing some way down the garden. He was staring back at her. She turned and, looking her teacher straight in the eyes, she replied, "Actually, miss, so have I."

Chapter W

Abigail hurried through the wings onto the stage to take her position. As she went, the scent from the basket of flowers became stronger and stronger to the point where it was nearly overpowering. Rather than being offputting, this somehow made Abigail incredibly relaxed. Probably more relaxed than she'd ever been in her whole life, in fact. She stepped out onto the stage and thought, 'Yes, *this* is where I'm meant to be. *This* is what I'm meant to do.'

From Abigail's point of view, the evening could not have been much more of a success. She remembered every word of every line. She was right on cue every time. She was almost faultless and, although the boy playing Higgins was also extremely good, there was no doubt in anyone's mind who the real star of the piece was.

There were only one or two hairy moments when, during the Ambassador's reception scene, her paste tiara came unclipped from her hair and fell down over her eyes. She ended up looking like a cross between Elton John and a drunken Queen of the Prom.

Even this mishap, did not really faze her and she soon regained her composure.

As the curtain fell for the final time after the entire cast had taken four calls, everyone was jubilant. They were all hugging each other. Miss Diamond was dabbing at her eyes with her lavender scented lace handkerchief. Mr. Alphabet came backstage and shook the hand of each cast member and back stage helper. He took Abigail's hand in his and shook it so hard that she thought it might drop off. "You were marvellous, my dear, absolutely marvellous. I can't tell you how proud you have made us all." Glancing over the girl's shoulder, he said, "Ah, and here's someone who's prouder than all of us put together."

Abigail turned and saw her father coming towards her stuffing his hankie in his pocket. "What did you think, Daddy? Was it o.k.?"

Her father couldn't answer. He couldn't speak. He merely nodded and took his daughter in his arms. When the melon-sized lump in his throat had gone down to the size of a lemon, he managed to say, "O.k., love? It was a bit more than o.k. You were brilliant." He pulled back and smiled at her. "My little star is going to be a big star."

"Do you know, Mr. Ayres, I think you might have a point there," Mr. Alphabet agreed.

Anthony addressed his daughter again, "By the way, where did you get those lovely flowers at this time of year? Let's have another look at them."

Abigail stood on tiptoes and whispered in her father's ear. "Grey, the old gardener, grew them specially for me and they really helped me, you know." Then speaking more normally, she said, "They must be around here somewhere." They looked around quickly and asked a few of the other cast members but no-one remembered seeing the flowers after the end of the first act.

"I'd better go and change out of this get-up. The game'd be a bit up if I went home with all this make-up on, wouldn't it?" she laughed.

Since Mr. Alphabet was still standing with them, Abigail's father looked a bit sheepish. He didn't really want to make it too obvious that there had to be so many secrets in their house. Nevertheless, he smiled at his daughter. "Just a bit, love. I might go and find Grey while you're getting cleaned up. I'd like to thank him for what he did for you."

"O.k., Daddy. But don't expect much. He's a bit, you know, funny."

"I think I can cope with 'funny', don't you?"

They smiled at each other and then set off in opposite directions. Her father out of the main entrance and into the garden to look for the old man. Abigail to the classroom at the back of the school where she had left all of her stuff.

In the empty classroom cum dressing room, Sally was waiting for her. "Well, Ayres, not bad, I suppose."

For a moment, Abigail was shocked and upset by this rather understated comment until she looked up at her friend's face. Sally was smiling more broadly than Abigail had ever seen anyone smile. The bigger girl gave Abigail such a tight hug that she thought she might be going to suffocate and that that performance would have been her first and her last.

Suddenly the door burst open and the other girls from the play tumbled in. They were shocked to see 'The Sturgeon' hugging someone. Displays of affection were not something they had ever associated with her.

Sally, noticing the shocked looks on the faces of the other girls, quickly pulled at the zip on Abigail's dress. "I can't seem to get this undone, no matter which way I try. Hold on, I'll give it another go." She moved round to the back of Abigail and undid the dress with a feigned struggle. "There we are, you're free!"

"Thanks, Sal." Both girls knew that there was more to Abigail's gratitude than simply being helped out of her frock. "I'd better hurry up and get changed because I don't expect Dad'll be long with Grey." She explained to them all where her father had gone.

"I bet he's on his way back now," put in Sally. "You know what an old misery Grey can be. He won't give your Dad more than about two seconds if I know him." Sally had had a good few run-ins with the gardener during the course of the term.

"That's not nice, Sal. He really helped me with those flowers. Don't know what magic potion he put on them but they certainly worked the trick for me. Maybe we've all been wrong about him all along."

"Doubt it!" Sal was not going to be so easily convinced. "Anyway, I don't see what was wrong with the lovely flowers I got for you in the first place....Where are they by the way?"

Mrs. Evans and her conscripts had cleared up most of the debris from the interval refreshments, leaving very little to do at the end of the show. Once she had given them their orders, she headed off to her office claiming that there was paperwork which needed to be done.

"Can't wait for a sit down," she mumbled to herself as she trudged the lengthy corridor. "Not funny all these late nights when you're over sixty..."

"What's 'over sixty'?" Mr. Alphabet was, unbeknownst to her, walking along behind.

"Er..erm..over sixty...over sixty...teas served. Yes, that's it. Over sixty teas served in the interval."

Mr. Alphabet smiled. He had heard every word of Mrs. Evans mutterings but was not about to let on to her. It amused him intensely that she tried to keep her exact age a secret. She seemed to forget that he knew precisely how old she was since she'd had to write down her date of birth on the forms which *she* introduced. Mr. Alphabet had not been at all concerned about having everyone's personal details on file but she had insisted, claiming that it was important to keep accurate records on everyone. He conceded, but was well aware that the main reason for his secretary wanting such information was that she was almost pathologically nosy. It entertained him, and frustrated Mrs. Evans, that the data on every member of staff in the school was accurate except for one person. Him. He was the only one who was unable to provide any of the particulars required.

As they entered his office, Mr. Alphabet was about to congratulate his secretary on her achievement and her inimitable organisational ability, which could not be denied, but his words were cut off by her gasp of disgust. "Look at this mess! Just look at it! Those children are unbelievable. Do you think they leave their bedrooms like this?" Luckily this was a purely rhetorical question because Mr. Alphabet feared that the answer would, in fact, have been yes. Having taken a walk through the dormitory once or twice, he was well aware of the mess that could be created by children this age.

The headmaster noticed Mrs. Evans's face darken further. She had obviously had the thought that the same fate might have been meted out on her own office and she hurried to the connecting door. With a sigh of relief she stepped into her office and looked around for evidence of interlopers. Thankfully nothing seemed to be out of place except…. "Someone's opened that window. Now why on earth would anyone want to do that in the middle of December?"

Without waiting for an answer, she hurried around the back of the desk to fasten the window to. It was not until her foot crunched heavily down into the basket of dried flowers that she even noticed they were there. By then it was too late. In her haste to extract herself, she managed to get the woven handle of the basket wrapped around her ankle and hopped out from behind the desk shedding crushed petals as she went.

"Get this thing off me," she shouted. "Whoever's put this here will have me to answer to. Don't just stand there grinning, man, help me." She tried to move over towards Mr. Alphabet but as she did so, she turned awkwardly and lost her balance. The next thing he knew, Mr. Alphabet was standing looking down at a prone Mrs. Evans covered in dusty petals and confusion.

Sadly, this was exactly what he needed to ease the tension which he had been feeling all evening and so he began to laugh. And laugh. And laugh. He laughed so much that he thought he would never be able to stop. The more Mrs. Evans shouted at him from her disadvantage point, the more he laughed. "Wait 'til I get up, Mr. so-called Alphabet. You'll be laughing on the other side of your face then."

The headmaster was only brought to his senses by the sound of feet coming along the corridor. Evidently his laughter had raised the attention of others who were now coming to see if they could join in the joke.

Realising that it would be a grave slight on Mrs. Evans dignity if she were to be seen lying on her office floor decked out like some curious pagan spring sacrifice, he quickly helped her to her feet and just managed to extricate her foot from the basket as the door opened.

"Are you all right, Mum?" enquired Christine. "What's going on in here?"

"I'm fine," said Mrs. Evans rubbing her ankle. "I'd be all that much better if this ignorantest of all men could tell the difference between what's funny and what's not."

Christine simply raised her eyebrows towards Mr. Alphabet. She knew not to press her mother when she was in this kind of mood.

"I'm sorry, Mrs. Evans. But you must admit…"

"I admit nothing. I think you've got a rotten cheek and only slightly less cheek than the wastrel who left the thing here in the first place. It was like a bobby trap behind that desk!"

" 'Booby', Mrs. Evans."

"Humph! Well there's no need for that. Booby, indeed. All I did was fall over a basket of rubbish what shouldn't have been there in the first place and now I get called a booby." Seeing her husband standing behind Christine, she took his arm and marched him out of the office. "Come on, Mr. Campbell, we don't have to stand here and be insulted like this."

Mr. Alphabet opened his mouth to explain the misunderstanding but was silenced by Christine's shake of the head. She mouthed the words 'no point' across at him.

"You're right, Christine. I should know by now that your mother does not take at all kindly to be laughed at, nor to being corrected."

"Don't worry. She'll get over it. You know her bark's worse than her bite, don't you?"

179

"It's a good job it is, frankly, because, if not, I'd be a headmaster with no head by now!"

While Sal's dried flowers were being finally done to death by Mrs. Evans, Abigail was scrubbing at her face to try and get the heavy pan stick off. This was a part of the acting profession which she was not overly keen on. By the time she had finished, her face was exhibiting what some might term a healthy glow and others might call a red-raw look.

Finally she was ready to go off and meet up with her Dad. She went in search of him in the entrance hall which seemed to be the most logical meeting point but there was no sign of him. Next, she tried the main hall and stage area. Only the children who were stage hands and cleaners in there. After about ten minutes she had pretty much covered the ground floor of the main school and was beginning to get worried.

Robbie and Govinder were just leaving the cloakroom where Gov had been getting ready to go home. "All right, Beeg?" asked Robbie. "What's up?"

"I can't find my Dad. He was supposed to wait for me. I know I took a long time getting that muck off my face but even so, I don't think he'd have gone off without me."

"I doubt it." Robbie knew how reliable Mr. Ayres was. "Where did he say he'd meet you?"

"Well, he didn't exactly. He said he was going off to thank Grey for the flowers and he'd see me when I was ready. But that was ages ago. I'm sure he wouldn't have been with Grey that long."

"You never know, I suppose. Let's go and have a look outside, shall we?"

"It's pitch black, though."

"Come on, Beeg. Its' not like you to be a scaredy-cat."

"I'm not scared. I just don't think we'll be able to see anything, that's all." Abigail wanted to put the boys off going outside but was not keen to show them how frightened she really was.

Her bluff was called, however, by Govinder. "I've got a torch here, somewhere," he said rummaging in his bag which seemed to contain everything bar the kitchen sink.

"Oh good!" Abigail's teeth were gritted. "Let's hope you can find it" Another fib!

Eventually Gov pulled out a slim black rod from his bag. "Ta-na!...Right, let's go!"

Before she could say 'Actually, d'you know what, I'd rather not' the boys were out of the front door and racing down the garden towards Grey's house.

Abigail's wish not to be excluded from an adventure sent her out after her two friends. "Wait for me, you two!"

The three friends reached the picket fence surrounding Grey's private garden and approached the little house on tip-toe not wanting to alert Grey. Or, more to the point, not wanting to alert Fritzi.

"Give me a bit of a bunk up, Gov, so I can look through the window and see if Beeg's Dad's still in there," Robbie hissed to his friend. Govinder handed the torch to Abigail and bent down to take Robbie's bent leg. No matter how much he struggled, however, and how much effort he put in, he simply couldn't lift the bigger boy off the floor. Abigail stood, hands on hips, watching and marvelling at how two extremely intelligent boys could actually be quite dense at times.

"Could I make a suggestion, guys?" she whispered. "Why doesn't Robbie lift Gov up on the grounds that he's about half the size?!"

The boys embarrassedly changed positions and Gov was soon hanging onto the window sill peering into Grey's living room. Through the gloom, Govinder could make out that the room was full. Full of books, ornaments, silver things, furniture, lamps. Only one lamp was shining, however, over the large carved oak chair where the old gardener was sitting with an enormous book in his hand. He was wearing clothes the like of which he had never been seen to wear before. He almost didn't look like the same person that the children had known for the last three months. "Wow!" exclaimed Gov.

"Wow, what? What is it? What are they doing?" Robbie was anxious both to know what his friend had seen and to lower him to the ground because, light as Govinder was, it was still an awkward way to lift someone and his arms were starting to tire.

"What are who doing?" Govinder, to Abigail's exasperation, seemed to have forgotten what they were there for.

"Grey and my Dad, of course."

"Oh, he's not in there. You're Dad's not in there. It's just Grey on his own." This was the point at which Robbie's arms finally gave way. Not just his arms, in fact, but his legs, his back, his whole body. The two boys came tumbling down to the ground in a noisy heap.

"Ow, Gov. You've got your foot in my ear, you idiot!"

"It's not my fault. If you hadn't dropped me…"

"Who's there?" A voice bellowed from inside the house

"Quick, you two, get up. We'd better run for it." Now Abigail was no longer reticent about showing how truly scared she was.

The boys scrambled to their feet. We'll never make it up to the school before he sees us and then we'll be in the biggest trouble imaginable.

"Well, what can we do? Where can we hide? There's nowhere round here."

"Yes there is," Robbie told her. "We'll hide in the old hot-house. He'll never think that we'll go there. 'Specially not in the dark. Come on, quick!" The boy led the way speedily away from Grey's house.

As they rounded the back of the laurels, Robbie and Govinder halted. Abigail soon joined them and with hands on knees and her body bent over she tried to catch her breath. The air was so cold that it felt like needles going down into her lungs.

Nobody spoke. All three were breathing heavily but almost noiselessly, listening out all the time for the sound of approaching footsteps.

The sound that they heard, however, was not of the gardener marching over to tell them off. Nor was it the sound of the little dog yapping. Nor was it the sound of their hearts pounding in their chests. The sound that they heard was much more chilling. It was a sort of whimpering. A little like a baby crying or a kitten mewling. Or was it just the wind squealing through the laurels?

The three friends looked at one another. "What on earth's that?" Robbie questioned the other two.

"Dunno. Shhh, let's listen."

The noise had stopped, however. "Oh, it was just the wind, I think." Abigail tried to reassure herself as much as the others.

This time there was no show of bravado from Robbie. "I guess you're right. Shall we go then?" The friends stood up from where they had been crouching.

"Good idea. The sooner we're out of this rotten garden the…." Govinder's words were interrupted by the strange sound starting up again.

"That's not wind, Beeg, that's a person. And the noise is not coming from the laurels. It's coming from inside the hot-house. Someone's in there…and they don't sound exactly happy."

All the stories which they had heard about men going down to the hot-house and never returning came flooding back to them.

"It can't be." Govinder tried desperately to be rational. "No-one's allowed in there, you know that."

"Of course I know. But that doesn't alter the fact that right now, right this minute someone is in that spooky place and they sound like they need help."

The other two could not believe what Robbie was implying. "You're not thinking of going in there to take a look are you?" Govinder voiced the thoughts of both of them.

"Well, what do you suggest? Leave whoever's in there to suffer? More to the point, go away never knowing what it was we really heard?" Robbie's courage seemed to have returned from somewhere. "I'll go on my own if you two don't want to go with me." He knew that his friends would not desert him and leave him to whatever fate had befallen the others who had gone into the place alone.

"All right," they agreed reluctantly.

"Can we just stand near the door and look in though," Abigail asked. "We don't really have to go all the way in, do we?"

"No, we don't, Beeg. Anyway, you can stay outside and me and Gov'll go in if we have to." Govinder looked less than impressed about being volunteered into such activity but was anxious to get on with the task and get back up to the safety of the school.

"I'm still sure it's nothing, anyway," Gov told his pals.

"O.k., let's go. Ready, Beeg?"

"Ready."

As they set off they heard the sound of a door banging from the direction of Grey's house and realised that he must have given up his hunt for them. Momentarily they were relieved. At least that was one less thing to worry about.

Their relief was immediately dispelled though when they reached the hot-house door and Govinder shone his torch inside. The sight that greeted them was shocking and ghastly. It was a sight that would be imprinted on Abigail's mind for the rest of her life.

183

Chapter X

By the time the children saw him, Mr. Ayres was submerged more or less up to the shoulders in green slime. His eyes were closed. His face as pale as the slime was dark. It looked like he was struggling to breathe.

"Daddy!" Abigail immediately burst into tears.

Anthony Ayres just about managed to open his eyes and look at his daughter. He struggled a little to try and free himself from the mud but the more he struggled, the more he sank.

"Don't move, Mr. Ayres. Stay where you are. We'll get you out. Wait outside, Beeg."

"No, no," she sobbed. "I'm staying here. Oh Daddy, Daddy!" At this Mr. Ayres began to struggle again. And to sink further.

"Please, Beeg," Robbie insisted in whispered tones. "I think you're Dad'll be calmer if you're not in here. Really."

"O..O.k. You'll get him out, Rob, won't you?"

"Sure. Of course we will. No worries." His words were a lot more confident than his tone. "Maybe you could go up to the school and fetch some help?"

"No. I'm not leaving. I'll wait outside but I'm not going any further." She started to sob again.

"O.k. O.k. Don't worry. I've seen a rope in there and I'm sure we'll be able to get him out with that."

Robbie turned and went back to where Govinder was unlooping the rope from its hook. Under his breath, not wishing to alarm either of the Ayres, he asked Gov, "How are we going to do this?"

"Not sure, Rob. We need to try and get it under his arms somehow. It's not going to be easy because we can hardly see his arms now. But let's just give it a go, anyway."

Fortunately Mr. Ayres was close enough to the wooden walkway that Govinder could lie down and reach over to him while Robbie sat on his legs to make sure that he too didn't slip face first into the horrible green gunk. Slowly Govinder reached his hand down into the freezing cold slime and it was then that he realised the true gravity of the situation. Not only was Mr. Ayres stuck and gradually sinking but his body temperature was obviously plummeting. Neither of the boys had realised this at first because they had, of course, got so hot from running and general excitement that they hadn't even noticed how cold the night had become.

"This is not good, Rob." Robbie did not need to see his friends face to understand exactly how concerned he was. "I'm going to try once to get this rope round and if I can't do it, one of us is going to have to go for help and hope that in the meantime he doesn't slip any further in."

Govinder managed to feel through the slime and pass the end of the rope under Mr. Ayres armpit. Reaching around the back of the man to pull the line through to the other arm was a different story, however. He struggled and struggled to join his hands at the back of the trapped man but, slight as Abigail's father was, the small boy simply could not reach around.

"Let me have a go," Robbie said. "I'm taller than you."

Govinder sat up and looked at his friend. "You are, yes. And you're much heavier and if I'm sitting on your legs and you start to slide in there, we're all going in together!...Nope, it's no good, we're going to have to get help."

Abigail, who had been standing outside the door, trying to make out in vain what the boys were saying, came back in at this point.

"You said you'd get him out! You said...You said...Oh Daddy!..." The tears were flooding down her face.

Once more her father made what looked like a superhuman effort to open his eyes and he gave one last fight to free himself. The result of all this struggle was that now his neck and chin were completely submerged and the slime was up under his bottom lip.

Govinder shot to his feet. "That's it. I'm going for help."

"It's too far up to school," Robbie told him.

"I'm not going to school. I'm going to get Grey." He picked up his little torch and ran off into the dark.

As the school had begun to empty of parents, teachers and children, Mr. Alphabet realised that it was some considerable time since he had seen Abigail and her father. He felt sure that they would not have gone home without saying goodbye to him and decided that they must both still be talking to Grey. Full of curiosity about such an unlikely event, Mr. Alphabet convinced himself that it would be good if he too went and gave Grey his personal thanks for the wonderful flowers which he had provided for the play.

He was surprised as he drew close to Grey's house to see Govinder Gohil running for the same place as though his life depended on it.

The little boy hammered on the gardener's heavy front door. After a few seconds a light went on in the cottage and a sleepy voice came from inside. "Wer sind Sie? Was wollen Sie?"

"Herr Grau, Sie muessen uns helfen? Schnell, schnell!"

Grey came out of his front door wearing what must have once been a very smart burgundy robe and Mr. Alphabet could just make out the remains of a gold crest on the breast pocket. Some very tatty pyjama bottoms were poking out from underneath the robe and the whole effect was somewhat incongruous.

"Bist du verrueckt? Es ist fast Mitternacht, weisst du!"

"I know it's nearly midnight, Mr. Grey, but we have a real emergency on our hands. It's Abigail's Dad. He's fallen into that stuff in the hot-house and he can't get out. I've tried pulling him out with a rope and I can't and I think he might drown and oh.....poor Abi." Govinder broke down.

Mr. Alphabet came up behind the distressed boy and put out a reassuring hand. Grey meanwhile was down the garden path like lightning with Fritzi yapping at his heels.

"Come on, Govinder, let's go and see how we can help, shall we?" Mr. Alphabet's tone totally belied his true feelings. As far as he knew, he had never in his life felt so afraid. "We need to be really strong for Abigail at the moment, o.k.?"

The boy looked up at him and wiped away his tears.

"O.k." He was running off after Grey before Mr. Alphabet could say another word.

When Govinder and the headmaster arrived at the hot-house, Grey was already bending over a very sick looking Anthony Ayres trying to feed the rope around his back. This was not the most pleasant task in the world since it involved Grey pushing his face almost under the slime but he seemed completely oblivious to the fact.

"Blugh thuh tugch over hugh."

"What did he say?" Govinder was unable to make out what the gardener was mumbling through a mouthful of slime.

"I think maybe he said 'bring that torch over here'," Mr. Alphabet suggested.

"Oh right! Yes, straight away."

In his anxiety to be of help, Gov ran over and shone the torch straight into Grey's face.

"Uuuuuuuuuuuuugh! Nugh in mugh fughce, Ughdiught!"

"Shine the torch on Mr. Ayres, Govinder. I think you might be blinding Grey."

"Sorry, sorry!" the boy said, moving the beam onto Abigail's unconscious father. "Oh, he really doesn't look too good at all, does he, sir?"

Mr. Alphabet noticed the desperate look on Abigail's face. "I'm sure that it's only the torch light making him look worse. I'm sure he's going to be just fine." He turned to Robbie. "Could you run up to the school and call an ambulance. No, fire brigade. No, police. Oh I don't know!....Yes, I do. See if you can find Mrs. Evans's daughter. She's a police woman. She might know what to do and who to call. Quick Robbie. Find her and tell her what's happened."

Robbie leapt to his feet and Mr. Alphabet followed him out of the hot-house. "Fast as you can now, Robbie. I don't think we've got much time."

"But, sir, I thought you said he was going to…"

"Never mind what I said, Robbie. Just run like mad."

Robbie felt himself propelled up the garden by the force of Mr. Alphabet's large hand on his back.

As he reached the school entrance, he practically collided with Mrs. Evans, Christine and Sally Sturgeon, who were all leaving at the same time.

"Miss….Miss…" He addressed Christine. "You've got to come quick….." Robbie bent over, unable to catch his breath.

"Come where? What on earth's happened?" Christine asked.

"Hot-house…..Beeg….Dad…."

"What are you burbling on about boy? What's 'Beeg'?" Mrs. Evans was not impressed by the boy's incoherence.

"Beeg's Abigail Ayres, miss," Sally informed her. "What's happened Rob? Is it Abi? What?"

Robbie merely shook his head and repeated the word "Hot-house…Hot-house…"

"Come on then, Mum. Where is this hot-house?"

Mrs. Evans looked at her daughter in astonishment. "You don't mean to tell me that you actually believe this little monster? He's had me on a line more times than I care to mention. Full of tricks, that one."

"Full of tricks he may be, Mum, but I'm guessing by the look of him that this isn't one of them." Robbie was by now flat out on the floor wheezing heavily. It was times like this that he wished he'd taken up Running instead of Russian.

Christine continued, "If you won't show me the way to the hot-house, I'm going to have to find it for myself in the dark."

She was about to set off when Sally spoke up. "I'll show you, miss. Follow me."

The girl and the police woman started down the path and could soon pick out the dancing light of Govinder's torch in the otherwise pitch dark glasshouse.

Mr. Alphabet was at the door waiting to meet them. "He's back there." He pointed to where Grey was kneeling in front of Mr. Ayres making an elaborate knot in the thick rope.

"*Who's* back there?"

"What's happened?"

"Didn't Robbie tell you?" Mr. Alphabet asked.

"He wasn't really in much of a position to speak, to be honest," Christine told him.

Mr. Alphabet did not have time to be puzzled. "Abigail's father has fallen into the slime in here and we can't get him out. Grey's managed to get a rope round him but I don't know if we'll be strong enough to pull him out."

"I'll call for help," Christine said, removing a phone roughly the size of a house brick from her bag. She quickly made her call and the three of them inched their way carefully along the wooden walkway. One person in the mire was quite enough for one evening.

"Stand back," Grey said as they drew close. "I'm going to try to tug him out." He heaved on the rope with all his might. He heaved so hard that he was nearly bending over backwards with the effort. He heaved and heaved and heaved some more. But nothing. Mr. Ayres had not moved one little bit.

"It's no good, mister. I can't seem to shift 'im." Grey told his boss.

"What are we going to do, sir?" Govinder asked.

It was times like this that Mr. Alphabet rather wished that he were not in charge and could hand over the responsibility to someone else. "Erm…er…" Then it came to him. "Lawnmower!"

Under normal circumstances someone would have been sure to tell him that this was no time to be mowing the lawn but matters were a bit too serious for such jokes.

"Get the lawnmower, Grey. We'll back it up to the door of the hot-house and tow him out." He moved towards the gardener. "I'll hold him steady while you go and get the machine….It's got lights on it, by the way, hasn't it?"

"It's got lights, gears, the works. There's some as didn't want me to have such a fancy machine, if you remember rightly, mister." Grey was referring to Mrs. Evans with whom he had had many a long argument about the purchase of the new piece of equipment. "Well, they'll be eating their words, now, won't they?"

"Just get the machine, Grey. This is not a point-scoring exercise! Now go, man!"

Mr. Alphabet took up the strain on the rope and the gardener rushed off to get his favourite toy. The shed it was kept in was very close and within a matter of a couple of minutes he was back and making more professional looking loops in the rope to attach it to the lawnmower.

"Now gently does it, Grey," Christine told him. "We don't want the man to be any more injured than he already is, do we?"

"I'm not an idiot, young lady, in spite of what your mother might 'ave told you."

Christine knew that to rise to this argument was futile and turned instead to Mr. Alphabet. "You'd better stay where you are and try to take some of the strain on the rope while Grey edges the mower forward….O.K. Grey. When you're ready…"

Grey began to gently rev the engine of the lawnmower and riding the clutch expertly he moved very slowly forward.

As the rope started to tighten around his back, Mr. Ayres gave a loud grunt as though expelling every last bit of air from his already compressed lungs.

"Stop, stop! You're hurting him." Abigail began to run forward but was held back by Christine Campbell who was extremely grateful at that moment for the "Arrest and Restraint" training course which she had been sent on the year before.

"If we don't get him out, he's going to be more than hurt, I'm afraid, Abi. And if you get too close, you'll be ending up in there with him. So stand back and promise me you won't move."

"O.k."

"Promise?"

"O.k. I promise."

The rope between the mower and the sinking man was now taut. Mr. Alphabet was having difficulty standing upright and taking some of the pressure off Abigail's father.

"Right, Grey," Christine called out. "Forward now…gently…gently."

As Grey and the mower moved inch by inch away from the hot-house door, the others saw Mr. Ayres slowly lifting out of the mud. First his mouth became visible, then his chin, his neck, his shoulders. He was soon clear of the slime from the waist up.

Grey let the clutch out one final time and the onlookers suddenly heard a giant slurp. Mr. Ayres was lying face down on the wooden walkway.

Within a split second another loud sound was heard. This time it was a thud. Everyone except Mr. Ayres looked to where the noise had come from and saw Abigail lying on the floor near the door. She had fainted clean away.

Christine spoke to Mr. Alphabet. "It looks like there'll be more than one member of the Ayres household going of to hospital this evening."

"Yes and I think that the unfortunate duty falls to me of telling the third member of the family exactly what's happened."

Chapter Y

Mr. Alphabet made sure that Abigail and her father were safely installed in the hospital and went off to break the news to Eleanor Ayres.

Within forty minutes he was back at the hospital.

"That was a bit quick," Mrs. Evans scolded him. "I hope you weren't a bit short with the poor woman, like you usually are."

"Frankly, Mrs. Evans, 'poor' and 'woman' are not words which should be used together when referring to Mrs. Eleanor Ayres. And if anyone was short during our exchange it was certainly not me." Mr. Alphabet had clearly come off the worse from his brief meeting with Abigail's mother.

"Where is she, anyway?" Christine was puzzled that Eleanor had not come back to the hospital in the taxi with Mr. Alphabet.

"At home."

"At home? What on earth's she doing there?"

"Smoking and playing a computer game, from what I could see."

"But did you tell her that her husband and daughter were in hospital and that her husband was apparently in a coma?"

"No, Christine. I went round there, discussed the political situation in the Middle East and came away again!...Of course, I told her what had happened."

"All right, all right. No need to get all uppity," Mrs. Evans jumped in. It was perfectly all right for her to have a go at her daughter but it seemed that Christine was not fair game for all and sundry.

"Sorry, but she has made me so mad, I can't tell you." Mr. Alphabet was distinctly unimpressed with Eleanor's behaviour. "She just asked me to call her if there was any change in their condition but wait for this…this is the best bit….as I was leaving she was muttering about needing to check her husband's life insurance policy and will. Now, can you believe the gall of the woman?"

"Crikey! She really does sound like a nasty piece of work." Christine was shocked.

"That would be the most polite way of putting it, I think. And to say that there's no love lost between her and her husband and daughter would be the understatement of the year!…Anyway, let's go and see the patients, shall we? Are they still in Casualty?"

"Yes, but they're moving Mr. Ayres to Intensive Care. They've said that they'd like to keep Abigail in over night too to monitor her but there are no beds so it looks like she'll be going home."

"Over my dead body will she be going home!" Christine and Mr. Alphabet turned to Mrs. Evans in surprise. "What? What you looking at me like that for? You think I'd let a girl go home to a mother like that? Woman doesn't deserve to have children." She looked at Mr. Alphabet. "Oh, I know. You think I'm hard and that but that's only in my job. I wouldn't want to see anyone suffer, leave alone a nice girl like young Abigail Ayres."

Mr. Alphabet didn't know what to say. He was more than a little touched by Mrs. Evans compassion.

"What can we do with her though?"

"Obvious! Take her back to the school. I can make up another bed in the girl's dorm and she can stay there tonight."

"What about tomorrow, though?"

"You know what they say, the sun'll come out tomorrow."

"Meaning?" As usual, Mrs. Evans had confounded her employer with her strange little sayings.

"Meaning nothing. I just like the sound of it!" She laughed and the other two joined in.

They made sure that Mr. Ayres was safely transferred to a bed in the Intensive Care Unit and left the nurses gently bathing him to try to remove the green slime which seemed to have almost embedded itself in his skin. It was time to take Abigail back to the school. By now, it was almost four thirty in the morning and Abigail was insistent that she wouldn't be able to sleep and that she might as well not go to bed anyway because it would soon be getting up time and that she wanted to go back to see her Daddy. The moment that her head touched the fluffy school pillow, however, exhaustion overcame her and she was asleep within seconds.

She was awoken five hours later by the sound of "We like sheep" from Handel's Messiah. This was Govinder Gohil's rather high-brow choice of Christmas music and Abigail always thought that the words sounded more like a Welsh hill-farmer's song than some highly religious choral music. She leapt up with such a start on hearing the school 'bell'. For an instant she had no idea why she should be in a school dorm, why she should have slept until after the start of the first lesson, why her head was banging so much. Then the events of the previous night came flooding back. She experienced that dreadful sinking feeling and realised that, quite possibly, her life would never be the same again. She began to cry and despite every effort she made to convince herself that really it might not be as bad as she was fearing, she could do nothing to stop feeling utterly wretched.

Robbie, who was sitting on the other side of the partition into the boys' dorm, came rushing in. "Hey, Beeg, come on. There's no need to get so upset. Everything's all sorted."

"What's sorted? Is Daddy all right?"

The girl's momentarily raised hopes were dashed when she looked into Robbie's eyes. "Mr. A. told me the hospital have said that he's stable and that he's certainly out of immediate danger."

"Did they say when they expect him to wake up?"

"Er…no…er…I don't think so."

Abigail began to wail again. "He's not going to wake up is he? Oh, what am I going to do? I can't carry on without my Daddy."

Mr. Alphabet entered the dorm at that moment and took the distraught girl in his arms. "You won't have to carry on without him. I'm sure that he'll come round and probably very soon. And even if it takes a little while, we'll look after you here, you mustn't worry."

Abigail knew nothing of what had gone on between Mr. Alphabet and her mother the night before but she was certainly relieved that he seemed to understand her position completely.

Still concerned about her father though, she asked, "If people don't come round quickly, that means they're going to die, doesn't it?"

193

"Certainly not, thank you very much! Look at me!" Mr. Alphabet smiled at his pupil but she did not smile back.

"Yes, but you don't remember anything or anybody from before, do you? That means…." Again she started to sniff. "That means that he won't remember who I am." The tears were flowing strongly again now.

Mr. Alphabet took her face in his hands. "Look at me, Abigail." Slowly she lifted her red eyes. "If I'd had a daughter as lovely, kind and considerate as you, there is no way that I would ever have forgotten about her." Mr. Alphabet could not be certain that what he was saying was the absolute truth but at that moment he felt it so strongly that he didn't stop to question his own words.

Abigail managed to squeeze out a tiny smile.

"That's my girl. Now go and wash your face and have some breakfast. You're going to need some sustenance because, don't forget that you've got another star performance to give this evening."

"Oh no! I don't think I could possibly…"

"Hold it right there, young lady. What do you think your father would want? Would he want you to sit around moping when what you should be doing is getting up and entertaining everyone, getting up and working towards the goal that you've always had?"

Abigail knew that the headmaster was right. The last thing her father would want was to feel that he had come between her and her ambition. She simply looked up at Mr. Alphabet, nodded and set off to the bathroom to clean herself up after last night's little adventure.

———————————————

Ten minutes later, Mr. Alphabet was sitting in his office with his head in his hands when Mrs. Evans came in carrying his morning tea tray.

"Whatever's the matter?" she asked him.

"Oh, Enid. I've done it again, haven't I? I've promised something which I'm really not sure I can deliver."

"What are you talking about?"

"I'm talking about young Abigail Ayres. I've told her that we'll look after her here until her father comes round but how on earth am I going to get this one past her mother?

I know that the girl doesn't want to go home but if I keep her here, Mrs. Ayres could have me for all sorts of things like…I don't know…like abduction or kidnapping or something dreadful…"

Unlike over the incident with Robbie, Mrs. Evans made no attempt to admonish the headmaster for his generous promise. Quite the contrary, in fact. "If she tries any such thing, she'll have me to answer to. Dreadful woman. Dreadful!"

"I appreciate your support, Enid, but I'm not sure how much practical use it is." He thought for a moment or two. "No, it's no good. I'll just have to go to Abigail and tell her that really she's going to have to go home. She's going to be devastated."

"Stop right there. This is not like you! Since when did you ever give up on something without even trying? You haven't even spoken to the woman yet." Mrs. Evans was adamant. "You've wriggled your way out of worse things than this before now. You might as well put all your clever talk to some use, hadn't you? And remember what they say 'it ain't over until the fat laddie sings.'"

Mr. Alphabet was convulsed at this, picturing a rather portly Scottish boy dressed up in a kilt singing his heart out about his 'Bonnie wee lassie'.

As usual, Mrs. Evans was deeply unimpressed by this show of hilarity. "If all you're going to do is laugh then I'm off. Don't come to me snivelling for help, that's all I can say."

She stalked out but Mr. Alphabet was unable to call her back since he was once again overtaken by the vision of the kilted minstrel. "Fat laddie," he chuckled to himself. "Priceless!"

He picked up the telephone and began to dial Eleanor Ayres number. 'Maybe she won't be there,' he thought. 'Maybe I won't have to speak to her and can just leave a message…' After three short rings, however, the receiver was lifted at the other end.

"Hello?"

'Ugh! That woman really does have an awful voice. If anything was going to make you throw yourself into deadly green slime, it'd be that,' thought Mr. Alphabet flippantly.

"Mrs. Ayres? Mr. Alphabet."

The voice dropped a few tones. "Oh, hello."

He thought he'd better stick to the convention that she actually was remotely concerned about her family. "Don't worry. I'm not calling with bad news….It's just…I…well…"

195

"Can you get to the point, please? Only I've got someone coming round to have a look at Anthony's print collection. I mean, if he's not going to be bringing money in, I'm going to have to find a way of paying for all the bills, aren't I?"

Mr. Alphabet's jaw dropped so that it nearly hit the desk. This was possibly the most unbelievable woman that ever walked the earth. Strangely enough though, her cold, calculating behaviour spurred him on. "I have a proposal for you. I understand how distraught and upset you must be feeling at the moment..." Here he paused and his silence spoke far more than his words ever could. "...and I understand that it's the most difficult thing in the world to have to be strong for both your daughter and yourself. So, I was wondering if we here at the Academy might be given the honour of looking after Abigail while your husband is in hospital and later during his recuperation period. Obviously, you realise that this is only a suggestion to alleviate some of your burden but clearly, if you would like your daughter with you at this awful time, then..."

Eleanor Ayres had no need to think about this offer. "Sounds fine to me. As long as you don't expect any money out of me. As I said, I can barely make ends meet as it is."

"Of course not. We'd be only too glad to offer our support in any way we can and that includes financial. You will, naturally, not be required to pay Abigail's school fees until such time as your husband fully recovers."

"If he ever does. I could be nursing a cripple for the rest of my life. Fine life that's going to be for me. And will I get any thanks for it? I doubt it. And another..."

Mr. Alphabet could tolerate no more of this. "Well, as ever, Mrs. Ayres it's been a pleasure and an education speaking to you. We will, no doubt, remain in touch over the coming weeks. I wish you everything that you deserve." Mr. Alphabet was the expert in double meaning. "Goodbye, now."

He did not wait for her to answer him and the phone went down with such a crash that it brought Mrs. Evans scuttling in from her adjacent office. "She didn't buy your suggestion then?" His secretary seemed to have forgotten her earlier indignation.

"Oh, she bought it all right. But I tell you what, Mrs. Evans, if I never have to speak to her again, it will be too soon!"

Seeing the thunderous look in her employer's eyes, Mrs. Evans knew not to press the matter any further and left the room almost as quickly as she had entered it.

The remainder of the Christmas term passed without great event. Abigail quickly slipped into the life of a boarder and was, in many respects overjoyed because she got to spend so much more time with her friends. A rota was established for people taking her to and from the hospital so that she could see her father every day. Every evening, she would sit by his unconscious figure in the hospital bed and tell him the small things which had happened during the day. She thought to herself that, ironically, this was the most she had ever been able to speak to her father privately in her whole life.

Grey got on with his few winter jobs around the garden but otherwise made himself quite scarce. It was as though he was in some way ashamed of the events on the night when Mr. Ayres had come to see him but had never quite made it to his cottage. But surely he wasn't to blame for the accident, was he?

Darren Darby spent many hours poring over his budget sheets trying to make allowances in the school's already tight finances for an extra full boarding scholarship.

The Christmas party was a huge success and was the proof for Mr. Alphabet that the feeling of community in the school was going from strength to strength. It really seemed that his original plan was coming to fruition.

It was the day before the holidays, then, when Abigail entered the drama room for the final lesson. She was surprised to see Mr. Alphabet standing there waiting for her along with Miss Diamond.

"Abigail, Miss Diamond has something she'd like to put to you."

All sorts of things went through Abigail's mind. Were they going to send her away to another school? Was she going to be asked to give up acting because she was so rubbish at it? Surely it wouldn't matter that she had fluffed one or two lines on the second night of the play?

Mr. Alphabet laughed. "Don't look so worried, Abigail. Not all news is bad news, you know." He turned to the drama teacher. "Perhaps you had better enlighten her, Miss Diamond."

Daphne Diamond picked something up from her desk and handed it to Abigail. It was an advertisement cut from a newspaper. Abigail looked at the paper and then back at her teacher and back to the paper. Her head was moving up and down like someone watching a professional tennis match. "What has this got to do with me?" she asked finally.

197

"I should have thought that was obvious, Abigail," Mr. Alphabet replied. "It's an advert for auditions for people to star in a show. They're looking for a whole new family for the show and Miss Diamond thinks that you'd be perfect for the teenage girl."

"But I bet millions of people watch this show. I'd never get the part. I've had no training or anything. It'd be a waste of time."

"I could answer all of those points reasonably logically, Abigail, but I'm not going to. All I'm going to ask is that you give it a try. Trust me and give it a try." Miss Diamond's wonderfully calming lavender scent seemed to fill the room.

"O.k. I'll do it. But I'm really scared, mind."

"I know you are, my dear. Imagine, though what your feeling will be when you get the part."

"If," Abigail corrected her teacher.

"As I said, when." Miss Diamond smiled down at the girl.

"Miss Diamond has kindly agreed to come in every day over the Christmas holidays and give you some coaching ready for the auditions on the sixth of January. Isn't that kind of her?"

"Very kind. Thanks so much, miss. I'll really try not let you down."

"It's never a question of letting anyone down, Abigail. Everything you do, you must do for yourself."

At that moment, the door burst open. "I can't stand it any more. Have you asked her yet?" Robbie was beside himself. He had been straining in vain to hear through the thick drama room door.

"You mean you knew about this?" Abigail asked her friend.

Miss Diamond enlightened the girl. "It was Robbie who found the advert, my dear, but he thought that if he put it to you himself, you'd just poo-poo the idea, so he came to me instead."

"You sneak!"

"Never mind that. Are you going to do it then?"

"She is going to give it a try, Robbie, yes," Mr. Alphabet responded for Abigail.

"Hooray!" Robbie took his friend's hands in his own and dancing her around, he chanted, "Beeg's going to be on the telly! Beeg's going to be on the telly!"

Chapter Z

The first week of the Christmas holidays was spent with intensive acting work every morning from nine until one. Abigail was put through exercises which she'd never had to undergo before. She was a tree, she was an orange, she was an alien. She was happy, she was sad, she was dismal, she was mildly disconcerted. All of these emotions needed to be practised, according to Miss Diamond. Although from the snippets of this type of show which Abigail had seen, 'mildly disconcerted' didn't often seem to feature in the programme.

At one o'clock on Christmas Eve, Abigail and Miss Diamond were in the main entrance hall of the school. "Right then, my dear. Two days off from acting lessons. So we resume on the twenty-seventh at nine a.m. Agreed?"

"Agreed…Erm, miss, …er…what'll you be doing tomorrow."

Miss Diamond was wrapping her large lilac scarf around herself. "Oh, the same as everyone else I expect. Eating more than I need, sleeping more than I need. You know, the usual."

Abigail looked sad. "Will you be having a lot of friends round? Will you be having a party?"

"I might meet up with a few people, yes. We'll see."

Abigail could see that Miss Diamond was anxious to get off. 'Perhaps she's got lots of preparation to do for her Christmas dinner, or perhaps I'm getting on her nerves.' The girl made a conscious effort to smile broadly at her teacher.

"Well, miss, have a lovely day. A very merry Christmas."

Miss Diamond reached out and touched Abigail's head. "And to you, my dear, and to you."

199

As she watched Miss Diamond gliding down the school path away from her, Abigail felt low and alone for the first time since her father's accident. It was going to be terrible not spending Christmas Day with him. There was, of course, the benefit of not having to see her mother and suffer the indignity of being given presents which were then taken back by the end of the day because of some supposed misdemeanour which Abigail had committed. This happened almost every year. Every year her mother told her that the toys and clothes on which she had spent her 'hard-earned money' were going to be given to the children's ward at the hospital rather than to her ungrateful daughter. One year, however, Eleanor Ayres had, in error, left out the receipt for the refund which she had received from the toy department in Dorrid's. Coincidentally along with that receipt was one for roughly the same amount for the purchase of a very expensive two-piece ladies outfit from the same store.

So, it was really going to be a relief not to have to go through that charade again this year. Nevertheless, much as she liked Mr. Alphabet, dinner alone with him on Christmas Day was not the most appealing prospect in the world.

Abigail managed to fill most of her afternoon mooching around the school. It was very dark everywhere and looked remarkably dull because there were no Christmas decorations to be seen. In the end she gave up on the mooching, as she figured it was slightly too depressing and went up very early to the dorm. She was quickly asleep and in spite of her down mood, slept solidly through until seven the following morning.

Unfortunately, the long sleep did not seem to have improved her mood and she made her way down to the school kitchens with a leaden heart. As she descended the stairs, however, through the gloom there was a curious light coming up from the entrance hall. She began to skip down the stairs and was soon at the bottom where a huge heavily decorated Christmas tree was standing. It was the most impressive tree she had ever seen and completely put in the shade the moth-eaten plastic effort which was dragged down from the loft in the Ayres' house every year. The decorations too were like nothing she'd ever seen. There were no cheap tacky bits of tinsel, no baubles with dents in tied up with manky bits of cotton, no string of garish coloured lights which every year caused an argument because it took forever to locate the one which was not working, no ancient doll on the top that looked more like a fairy grandmother than a fairy godmother. This tree was covered in tiny wooden toys all beautifully painted. The little white lights twinkled delicately in the gloom of the great hallway. At the top of the tree was a large wooden star painted in what looked like real gold.

The whole effect was amazing.

Still more amazing was the sight of Mr. Alphabet, Grey, Mrs. Evans and Mr. Campbell, Christine and Stephen, Darren Darby, Daphne Diamond, the Redovitch family, the Gohil family, Sally Sturgeon. They were all waiting there for her she realised.

"Happy Christmas, Abigail," they cried in unison.

This was almost the best Christmas present anyone could possibly have given her. She began to cry. "Oh, oh, I'm sorry. I'm not really sad. I'm really happy, oh....."

"That's good, my dear, remember what that feels like. You might be able to use that in the audition." It seemed that Miss Diamond was never off duty.

It was the best Christmas Day that Abigail had ever experienced. Only one thing would have made the day more perfect, having her father there to share it with her. She felt sure, though, that he would have been delighted if he could have seen her enjoying herself with so many friends.

At about half three when Abigail had just given her own, rather amusing version, of the Queen's speech, accompanied by Robbie and Govinder's fanfare played on imaginary trumpets, Mrs. Evans and Mr. Alphabet were in the kitchens beginning the big clear up campaign.

"Can you believe that that awful woman has not even been an eye today?" Mrs. Evans asked her boss.

" 'Been an eye', Enid? That's a new one on me, I'm afraid. You'll have to explain."

"I mean, Abigail's so-called mother has not even called or anything today. What with it being Christmas and everything, I thought that she might at least have put herself out a little....Still, some people don't know when they're well off, do they?"

"I suppose that they don't, Enid," Mr. Alphabet said. He considered, not for the first time, just how well off *he* was and how differently his life could have turned out had he not chanced to meet so many great, if occasionally infuriating, people.

For all those involved in the great Academy Christmas Day party, most of Boxing Day was spent recuperating and it was straight back into action for Abigail and Miss Diamond the following day.

As audition day approached, Abigail became increasingly nervous. "What about if they think I'm useless? What about if they just don't like me? I've never done this before, what about if I'm rubbish?"

"What about, what about, what about! Have you thought maybe what about if you succeed, what about if you bowl them over, what about if their show couldn't possibly go on without you?" Miss Diamond smiled at her frightened pupil. "Look, if the worst comes to the worst, you will have tried. And what a story to tell your Daddy when he wakes up. He'll be so proud."

Abigail remembered her father's words 'the fact that you've even been brave enough to put yourself up for the part goes a long way in my book'. "You know what, you're right," she told her teacher as they parted the evening before the audition.

"That's the spirit! Right, eight thirty tomorrow morning then?"

"Eight thirty it is! See you then."

As she watched her teacher stride away down the gravel drive, Abigail knew that there was no chance of her getting a wink of sleep that night. Adrenalin seemed to be rushing through every part of her body. Her mind was going over and over everything that Miss Diamond had told her over the last few weeks. "Breathe, Abigail. Remember, you *are* this person. Remember, they need you more than you need them. Remember, you are on your own, you're not in a room full of people. Remember…Remember…Remember…"

"Aggghhhhh!" Her scream echoed around the entrance hall.

Grey appeared from nowhere. "You all right, miss?"

"Oh, Grey. You startled me. Yes, yes, I'm fine. Just a bit scared about tomorrow. Don't tell anyone, but I've got this audition tomorrow and I'm really, really nervous."

"Ah, I see."

"I can't seem to think about anything else. My head's going round and round and round."

"Tell you what, miss, why don't you come for a little walk with me round me garden? Might make you feel a bit better to get some fresh air."

This was most unlike Grey. Abigail was amazed. She was also a bit scared, if the truth be told. "Erm..well…er…" Not wishing to seem rude, she agreed to his suggestion. "O.k. then, maybe just for five minutes."

Grey set off apace down the garden towards the hot-house. 'Is he mad?' Abigail thought. She hadn't been near the place since the night of her father's accident. "Mr.

Grey, Mr. Grey…" She ran along behind him trying to get his attention. 'For a man with a stick he can't half shift!' she said to herself. She tried calling him again. "Mr. Grey!" Still he pressed on and before she knew it he was opening the door of the greenhouse and stepping inside.

As Abigail approached the door, she began to realise that there was the most horrific smell coming from inside. "Ugh horse pooh!....MR. GREY!" she shouted as loudly as she possibly could. Nothing. No response whatsoever. "I can't go in there. I'll be sick. It stinks." Already she could feel her lunchtime lasagne making its way back up her throat.

She was in a real dilemma because she didn't want to seem rude and annoy Grey but she also didn't really want to lose her lunch. Suddenly she saw Grey staring at her from underneath…..the most incredible flower she had ever seen. It was a deep, deep pink, shaped like a bell and at least as tall as Abigail herself.

Grey was beckoning her. Luckily, as she had left the school, she had picked up her Daddy's tartan scarf as a precaution against the cold and she now wrapped it around her nose and mouth in an attempt to stave off at least some of the dreadful stench.

She made her careful way along the wooden walkway to where Grey was standing at the back of the hot-house. She drew nearer to the flower and its beauty got more and more unbelievable. It was mesmerising, so much so that she almost completely forgot about the smell. Only almost.

The two of them stood motionless before the immense blossom for a couple of minutes. "All right, miss, let's go out now, shall we?"

Abigail didn't want to lower the scarf so she simply nodded and followed Grey from the building.

When they were outside she ripped the scarf down and a string of questions came tumbling from her mouth. "What is that flower? Why's there only one of them? And where's the smell of horse doo-doos coming from?! It's a shame you have to go through that stink to see something so lovely, isn't it?"

"Ah well, miss, that's how life is. Sometimes to get to what we really wants, we has to go through some things we don't really like." Without another word, Grey headed off for his little cottage and somehow, Abigail knew she had been dismissed.

The next morning, Miss Diamond was at the school at seven o'clock. It was not only Abigail who was nervous about this audition day.

At eight thirty precisely, the taxi arrived and Abigail was delighted to see Mr. Alphabet getting ready to go with them to the studios. "I hope you don't mind me coming along for the ride, dear. I just thought I'd see what it was all about."

Abigail tried to disguise her pride with nonchalance. "Don't mind at all. It'll be interesting for you, I dare say."

The headmaster smiled at her. "I dare say!"

As the car pulled away from the school gates, Abigail noticed Grey standing with Fritzi near one of the large oak trees. He raised his hand in a small wave, turned and made his way back down the garden. Abigail looked back at her two teachers and began to tell them about the curious incident with Grey and the flower the previous evening. "How does he grow things like that, Mr. A? How come it's growing in winter, anyway?"

"Abigail, I have no idea."

"There's more to him than meets the eye, I think."

"I think you're probably right, my dear."

Twenty-six minutes after setting out from the Academy, the taxi was pulling up outside the enormous television building.

"Oh, no,no! I can't do it. I really can't. Look at all those people. Look how big it all is. Look!"

"I know, my dear," Mr. Alphabet rested a reassuring hand on her arm, "but we're here now so we might as well at least go inside."

They got out of the taxi and entered the lofty marble and glass reception area. The receptionist quickly directed them to the part of the building where the audition studio was. His directions were a little too brief, however, because they found themselves wandering down corridor after corridor lined with pale wooden doors. Doors giving no indication as to what might be going on inside.

"This is a bit like being in one of those new towns where every road and every roundabout looks the same. I drove round and round one of those for two and a half hours once and never found a single person to ask directions." Miss Diamond was not at her most confident behind the wheel of a car.

At the end of one of these identical corridors behind one of the identical doors, they could hear raised voices. "I think we're just going to have to knock on here and ask…"

Mr. Alphabet's words were cut short. The door was flung open and a giant of a man stepped out.

Abigail and her two teachers stood motionless as this huge man looked down at her. "Cen I help you? Vot do you vont? Zere is no exit zis vay."

"Oh..n..no," Abigail stammered. "We're not looking for the exit. We...we're looking for an audition studio...it's for that family...you know, that new family in that show..." She ground to a halt, fully aware that she was not exactly making herself clear.

"Ah, yes. I know it. In fact I am ze executive producer." The man's demeanour changed completely as he held out his hand to Abigail. "Allow me to introduce myself. My name is Zappa. Zoltan Zappa."

Abigail, Miss Diamond and Mr. Zappa all turned around as they heard Mr. Alphabet fall back against the now closed office door. "Are you all right, Mr. A? You don't half look pale." Abigail was worried.

Mr. Alphabet had his hand over his forehead. "I'm fine, I'm fine. I just felt a bit dizzy there for a moment." For the first time, Mr. Zappa took a close look at Mr. Alphabet and as quickly as he had come out of the office, he set off down the corridor.

"Follow me," the giant called over his shoulder.

Mr. Alphabet had pulled himself together. "Just a minute, sir, just a minute. Don't I know you?"

Zoltan Zappa stopped in his tracks, his face darkened and slowly he turned to look Mr. Alphabet hard in the eyes. Very slowly he said, "I really don't sink so. Do you?"

A shiver ran the length of Abigail's spine as she watched Mr. Alphabet visibly wither before this monster. Never had she heard anyone speak in such a threatening tone about something so minor.

In a flash the menace was gone from Mr. Zappa's face. "Kom, qvickly. Ve don't vant to be late, now, do ve?"

They followed Mr. Zappa through the rabbit warren passing once again through the lofty reception area and finally ending up at completely the opposite end of the building.

"You take a seat and vait until zey call your name." Mr. Zappa pushed open the double doors and, ducking to avoid bumping his head, he entered the studio.

There were about fifty girls sitting waiting in the corridor. Abigail's heart was in her boots. As the minutes past, she kept hearing her mother's voice in her head. "You're just like your father, you are. You'll never make anything of yourself, my girl. Don't even bother trying. You'll never..."

"Abigail, Abigail!" Miss Diamond was calling her name. Abigail realised she must have really gone off into a day dream.

"What? What is it?"

"Abigail, this is it. It's your turn, now."

Epilogue

It was a scorching hot evening. Mr. Ayres was lying, still unconscious, in bed in his small room in Hope House Hospital. He had been there for five months now. His condition was deemed to be stable. He neither got better, nor did he get worse.

There had been a hot spell of weather for some three weeks now and the nurses, in spite of their best efforts, found it almost impossible to keep the heat down in his room. This evening, the room was particularly stifling because today Mr. Ayres had more than one visitor. In fact, his room was packed to bursting. There was Abigail, Mr. Alphabet, Miss Diamond, Robbie Redovitch and his whole family, Mrs. Evans, Christine Campbell and Inspector Spencer. In fact, it seemed like everyone that Abigail knew was crowded into that tiny side ward.

Everyone except for one person, that is.

On the other side of town, Eleanor Ayres was sitting in her large ordinary living room in her ordinary semi-detached house. The windows were firmly closed, in spite of the heat, and the heavy curtains were pulled across them to cut out any chinks of sunlight which might interfere with her viewing of the soap opera through which she lived her life. She lit up her cigarette and flicked the remote control.

The continuity man was pouring out what Eleanor called his 'usual drivel' to fill in time before that familiar drumbeat heralded the opening of the theme tune. "...that we're all looking forward to is the introduction of a new family into the world of 'Riversiders'. The father is played by that well known actor..."

'He must have a lot of time to kill this evening,' thought Eleanor. 'Who cares, who's in it. Just get on with it.'

"..and finally, their teenage daughter played by promising newcomer, Abigail Ayres. This is Abigail's first television…"

Eleanor leapt off the sofa, more because she had dropped hot ash all over her trousers than for any other reason.

'Fancy that. What a coincidence,' she thought as she trod the ash into the already grey carpet.

The short opening music of the programme was soon over. Eleanor watched as a dilapidated car pulled up outside a small house on the screen and from the back of the car emerged….

"AAAAAAAAAAAAGGGGGGGGGGGGGGGGHHHHHHHHHHHHHH!!!!"

Some three miles away in the hospital, the nurses had wheeled a large television into the small side ward for this evening and everyone in the room had their eyes rooted to it.

Everyone except Anthony Ayres, that is. He lay immobile and unseeing in his bed, as always. Abigail sat on the bed with him and held his limp hand in hers.

The 'Riversiders' theme music subsided and as Abigail stepped out of the car on the screen, Mr. Alphabet looked round. "Did anyone just hear a scream then? Something like a witch being tortured?" No-one answered. "Must just be me then." He turned back to watch Abigail's first words on television.

"I think I'm going to like this," Abigail's character said.

The whole room cheered and clapped. They turned to congratulate Abigail but when they looked at her, they saw that tears were flowing down her face.

"Whatever's..?" began Mr. Alphabet. He stopped and his gaze followed Abigail's to where her father was lying.

Anthony Ayres, eyes open, was smiling up at his daughter and clutching her hand as if he would never let it go again.

Printed in Great
Britain
by Amazon

32031629R00125